Under the Surface

A novel
by
Paula Marais

Logogog

Under the Surface

A novel
by
Paula Marais

To Cole, my animal whisperer
and beauty connoisseur

"Falsehood flies, and the Truth
Comes limping after it."
– **Jonathan Swift**

~

"Travel far enough, you meet yourself."
– **David Mitchell,** *Cloud Atlas*

~

"Leis go brown, tectonic plates shift,
Deep currents move,
Islands vanish, rooms get forgotten."
– **Joan Didion,** *The Year of Magical Thinking*

Chapter 1

19 December 2004. Sunday. 07h00.

When it's Daniel and not a stranger who dies in his arms
this time, Dr Jay Gifford knows he will have to get away.
Waiting silently as the first claws of daylight scratch
through the curtains, Jay strokes the thin strands of his
brother's remaining hair. Daniel seems to be asleep, peaceful
for the first time in months since the melanoma was
diagnosed. By Jay. How Jay had hated himself for his
knowledge. But not as much as Daniel had. He'd
pummelled Jay, leaving fist-sized bruises on his chest.

"You *always* win, Jay, always."

And even when Jay was out climbing in the
mountains, forcing himself upwards against the rock with
the sheer strength of his stamina and will, he'd ached. Yet he
hadn't resented this. It made him feel alive. And alive he felt
guilty. There was nothing else to feel. He wonders if now
the guilt will fade. When the grief sets in.

Below his window, Jay can hear the sound of the 93
bus passing, a bicycle bell ringing shrilly. A shriek of tyres.
Curses. *Fuck* and *bastard* and *don't you even look where you're
going, you stupid git?*

Jay can't move. He's lost feeling in the arm where he's cradled Daniel for hours. But he feels oddly reassured by the normalness of the day's wake-up call. He and Daniel used to fight. Five years' difference and nothing much in common but their parents. That and a thing for the same type of girls. And this didn't get them anywhere either. Daniel panting over Kerese at the dinner table, making inane remarks that for reasons Jay could never understand seemed to charm her. They'd argue in the car on the way home. *Go easy on Dan,* Kerese would say. *He doesn't mean anything by it. Actually, I think he's quite sweet.*

But Dan wasn't sweet; he was ruthless, determined, and about to take on the world. Jay's world. Was Jay in his rights to feel threatened by him then? And what about now? For Jay, it was never about winning. Not like it was for Daniel. Competitive from the first moment. Hitting tennis balls for hours on the garage door, until they spun just right, bouncing perfectly. Perfectly enough, he believed, to win every match. And then the gloating as Daniel relished his victory for hours after the event, not realising how Jay had decided to let him win by purposely missing the odd shot. They'd sit with the family as Dan made snide remarks about Jay's lack of form, lack of fitness. Passing the rhubarb crumble to Jay, Daniel wondered aloud if Jay might improve his game if he lost a bit of weight. Pensive. Seemingly concerned. And their mother would smile tolerantly.

"Now boys ..."

~

The melanoma hadn't changed everything. But it had changed enough. To be twenty-seven and dying can give you some perspective. They didn't apologise. Not for anything. Not for the fights, or for Jay's Honda abandoned in a ditch filled with murky storm water in the middle of winter. Not for the tattletales, or the vomit on the carpet of Jay's new apartment. And certainly not for the stray thoughts that crossed Jay's mind that he was somehow better than Daniel. They were brothers. And for once, they were going to pool their efforts to fight this thing.

Jay didn't want to perform the operation, but Daniel had insisted.

"You're so good at everything, why not for once be good at something for me? And if I do have a seizure, then you'll just have to make a plan. I'm not giving up that easily, Jay."

So, they prolonged the inevitable with operations and chemo. Radiotherapy. And for the one time that it really, truly counted, Jay just wasn't good enough. He looks at his brother's face, so much like his own. His sharp, almost pointy nose. His sallow cheeks that once loved the sun – before all of this. The thin upper lip, and full lower one, so red that they almost look dabbed with lipstick.

Jay feels a sob rising in his throat. His dead brother is lying in his arms and this time it *is* all over.

The bedroom door swings open.

"Jay?"

His mother is already dressed, her make-up immaculate. She doesn't so much peer around the door as dominate it.

"Would you like me to take over now so you can have a rest?" she asks.

"He's gone, Mum."

She pales, her face registering the shock. "But you didn't call me."

"I was going to, but he just slipped away now in his sleep."

Jay feels the tears on his cheeks. Is this where he hands over? His grief, his brother, transferred like a baton in a relay race? But his mother has her arms around both of them. "My boys. My poor boys." She showers them both with kisses. "Thank God your father won't remember any of this," she says. "Thank God."

"I'll have to wake Nina," Jay says.

His mother nods. She's manoeuvred herself so that Dan is lying against her chest, freeing Jay. His arm stings, the blood returning to it in agonising needle bursts. He rubs his wrist half-heartedly, for the feeling reminds him of what Daniel no longer has. Leaving his mother alone with his brother, Jay walks down the passage. He isn't wearing any slippers and the laminate flooring under his feet is icy. How will he tell Nina? She'd flown back from Thailand to wait for their brother to die. Every morning she and Jay have looked at each other, waiting. *Has it happened yet?* Dan, though birdlike, has been fighting the morphine, fighting for life. Giving up, giving in, didn't ever come easily to him.

Jay knocks, then pushes the door open. Nina is squirrelled under the duvet; he can just see her spiky black head against the pillow.

"Dan," she murmurs, then sits up suddenly as the realisation dawns. "When?" she asks.

"About half an hour ago," Jay replies.

"I'm so glad," she says. "He left us weeks ago."

And Jay isn't shocked. He knows what she means. What was Dan without that gleam in his eyes, the darting gaze appraising everything?

"I'll get dressed," she says. "You hungry, Jay? I can make banana pancakes?"

Chapter 2
23 December 2004. Thursday. 21h00.

Jay shifts uncomfortably. His legs have always been too long for these damn aeroplane seats, but Nina insisted on economy. He should have just bitten the bullet and paid for her upgrade. What the hell was he doing? Kerese is asleep against his shoulder, and he needs to pee. He's never left the UK and now he's on a plane to Bangkok with his crazy sister and a woman he's not all that sure he loves anymore. It had seemed a good idea at the time.

"Of course you need a break, Jay," his mother said. "And I don't want to celebrate Christmas this year anyway. What's there to celebrate?"

"You could come with us," Jay had offered.

"What, and leave your father? At Christmas?"

Jay didn't bother to contradict her; his father's mind was so far gone he wouldn't know otherwise. His mother wanted to be alone. That much was obvious. Leaving her house, with its almost tangible smell of illness, he should have felt liberated. But leaving had seemed rather like abandoning Daniel. Dropping his suitcase next to the door of his terraced house in Putney, he'd been too exhausted to move. He'd popped a beer, and watched the footie, trying to go into a state of numbness.

The house was too quiet. He should have fetched Nelson from the kennels and now it was too late. Kerese would come round after work. She'd curl her lithe body around him, and while they were naked, he would forget. But only temporarily. He was realising more and more that they couldn't really talk to each other. They were great at sex. But not that great at anything else. She didn't even like Nelson.

Jay turns his shoulder to extricate himself from Kerese.

"Jay?" she says.

"I need a slash," he says, knowing his crassness will irritate her.

She turns her back to him, adjusting the travel pillow hooked around her neck. He walks to the back of the plane, glad to stretch out. He finds an empty cubicle, locking the door. His mother was right. There wasn't anything to celebrate this Christmas.

~

Thailand was Nina's idea. "What do you want to go to Snowdonia for? It's the middle of winter."

"I like Snowdonia," Jay said.

"There's some of the best climbing in the world in Krabi and Koh Phi Phi. I can get you a deal at the Phi Phi Paradise. Live a little, Jay. You've been stuck at sickbeds for more than two months."

"In case you've forgotten, I do sickbeds for a living."

"And even if I ignore how heartless that sounds, that's all the more reason to get away."

"I'm sure it will be nice for Nina to show you her new life, dear," his mother added.

It was hard not to feel cornered. He deserved a holiday; that much was true. But a holiday halfway across the world in a place he knew almost nothing about would not have been his choice. He wasn't an adventurer at heart. Not really. Nina was always the one to bash around the world, only to return completely penniless with reams of photos, usually showing her doped up, wearing tie-dye and nose rings and sunning herself against an exotic backdrop. He wasn't sure if they made him even vaguely envious. When he was honest with himself, he recognised how terrified he was of being out of his element. Familiarity may have bred contempt to others. But never to him.

Kerese, of course, started packing her bags before the decision was even properly finalised. She'd booked a tanning session for straight after the funeral, and was surprisingly put out when he made her cancel it.

"But Daniel would understand I need to look good," she said.

"Daniel's dead, Kerese. That's why we're going to his funeral."

~

As people queued at the buffet station that the family had laid out in the dining room, Kerese's sulking was almost tangible. He looked over at her, wondering if she would snap out of it. And eventually she did. Jay found her discussing travel tips with Nina, her glass of Merlot almost empty. She smiled at him, offering him a sensuous sip. He could never accuse Kerese of prolonging a disagreement, but she would never agree that she was wrong. And that's where they were more alike than he usually liked to admit.

The endless condolences were tiring. He drank more than was good for him. Whiskey. Wine. The odd tequila. Then tried to sober up with instant coffee that was so old it had hardened in his mother's cupboard.

"I never drink the stuff, dear. Dig around and see what you can find. I can't promise anything, though."

He missed Daniel. Dan had always been the family glue, the halfway mark between Nina's eccentricity and his predictability. He'd never told him. There were lots of things they hadn't said, despite his vigils at Dan's bedside. They'd talked about football. Reminisced about their father, an illustrious surgeon, and how knowing about his early-onset Alzheimer's would have destroyed him emotionally. Nina. *Will she ever stay in one place for longer than a few months?* Kerese. *I've always wished I could have shagged her, Jay. Just once. Is she any good?* Death. *I'm planning a great funeral. Make sure you get shit-faced. I would have. And don't feel bad about it. It's a great feeling to get pissed once in a while, not that you'd even remember it's been so long. Bury me with a bottle of Jack for the afterlife. And if Kerese is up for it before I go …*

Jay was shocked by Dan's nonchalance. It wasn't as if Dan was the first person he'd watched die. People died around him all the time. Colons riddled with tumours.

9

Tarred lungs. Mastectomies performed much too late. It was easier to separate the bodies from the patients. Not that it was always possible. Toddlers by the bedside. Distraught tears. Why me? And why not me? He'd prided himself on his calmness. His strength. It was just that he wasn't so sure he could be that strong again so soon.

~

So Thailand it is. Jay leans forward, feeling the warm water on his face. His skin feels dry, making his cheeks itch. How long has he been in here? Flushing, he swings the door open. Five people stand in a haphazard queue, looking peeved. He shrugs, then steps to the back of the plane to stretch his legs. This trip is out of character for him. But what's so great about his character anyway? Maybe it's taken Daniel's death to force him into this. A step out of his comfort zone. An exotic experience. And besides, it's only two weeks of his life. He doesn't have to come back again if he doesn't like it. *Live a little, Jay,* he hears Daniel say. *It's not as if I'm going to.*

And that's what decided him in the first place.

~

The plane lands at dusk. Jay feels disorientated. Unlike Kerese and Nina, he hasn't actually slept. The girls chatter excitedly in the immigration queue. They're so different from each other that Jay is often amazed they have anything at all to talk about. Nina is teaching Kerese some basic greetings, laughing at Kerese's pronunciation. *Sawat-dee …* And Nina was right. He should never have brought so many jumpers. Now he's going to have to lug them around at the bottom of his bag. Extra weight for nothing. Despite the air-conditioning, he's sweating. The carousel hums loudly; a lone suitcase catches, then topples so heavily the handle snaps. "Shit!" he hears behind him.

Of course his bag is the last to come. He's almost given up hope. Kerese and Nina stand outside, smoking. He's never seen Kerese smoke before. Yet she drags the cigarette to her lips with a practised air.

"Oh don't be such a fuddy-duddy, Jay. We're on holiday," she says before he even comments, but stubs it out anyway.

"The bus will leave soon," says Nina, tossing her cigarette onto the cement. It carries on burning until she squashes it with her sandal.

In distance, it can't be that far to the Kao San Road. But in the traffic, where lanes are irrelevant, intersections have no real meaning and highways have people driving in the wrong direction, time is a concept Jay has to relinquish. It takes two hours. Nina's already told them where they'll be staying – the Merry V. It's cheap. One-hundred-and-fifty baht for a double, with no bathroom. No bathroom? Even Kerese isn't happy about that, but is too exhausted to comment.

He needs a shower, and sends Nina into mild hysterics when she realises he's used the hose next to the toilet to clean himself.

"That isn't exactly what those hoses are for, Jay," she cackles.

He's left the toilet cubicle flooded, but at least he feels clean. Kerese finds the actual shower stall, stepping tentatively on the dirty floor with her flip-flops. There's no way she's taking them off.

~

They walk between a flurry of food sellers, assailed by the stench of sewage. Nina stops to buy a pineapple, offers them both a piece.

She grins at their hesitation.

"For God's sake, you two, it's just fruit."

The restaurants are nothing like Jay is used to. They're noisy joints, with beats pumping from out-of-tune stereos, and TVs showing fashion models, or football or Thai kickboxing. The plastic tables and chairs extend into the street, circumnavigated by mangy dogs fetching scraps from under them. Jay is more than a little hesitant as Nina leads the way.

"Oh come on, guys," she says, "I've never got food poisoning here. Not even once."

There's always a first time, thinks Jay, but he sits where he's told, watching the locals roar past on their motorcycles. Vendors push their bicycles past, their fruit on display in transparent plastic boxes. Jay observes the owners of the restaurant chatting, unconcerned by their clientele, as used dishes are cleaned in big bowls of water next to the street.

"I don't know what to order," he says helplessly, as he looks at the laminated sheet written entirely in Thai squiggles.

"I'll do it," says Nina.

She points at a few lines on the menu. The waitress nods, turning away quickly to where a cook is sweltering next to a gas stove.

"So you need to decide," Nina says, slurping a noodle, "whether you'll go up north to Chiang Mai or Pai, or travel with me tomorrow to the islands. I don't mind really. You decide what you want. But I need to start back at the dive school on Christmas. Trip to the Similan Islands. We've got a whole boatful of punters. Oversubscribed and understaffed. As always."

"Why would we choose to go north then?" Kerese asks.

"Hill trekking, Thai cooking, maybe even some elephant rides," says Nina, "but I don't really recommend the ellies. They're bloody uncomfortable and fart like troopers. Jay wouldn't like it. Much too unsophisticated."

Jay almost feels like rising to Nina's challenge and mounting a fucking elephant. He shudders to think what she thinks of him. His life so ordered, so organised. A perfectly appointed house (paid off), life insurance, a pension, a string of long-term monogamous relationships, his oncology practice and various articles published on lymphoma. And yet by his standards he has a good life. Apart from Daniel …

"Don't you at least want to spend Christmas together?" he asks, tentatively.

Perhaps Nina's right. Maybe he's just too afraid to go north without her. She seems so fearless, undaunted by the language gap, foreign alphabet and touts calling to them from their tuk-tuks.

Nina raises an eyebrow. "It's not going to bring Dan back," she says matter-of-factly. "In some ways, it's easier to forget it's Christmas here. I just can't do any more forced hours of reminiscing."

Jay nods, but her answer stings him.

"Don't look at me like that," she says. "What I mean to say is that it hurts too much. I just want to keep busy."

Kerese shifts. She's tied her blonde hair into a knot at her neck, and a thin layer of perspiration coats her forehead. Despite this, Jay thinks she looks beautiful. She takes his hand. "Well I don't know about you, Jay," says Kerese. "But I'm ready for a beach."

~

But getting to the beach is a plane journey, then a boat to Krabi Town. Nina refuses to take the ferry.

"We'll get our own boat from Chaofa Pier," she insists.

So it's two-and-a-half hours from Krabi to Koh Phi Phi by Thai longboat, their suitcases piled together. And each time a wave from a passing boat threatens, Kerese winces. "Can't they cover them with some plastic or something?" she asks.

But Jay is surprised to find he doesn't really care. As they leave the bustle of Krabi Town behind them, their driver uses one hand to steer them deeper. In his other he holds a banana, which he bites into with gusto. "Thailand, you like?" he asks, his mouth half-full of masticated fruit.

They nod.

"You need boat for snorkel?" he asks. "I know velly good place. Lots fish. Not deep. Plivate."

"Sounds good," says Jay, as Kerese frowns. She doesn't like to encourage *the locals*.

"Yes, velly good. Velly good. American?" he asks.

"British," Jay answers.

"Princess Diana. Yes?"

"Yes."

Jay wonders if he knows she's not around any longer, and hesitates to disappoint him. Nina is lying back; she's covered her face with a floppy pink hat, so you can just see the rose tattoos snaking up her arm. The other arm is a riot of curlicues that might possibly mean something.

"You like Leonardo?" their pilot asks.

Jay and Kerese look equally blank.

"Leonardo," the man repeats, lifting his sunglasses to study his passengers.

"He means DiCaprio," Nina mutters. "Unreasonably famous in these parts. *And* the movie was no match for the book."

Not asleep then.

"Sure," says Jay, "why not?"

"I take you. Maya Beach. Ko Phi Phi Leh. I cook for you. Good swimming."

"Right," says Jay.

"You like? I wait for you. Drop bags. We go."

Kerese looks about to twitch.

"Another day," says Jay. "Maybe. Today we need to rest."

"Rest," the man says, nodding. "Yes, good place for resting. Tomorrow. I find you. My name Aroon. You call me Harry."

Kerese rolls her eyes, then picks up a *Vogue*. She flips through it noisily and far too quickly to be taking anything in. But the man becomes suitably silent. He studies Kerese briefly, his face impassive.

Jay extends his hand into the water. The depth changes with alternating pools of darker greens and blues. *What a difference from London.* When they'd left it had been sleeting, leaving brown sludge on the roads, tyre tracks tracing through the deposits on the tar. He'd driven carefully, blocking out Kerese and Nina's chatter as he turned into the long-stay carpark.

But now the sun is soaking into him, his hand caressed by the deep, turquoise water. And he can't see a cloud. Not anywhere across the entire sky. The put-put-putttt of the longboat is hypnotic. He wonders how Daniel would have reacted if he were here with them. He'd probably have dived off the boat by now, splashing Kerese and making her shriek. Yet even then, Jay guesses Dan's spontaneity would have been infectious enough for her to forgive him. And maybe, just maybe, follow him into the water.

So Jay finds himself waving at their pilot to stop. And by the time the boat is silent and still, he's stripped off his shirt and kicked off his shoes. "Come on!" he shouts, but doesn't look back.

And under the water he can feel the bands of water against his skin, cool, then bath-water warm. They're actually above a coral garden, but he can't see much with the salt stinging his eyes. He has this strange sensation of not wanting to surface, as though to stay underwater he can breathe differently, be different. But like a cork, he does eventually bob back up and when he does, he finds that he is laughing.

"What's got into you, Jay?" Kerese says. She hasn't moved, but her mouth is pursed. It's Nina who gets up. She doesn't even bother to take off her clothes before she tumbles in after him. Her hair is pasted flat against her scalp, her shirt floating about her like a cloak. She swims towards him, vulnerable, he thinks, despite the harsh black etched into her skin. His little sister. Then, her hand is on his head pushing him under, taking him by surprise. And he has to swim under her to grab her legs and dunk her. But as soon as he lets her go, she pulls away from him with strong strokes. He chases after her but she dives down again, emerging on the other side of the boat.

"Hey Jay," she shouts. "I thought for a moment you'd turned into Daniel ... But the truth is Daniel would never have let *anyone* beat him."

~

By the time they approach the island of Koh Phi Phi Don, Jay and Nina are both dry. Stacked high above them like marble cake in grey, white and brown are the sheer limestone pinnacles that eventually brought Jay here. His jaw drops. The cliffs rise up out of the emerald waters, tufts of green poking out of the holes in the rock weathered by water and time. Stalactites reach their fingers towards the ocean. Tips of roots have been preserved in some of the rock and drip continuously. The rock closer to the sea is eroded like popped bubble plastic and conglomerate rock peppered with seashells dominates at the base. Jay can already feel his hands itching. *How long will it take to get unpacked? With Kerese – all day.*

"Jay?" Kerese says. "You're not going climbing this afternoon are you?"

"I don't know," he answers.

"I thought we could explore a bit together," she says.

He's already decided he'll leave her by the pool as soon as he can. What's got into him? He knows he's being selfish but despite a slight trace of guilt, he doesn't really care. He needs to climb. He just does. Jay studies Kerese. Even her flip-flops have kitten heels, for God's sake. It never used to bother him. But even as he thinks this he knows he's just making excuses.

Nina breaks the silence. "Kerese, why don't you come with me for a bit? You know Jay won't be happy until he gets his fix."

Kerese sighs then shrugs. "Sure," she says, "why not? You give me the grand tour."

Jay has never realised before how much he's underestimated Nina.

~

Their bungalow sits in a grove of palm trees, overlooking the white sand and crystal clear water of Loh Dalum a reasonable walk away. Actually, Jay wouldn't have described it as a bungalow; more of an apartment really. It's a combination of traditional Thai architecture on the outside and Western comforts inside, and at a bargain rate that Nina managed to negotiate. Jay and Kerese are on the second floor and from the window he can see the sails of two windsurfers as they curve around a rock face, then disappear.

"You need to head into Tonsai Village," Nina says. "Go find Tyt's Climbing Shop. It's pretty new, but they're the best people to speak to. And they'll set you up with someone to climb with."

So that's why he finds himself lugging his bag through the souvenir-adorned footpaths. Stalls nearby offer snorkelling tours, diving trips, postcards, kayak hire, Internet, long-distance telephone calls.

"You want loom?" a woman offers as she eyes the tog bag slung over his shoulder. Children dance around him. "Where you going? You want loom?"

Nina was right; since the ferry left at two thirty, the streets aren't nearly as busy as they were when they arrived. And since there are no cars, it isn't anything near as frenzied as Bangkok. Nevertheless, on the isthmus that made Phi Phi famous, it's still bustling. People on bicycles pass by, insistent rings alerting him to move out the way. When he darts into Tyt's, he's relieved and just a little disorientated.

The shop itself is narrow, an Aladdin's cave of climbing equipment and more than a small piece of heaven. Jay drops his bag, fingering one of the ropes. Edelweiss Sharp Double. 8.5 millimetres. Nice.

"You need equipment?"

Jay starts. The voice is American, or Canadian. He can never quite tell the difference.

"Sorry," she says. "Guess you didn't see me. It's a good rope. Longer rappels, less weight. Perdur treatment, so its thirty-three percent more abrasion-resistant than untreated 8.5 millimetres."

"I've got my own stuff," Jay answers, as he finds her gaze locked with his.

She's tall, almost as tall as he is. And her red hair reaches halfway down her back in tight ringlets. At her hairline is a light frosting of untamed frizz.

"Oh," she says, raising an eyebrow questioningly.

"I guess I was looking for some advice. Just got in on the boat."

"Left your girlfriend on the beach to get her hair braided?"

"Braided?" Jay is flustered, his face filling with crimson heat.

"Or maybe a massage. They do a mean massage on Loh Dalum."

Jay senses that she is teasing him, but he's already on the back foot. "I just need to climb," he blurts, "and I thought ..."

A wiry looking Thai man walks in with climbing ropes slung over his shoulder. He's shirtless and his upper body is sculpted by hours of endurance.

"I'm back," he says, acknowledging Jay, then touches her on the arm almost possessively. "Thanks for helping out."

She nods, then indicates Jay with a flick of her hand. "He *needs* to climb, Deng," she says, with the trace of a smirk. "What about Ao Ling? Or Drinkin' Wall?"

"You alone?" Deng asks.

"Yes."

"I can take you in half an hour. Single pitch today on Tonsai Tower. See how you do."

Jay's face must register his disappointment.

"It's a great wall," the woman says reassuringly. "Deng's a safety control freak anyways. You'll never get him to take you on a multi-pitch on Day One. Trust me, though, you're with the right man."

Jay studies her, then smiles. "You can watch us if you like," he says. "I might impress you."

But she simply turns towards the exit.

"I doubt it," Deng answers for her as she heads out the shop. "She doesn't impress easily."

Chapter 3

25 December 2004. Saturday. 07h00.

Nina's dive boat leaves early on Christmas morning. Jay and
Kerese watch the group loading up their tanks and BCDs,
then throw their bags onto the deck. Nina is wearing her
wetsuit, unzipped and hanging at the waist, her belly ring
glinting in the sunshine. Yesterday evening she'd
introduced them to her divemaster friends Kelly and
Thomas to show them around while she was in the Similans.

Together, they drink a few beers on the beach and
watch the sun go down before heading into Tonsai for a
weak attempt at Christmas Eve dinner. Eventually at a
farang hangout, they find some roast turkey. As Nina had
warned them, they would have done better with green
curry. The turkey is dry, served with limp lettuce and burnt
roast potatoes. Luckily there is ample vodka and gin, some
of which Nina had insisted they bring with them from the
duty-free.

By the time the dinner is over, they are far from
ready for bed, and end up at Kelly and Tom's bungalow
behind the dive centre.

Stretching out on their Mon Khwan mattresses, they light a few joints and pass them around. Lying back, Jay studies the photos stuck with Blu-Tack all over the walls. Snapshots of people and large images of stingrays, sharks and angelfish. The room has a studenty feeling to it, with Thai silk sarongs flung over the chairs and attached to the wall with drawing pins as makeshift curtains. It reminds Jay of his own temporary homes when he was studying at King's College. Thank God he's moved on from that.

Jay doesn't like the effect of the marijuana on him. It makes him light-headed and dizzy and not in a good way. "I'm going outside," he says, "I need some air."

Kerese giggles, her lithe body sprawled out in a way that would have suggested things to him if he didn't feel quite as nauseous as he did.

"Wait up," Kelly says, "I'll come with you."

Kelly has an Asian look about her. Her eyes are narrow and her bobbed hair, thick and straight, almost as though it had been ironed flat. She is a neat kind of person, with everything perfectly proportioned. Her nose. Her neck. Her waist.

"You need to relax, Jay," she says to him, dropping her butt in the dustbin at the door.

"This is me being relaxed," Jay returns.

"Nina said you were uptight," Kelly laughs.

"Nina said you were honest," says Jay, "at least we meet each other forewarned."

Kelly laughs again. "So you do have a sense of humour if you try," Kelly says.

24

"But I'm not sure you have any hope on the tact side of things," Jay answers, making her chuckle again.

"Touché," she answers.

"So where do you come from?" Jay asks her.

"Every place," Kelly answers, "I'm a woman of the world."

"Something tells me I'm not going to get much out of you," says Jay.

"What do you want to get out of me?" Kelly says, touching him on the thigh.

Gently removing her hand, he picks up some sand, letting it run through his fingers. Unchastened, Kelly leans forward. "Sometimes I think it's so dull to go through all the formalities," she says.

"You can't break the rules if you don't have any," Jay answers.

"But I bet you never break rules."

"You've just met me," Jay replies, "so don't take your first impressions for granted. But, you're right, there are some things I just won't do."

"Like fuck a stranger when your girlfriend is stoned ten metres away," says Kelly.

"Like that, yes."

Kelly sighs. "They always say the best men are taken," she says, tracing his jawline with her finger.

He shifts. Her hand drops. "So what about Tom?" Jay asks.

"What about him? There's a new crowd of divers in and he's already got his eye on the blonde chick with big boobs."

"So why stay with him?" Jay says.

"Why not? When it's good with him, it's fuckin' awesome – in all the ways that matter. We have some wild times."

"I don't doubt it," Jay replies, studying the clear sky above him.

It has been a long time since he saw stars like this, as though a whole new galaxy has opened up above him. "I saw the photos on your wall," he says, changing the subject.

"Good spotting, Sherlock," Kelly replies.

Jay doesn't flinch. Her abrasiveness didn't mask her insecurities. Not to him.

"Did you take them?" he asks.

"New hobby. When I moved here I bought a camera on Ebay," Kelly says. "I'm getting better. I also keep a regular journal, you know, to remember when I'm old and decrepit."

"Kerese is pretty good too," he says, "she's got a good eye."

"The happy couple," says Kelly.

If only she knew.

"I'm thirsty," Jay says, "got any water in that gallery of yours?"

"I may do," she says.

Jay pulls himself off the sand, then offers his hand to help Kelly up.

"Ever the gentleman," she says.

"I try," he says, bowing.

When they get back to the bungalow, Nina has passed out on the floor in the bedroom. Kerese stands up quickly. "Let's go, Jay," she says, "I'm tired."

Tom salutes them from the mat. "Sleep tight," he says, then farts loudly.

~

Despite her overindulgence the night before, Nina is as bouncy as a pogo stick. She leans over to Jay, kissing him on the cheek.

"Take care of yourselves, bro," she says.

"We will."

"I'll be back in a couple of days," she says, tossing the last bag onto the boat. "You guys have fun."

Typically, Nina doesn't look back.

Jay wonders how their genes could be so different. Apart from their hair colour, Nina looks nothing like him. She is short and stocky and her skin is dark even in winter. But what amazes him more is her confidence. She's comfortable in her less-than-perfect body and that's what people, especially men, respond to. There's never been a shortage on the romantic front. Jay knows now that's why Nina's so eager to get going. One of the group is a Brazilian travelling alone. And as she put it, he's rather dishy.

Jay stands next to Kerese on the beach watching a boat pulling a couple into the sky. They're hitched to a green and red parasail, and the woman screams as the boat slows and they start to drop.

"Now what?" asks Kerese.

Jay notices her hand lifting as though to grasp his, but then she drops it. "It doesn't feel much like Christmas really does it?" says Jay.

They've already opened a few presents together. The pile looked a bit meagre, partly because they didn't want to lug around too many things they weren't going to use and partly because they already opened some of the presents they knew they could. Jay's climbing shoes, for instance, which are already scuffed from Tonsai Tower, and Kerese's yellow bikini, which she is wearing at the moment. And he has to admit, she looks fantastic in it, he just forgot to tell her.

"I'm going to do Ao Ling later this afternoon," Jay says. "Deng is meeting me there with a few other climbers."

Kerese nods. She's told him she's happy to stretch out at the pool and read *The Da Vinci Code* but she doesn't want to spend the whole day on her own.

"Nina told me about a few places we could snorkel?" Jay suggests.

"Why not?" she says.

Kerese is a good swimmer. It just takes her a bit of time to warm up, before she can even dip a toe into the water. In happier times, Jay joked she was like a lizard with temperature control in direct relation to her sun intake. Now he won't say anything. She offends easily and he knows he's partly responsible; Kerese doesn't seem to have the self-assurance any longer to know when he's joking. It seems to him that everything he says is now taken as a criticism, even if it isn't meant that way.

"I was thinking about Pi Leh Bay," Jay says. "We'll need to get a longtail or a speedboat to get there because it's a thin bay with high cliffs on all sides. Nina mentioned there's a shelf at the entrance, which makes getting there in other boats impossible."

"We could always find our man from yesterday, Harry was it?" Kerese suggests.

"Or he could find us," says Jay meaningfully, because their pilot is sauntering across the beach, targeting them with the doggedness of a hungry seal.

"We go?" Harry says. "Koh Phi Phi Leh tour. Four hours."

"We wanted to go to Pi Leh Bay," says Jay.

"Yes. On Koh Phi Phi Leh. Where your friend? She come too, yes?"

"No," Jay says, "just the two of us."

"Two. No problem. No problem. You need mask and snorkel? I rent cheap-cheap."

After a few more negotiations, one of which is a radical drop in price, Jay and Kerese agree to meet Harry back on the beach. "I wait," Harry says, settling himself under a palm tree.

They've a few things they want to fetch. Sun cream. Their equipment. Swimming towels. Kerese's camera.

Jay wants to get going. Now that he's finally in Thailand, he realises he doesn't want to miss a moment. And he needs to get back in time for his climb.

Kerese seems to sense Jay's impatience, and rubs the sunscreen quickly onto her face. Her hands reach down her back, but not quite far enough.

"You need some help with that?" Jay asks to hurry her along. At first.

She hands him the bottle and as he touches her skin, he feels familiar twinges of desire, his eagerness to get back to the boat dissipating. Kerese's body is made for plunging necklines and open backs, her smooth unblemished contours goosebumping to his touch. He rounds her bottom barely covered by the skimpy bikini briefs, slipping his finger under the elastic. She turns slightly, accommodating him, and his finger probes gently.

"The boat," she murmurs.

"Will wait," Jay replies.

His other hand trails to her bikini strings, loosening them. She's trembling, her hands cupping him over his swimming trunks. He feels himself responding, willing her to untie the chord at his waist. Kerese is still turned away from him, but even with her hands behind her, she is able to slip his board shorts down. A little roughly, he pushes her forwards so her thighs are against the dressing table overlooking the Andaman Sea. She lurches towards the table, letting him go as she tries to balance herself. Above them, the fan is whirring, whisking the warm air to coat their bodies. Jay pushes her pants down, and his hands cup

30

her full breasts, half-exposed, half-covered by her bikini top. Kerese moans. He can feel her nipples hardening under his touch. She's leaning on one hand, her other hand guiding him to her moist centre. And then he is engulfed by her. Tight and liquid. His hand moves down between her legs, rubbing. Friction. Kerese has fallen forward; he can feel her shuddering, as though guiding him to the heart of her. And he lets her take him there.

~

When it's over, she stands upright. Turning towards him to kiss him. Her face is unreadable. Flushed. But he kisses her back. It's a kiss of longing. Of regret. Of memory.

"Thank you," he whispers, brushing his lips against her eyes. And he finds just a trace of a tear lurking there.

"There are worse things that could happen at Christmas," Kerese says, pulling away to tighten her bikini.

And Jay wonders how he should take this. In the end, he doesn't say anything. Instead, he dresses himself then slings their bag over his shoulder. With the other hand, he links his fingers with hers.

"Come on, Kerese," he says. "Let's go snorkelling."

~

In their absence, Harry has acquired some other day-trippers.

"You so long, I think you no come," he says to them, his head cocked.

"We're here aren't we?" Jay says.

Harry waves his hands in an expansive gesture.

"We fit in boat. No problem."

Jay helps Kerese, his hand sliding a little longer over her bottom than it needs to. She turns back, smiling at him.

Maybe, he thinks, *maybe Thailand is exactly what we need to get ourselves back on track.*

There's a couple on the boat with a toddler, and two girls who seem to be travelling together. At first they just nod at each other. Then one of the girls leans forward.

"I'm Rikke," she says, "and this is Margot."

Margot nods. She's wearing a colourful sundress, which does nothing to cover her generous cleavage. Margot lifts her shades to acknowledge Jay and Kerese, then slips them back down again. He can't see her eyes, so has no idea how she has reacted to them. Rikke on the other hand, is less penetrating and more vivacious. She's wearing a T-shirt with *Divers Do It Deep* emblazoned across her chest. Her legs are bare, slightly freckled with well-toned calves. On her lap is a camera in an underwater casing, which she is cleaning with a spray valve and tissue roll.

Margot doesn't talk much but unlike Rikke, her English is completely without any Scandinavian traces. She sounds more American, almost Vivien Leigh as Scarlett O'Hara. Although the actress was British, he recalls. He wonders where Margot comes from.

Jay stretches his hand out to the couple just nearby.

"Jay," he says, but doesn't bother to introduce Kerese, who is far too involved in her own conversation.

"Steve," the guy says, "and this is Laura. And Finn."

Laura smiles, then shifts as the little boy dives for her sunglasses. "No," she says to him, "those are Mommy's glasses. Where are Finn's glasses?"

"Gone," the child says as he throws out his hands, his face taking on an expression of extreme seriousness. "Finn crying."

Steve laughs good-humouredly, then pulls the little boy to him to douse him with sun lotion. Finn tries to pull away.

"Yucky," he says, "Hor-ble." He wipes his mouth with a grubby paw, then pats his tummy. "Juicey. Finn. Juicey."

Laura digs in her bag to pull out a sippy cup. He grabs it from her with both hands. "Say thank you."

"How old is he?" Jay asks.

"Two," Laura says. "He's a little menace, but we love him." She kisses Finn's head, adjusting his peaked cap, which is coming loose in the wind.

"On holiday?" Jay says.

"We've come to visit some friends of ours. They've been teaching in Thailand. Somewhere near Chiang Mai, but we're meeting up here in Koh Phi Phi for the Christmas holidays. Their plane's getting in this afternoon, so we're just passing the time of day," says Steve.

"Nice way to do it," says Jay. "You Australian?"

"Kiwi," corrects Laura, with just a trace of disapproval, or disappointment, Jay isn't sure which.

Jay's dying to get into the water, it looks so inviting, and he can already feel the back of his neck reddening. Leaning over to Harry, he asks how long they will be.

"No far. Pileh Wall. One hour snorkel," Harry says.

And the ride isn't much longer. Their first views of Koh Phi Phi Leh are breathtaking. Sheer limestone cliffs tower above the jungle and vanish into calm, clear seas. Harry pulls out his stock of fins and snorkels. He spits into the first one he picks up as though at target practice, then hands it to Laura. She is unable to hide her disgust, but Margot only laughs and takes the goggles from her.

"It's just saliva," she says, "Anyways, it'll keep the glass clear."

Laura grabs another mask off the pile before Harry can get to it. Jay unpacks their gear, handing Kerese her stuff. This time, having warmed up on the boat, she soon follows him into the water. Following the steep drop off, they swim together, making noises to attract each other if they see something along the soft coral wall. A hawksbill turtle moves away from the bubble coral where it has been eating and swims right up to Jay. As he begins to follow it, it scares and soon he can't keep up. In his haste, he swallows some saltwater and comes up coughing. Despite that he's smiling. *So this is what Nina was on about*, he thinks.

By the time he and Kerese get back to the boat, everybody has already removed their fins, their eyes ringed from the glass pressing on their faces. Laura and Steve have taken turns in the water, and neither has ventured far from the boat. But Rikke and Margot are ecstatic. They've seen a leopard shark – a little one, but close up. It hardly moved when they approached it, but they could see it lying like a carpet on the seabed with its open mouth facing the current.

"Sweet," says Steve, "They're nocturnal, and unlike other sharks, they can breathe without swimming. This is paradise, isn't it?"

Harry has cut them slices of pineapple, which takes the saltiness out of their mouths. He passes around a bottle of Coke and a few plastic cups. There aren't enough, so they have to share, and though the drink is warm from the sun, it's refreshing.

This ride, Jay is sitting next to Margot, who is rather uncommunicative. She offers little about herself except that she lived for some time in the American South. Neither does she ask Jay anything about himself, settling back instead to read *Life of Pi* while he is in the midst of a sentence. Clearly the plight of Piscine and his tiger Richard Parker is a lot more interesting than he is.

Slightly put out, Jay frowns.

"Oh don't worry about Margot," says Rikke, "she's like a man. A limited quota of words for each day. Unlike me."

She isn't joking. Rikke has enough words for the entire boat combined – in English and in Norwegian. And anyway, Jay is not convinced; Margot with her wavy blonde hair to the waist, slender hips and large breasts (which, he notices, don't quite fit her bikini halterneck and may possibly have received cosmetic help) is not at all like a man.

At Pi Leh Bay, the water is even calmer than along the wall. Harry uses the remains of the pineapple and the odd piece of banana to attract a host of fish. It seems to Jay that the marine life already knows the drill, as vivid parrotfish and sergeant majors rush to the boat as soon as they throw anchor.

"Good morning time," says Harry. "Afternoon velly much shady. Now, you swim."

Rikke chews on a banana, speaking as she eats, then jumps in still masticating.

Classy, Jay thinks, but tries to push the thought away. Not just her eating habits, but something about the way she speaks …

This time Margot stays on the boat with Laura and Finn, who's fallen asleep in her arms. She's covered his legs and arms with a sarong and he seems quite peaceful, sucking his thumb.

Steve is a marine biologist. Kerese and Jay follow him over the shallow coral as he points out a few of the colourful fish and puts names to them: harlequin sweetlips, cleaner wrasse, crocodile longtoms …

They reach Maya Bay on the opposite side of Pi Leh via a cave route from the eastern side of the island at Loh Samah Bay. Maya Bay is sheltered by one-hundred-metre-high cliffs on all sides but one, and Harry plans to bring the boat round to meet them.

Steve transfers Finn in his backpack, and he goes straight back to sleep, obviously lulled by the movement.

As they walk, he tells Jay that Maya Beach is actually made up of several beaches, some of which only exist at low tide.

"The whole bay is actually one big reef," Steve says.

Jay's relieved he doesn't eco-evangelise, because despite what Steve says, nothing can mar the beauty of the powdery, white sand, lapping crystalline waters and limestone karsts rising up haphazardly into the sky. He takes Kerese's hand and they wade into the water, feeling the silky soft sand between their toes. Under the water are large boulders encrusted with coral, and populated by darting fish of every colour imaginable.

When they come out the water, Finn is transferring buckets of sand into a hole that Steve is digging. Steve is barely keeping up with him. Laura calls them over, asking Kerese to take photos of the three of them with the cliffs in the background. She does, but Finn looks away every time the shutter clicks.

Though there are only a few boats when they arrive, within half an hour there are at least fifteen boats drowning out the silence with loud engines and screaming tourists throwing themselves overboard as they pretend to wrestle large sharks. It seems like a good time to leave.

"Such a shame," says Kerese, "but I guess a place like this can't be a secret forever."

Harry looks up from his banana and winks. "You come first person morning time," he says, "then just your secret."

Chapter 4

26 December 2004. Sunday. 08h00.

Jay swears he's woken by an earthquake. It's either that or a reaction to the muscle relaxants he took after torturing himself on Ao Ling. But he really doesn't think that's it. Lying under the sheet, he watches as the lamp next to the bed shakes. It's the strangest sensation, as though he is still and the whole world is moving around him. A glass topples from the shelf under the mirror, shattering.

Kerese jumps, sitting up.

"Jay?"

Sixty seconds and it's over.

"Was that an earthquake?" Kerese asks.

But even though he is wondering the same thing, he doesn't know the answer. It's over anyway, whatever it was.

He slips on his sandals to avoid the glass, then moves to bathroom to shower. Cold showers. Despite it being muggy already, he can't get used to them.

"I was thinking," says Kerese brightly, as she slips into the bathroom, "we should have an early breakfast on the beach. Go for a swim."

Jay washes the shampoo suds out of his hair.

"Good idea," he says.

Kerese is wearing a T-shirt that barely covers her bottom. After one and half days of lounging on the beach, her smooth legs are already the colour of caramel. And of course there were the tanning sessions. Jay thinks how different she looks from the girl at Tyt's. When he saw her again from a distance yesterday afternoon, she was hanging upside down from a rocky outcrop he hadn't yet learned the name of. Lean, and muscular, her pale skin was even more pallid against the stone wall. Mesmerised, he watched her confident manoeuvring, her speedy, almost reckless abseil back to the beach. When she walked past him, she waved her hands about, chatting excitedly to her climbing buddies. He wasn't sure that she ignored him so much as didn't actually see him.

Later at the Hungry Shark in Tonsai Village, he saw her again, drinking Sangthip with Coke. This time she did acknowledge him, raising a glass with a cheerful grin, which didn't earn him any favours with Kerese, despite the happy day they'd shared. And then Nina wasn't there to unruffle any feathers. Not, he reminded himself ruefully, that he couldn't fight his own battles. But it wasn't like Kerese to be insecure anyway.

Jay steps out the shower, rubbing himself vigorously with this towel.

"I'm going to shower after we swim," says Kerese, "get the salt out."

She still takes ages to get ready though, brushing her hair, packing her book, searching for a missing sandal. Jay paces, watching her every movement with increasing frustration.

Kerese notices.

"Why don't you walk down ahead," she says, "and get us a table. You could always order me a fruit shake." Jay nods, relieved to get going.

"Lots of pineapple please!" Kerese calls after him.

"Alright."

Passing the dive shop, he wonders if he should pop his head in. They haven't seen Kelly and Tom since the bungalow party. And at least they might know something about the shaking this morning.

Kelly's rinsing down a pile of regulators outside in a big trough. She peers behind him as though looking for someone else. Kerese, he supposes.

"Hey," she says. "Any regrets?"

"Every minute," he answers, with a smile. "But I guess I'll have to live with it."

"Guess so."

"What the hell happened this morning?"

"No idea. We thought it must have been an earthquake. Tectonic plates having a party."

"Should I be worried?"

"No idea. Probably not. Why worry about something you can't do anything about?"

Jay nods. This isn't his philosophy but he admires her for hers.

Kelly dumps the regulators in another trough as Tom comes round the corner with a pile of wetsuits.

"Jay my friend," he says, "you kids coming out with us this morning?"

Jay watches Tom drop the wetsuits on the concrete. There's something a little slimy about Tom, but he seems friendly enough.

"Where you going?" Jay asks.

"Kayaking round the peninsula. We've got a spare canoe, you can take the other one," he says, then pours some fresh water into the trough Kelly has emptied. He leans back stretching.

"It's another shit day in paradise."

Jay laughs.

"Sounds cool," he says. "I'll chat to Kerese."

"Well, we're off at nine. Meet us on the pier where the boats leave for Monkey Beach if you want to join us. We won't wait though if you're late. Time to get wet, hey Babe?"

"Sure," says Kelly, pulling out a Roxy wetsuit, and stretching it out in a patch of sunlight.

08h45

They found the Blue Banana themselves yesterday. Jay and Kerese's first discovery without Nina's intervention – their first mark on Thailand. Hanging all round the edge of the open-sided building, between the pillars, are the hammocks they lay in on Christmas day after their stop at Koh Phi Phi Leh. The owner, a British man with a stringy grey ponytail and a strong Durham twinge to his words, is here again.

"Mornin'," he says to Jay, offering his an empty table. "Breakfast?"

"Please," says Jay.

He asks for the fruit shakes and two orders of pancakes.

Yesterday, they watched the owner walking down one of the Tonsai footpaths. Six Thai girls, the youngest of whom was probably about fifteen, surrounded him coquettishly in all his bald-fringed, potbellied glory.

In the morning light, he looks even older, and his antics of the night before seem all the more sordid. Jay would like to talk to Nina about this inappropriate sex-fetish, but he knows she will laugh at him.

"You're such a prude, Jay," she would say. "Were any of those girls chained to him?"

But Jay, who has seen choice ripped from people by the Big C, knows this is a relative thing. People forced by necessity to make decisions often do.

"Jay!"

He hears his name being called behind him. Steve and Laura take the table next to them with another couple. Finn is sitting in the sand a short distance away, his body encased in a neon green and yellow body suit to protect him from the sun.

"Hey," he says, "you found each other."

He gestures to the new arrivals.

"Susan and Pete," Steve says, "fresh from Chiang Mai."

"Hi," Jay says, "didn't I see you guys climbing yesterday afternoon?"

"Trying to climb," Susan laughs. "We're not very experienced."

"Speak for yourself," says Pete, "I was a demon out there."

"Which explains the huge gash on your knee," she says, kissing him on the cheek.

"Choice place," says Pete. "What's good here?"

Jay sees Kerese ducking past a hammock and gestures her over. He introduces her.

Despite having met, they don't push the tables together. Jay can be edgy around strangers and often prefers just to *be*. No small talk. No camaraderie. He's just not always very good at it. But he does like to kayak, and the offer is far too tempting to turn down.

"So Tom said we should join him at nine," Jay explains, his face lighting up.

"No," says Kerese.

She declines with such finality that Jay is taken aback.

"What do you mean no?" he asks.

"I don't like Tom," Kerese says, "he's an uncouth lager lout. He creeps me out."

"You seemed fine with him the other day."

"Well, I was stoned and drunk, and now I'm sober as a judge."

Her voice is brittle, verging on meltdown. Jay looks at her, as her eyes well.

"Did something happen while I was outside?" he asks.

"Nothing I want to remember," she says. "It's fine, Jay. But please can we kayak on our own? Just the two of us?"

It's such a reversal of roles that Jay almost wants to laugh. Usually it's Kerese who is coaxing, cajoling. But he understands what it's like having to do something you don't want.

"That's fine," he says, "if that's what you'd prefer."

Kerese smiles, then sips her fruit shake.

"Did you notice the bay?" she asks thoughtfully. "The tide's going out much faster than it did yesterday."

She's right.

There's an old couple walking right into the bay, inspecting the rock pools, a stray dog dancing around their legs. A jogger bends to pick up a shell, stopping momentarily as he looks out to sea.

Finn toddles over to his parents' table.

"Fishies," he says. "Fishies flopping."

Jay raises an eyebrow.

"You can't explain nature sometimes, can you?" he comments.

They watch Laura walk after her son, then returns with him. Finn is holding an angelfish, cradling it in his arms.

"Finn catch fishy. Yes. Catch. Clever Finn."

The little boy tries to clap for himself, and ends up dropping the fish on Susan, who shrieks.

"Oopsy," says Finn, making the table laugh.

Jay slurps the last of his fruit shake.

"Jay!" says Kerese.

"Sorry. Well, if it's not kayaking now, where to next?"

"I need to email my mother," Kerese said. "A quick dip, then let's dash into Tonsai before all the terminals are taken."

09h00

"Well, I guess the newbies are chickening out," Tom says, as he pulls the second kayak under a palm tree.

"Seems so," says Kelly. "Bit surprised actually."

"Maybe Kerese is keeping Jay busy?" muses Tom.

He gestures to a local fisherman, then forms his fingers into a 'v' pointing at his eyes, the man's, then the kayak.

"You watch, I pay you when I get back."

The man nods.

"No-one will take it," says Kelly.

"Well, they definitely won't now," says Tom.

He hands Kelly a life jacket.

"No thanks," Kelly says. "I'm catching some rays. That thing will ruin my tan."

"Suit yourself," says Tom, shrugging. "Whatever you want, Babe."

09h30

Steve and Pete get into the speedboat.

"You sure, Susan?" Pete asks.

"Yeah, I'll flag it. Laura and I will keep the deckchairs warm."

"Don't kill yourselves out there," Laura says, "you're taking us to Joe's for dinner tonight."

"Ye of little faith," said Steve, "I'm a champion skier. And I'm going to ignore that smirk."

He nods to the driver. "Be good for Mommy, Finn," he says.

Finn hugs Laura, his arms circling her neck.

"Daddy go boat," says Finn. "Bye-bye Daddy."

09h50

Jay looks at his watch. Kerese is still typing away, but he's bored with the long-distance chitchat.

"Are you almost done?" he asks.

"Not long now. Why don't I meet you at the pool?"

Jay emerges, blinking before he pulls his sunglasses from his neck. It's hot, and windless. He wonders where Tom and Kelly are now. Stopping a moment at a kiosk, he considers a red T-shirt, haggling lower until he loses interest. The saleslady runs after him.

"You buy," she says, agreeing to his price.

"OK," says Jay with a nod. "OK I will."

09h58

Jay looks out to sea. There's something strange going on, as though a weird force has pulled a giant plug out the bathtub of Tonsai Bay. Water sucks backwards, leaving muddy holes, and stranded fish gasp for air, their eyes bulging. Jay watches a fisherman squat as he gathers crabs from the pockmarked sand. He looks across to a Japanese man, gesticulating wildly, but doesn't understand him. It's only then that he looks out further, to see an impenetrable wall of water advancing towards the beach. It's mesmerising, almost hypnotic. Jay watches the dirty grey stretching from one side of the beach right across to the other. It's roaring, rumbling like engines powering up.

At first Jay is rooted next to the deck chair. The wave doesn't seem threatening. Not really. But the horizon is blue-black, blocked out. A mass of froth and angry foam toppling, moving. Then everyone is screaming. Running.

Go, go. Before it's too late.

Jay starts to move. The wave is about half a mile out to sea, but it'll be at least twenty feet by the time it reaches him. He has thirty seconds at most. But despite this, he's indecisive as he watches Laura running towards the beach, towards Finn, scooping him up as he kicks and screams. Laura falls, then pulls herself up, as Susan calls to her. Then it's a blur as the heavy liquid swirls towards them, scooping up loungers and beach chairs and umbrellas. Boats. And people. He tries to run. The water foaming at his ankles, black as an exploded sewerage system. Jay needs to reach higher ground, and grabs onto trees for support. He can hear them snapping like toothpicks behind him. Someone screams, her cries piercing his eardrums. Then a frenzy of name calling and desperation. *Annabelle? Annabelle! Jason!* There's a queue of people down the footpath, pushing, shoving forward and Jay realises they're all going to be caught in it. And then everybody will drown in this inky blackness.

There's no escape but to climb. And he does. Surprised by his own agility, he shimmies up the trunk of a palm, leaning just enough to reach the window ledge of one of the apartment blocks. Already cabanas are crumbling into wood and tiles and lone pieces of furniture are drawn back to the sea. He can't stop to consider the people being sucked into the depths. It's too much to think about. He needs to escape. Kerese. He wonders where she is now. Glancing down, he looks into the crowd of terrified people hanging onto anything they can reach as the water washes through the footpath. There's a couple above him. Their faces ashen. The man leans down, offering Jay his hand, lifting him as though weightless to the searing metal. The first wave is washing back, a vortex of bodies and debris. Jay's leg throbs. He's cut it and he didn't even feel it happen. The blood pumps rhythmically onto the steel. For some reason, he's still carrying the red T-shirt. Ripping it, he binds the wound. Then looks at the couple across from him.

"Shit, shit, shit," the man repeats, his eyes glued to the scene below them.

Despite the torrents of water pulling back into the bay, the sky is as blue as the day they arrived. Jay's lost his flip-flops in the climb, and the roof is scorching his feet. He moves from one foot to the other, using the remains of the torn T-shirt to stand on. Jay's French is rudimentary, but he realises the girl is having difficulties. Her arms rotate in a panic. She shifts, watching the other people scattered on roofs in the distance.

"English?" the man asks.

Jay nods, noticing his accent change. Canadian? Actually Jay has no idea.

"Can you look away please," he says, pointing away from where his girlfriend is standing.

Jay does. He can hear the sound of a zip, then the flow of liquid against the corrugated iron. It tinkles. Stops. Continues. Stops.

Jay tries to focus on the chaos below them. A mattress has caught between two trees, and is protecting a white-haired man from being buffeted by the retreating tide. He's holding on with one arm, unmoving. Jay can see the awkward slant of his broken arm, but he is too far away to do anything about it.

The man calls to him again, gesturing for him to lie down. They need to disperse their body weight before the next wave envelopes the village. He lies. The iron is hot against his skin, his legs. The sun burns down. Hotter. Jay feels as though he is being cooked alive.

09h58

"Glad we chose to ski," says Steve shouting up from the water, "there isn't even a breath of wind."

"Maybe it'll pick up later," answers Pete. "You almost ready?"

"You no ski now," the boat pilot comments, a deep furrow appearing between his eyes.

He's right. In seconds, the water in the bay is draining away, and Steve can feel the ski hook into the sand.

"Get back in, bugger," says Pete.

Steve tugs at his skis. He's hoisting himself back into the boat when he notices two kayakers struggling with the current, being sucked out to sea as though magnetised. Then all of a sudden, they're riding a wave at breakneck speed.

"Check those nutters out," says Steve.

They stand up in the boat, seeing the canoe career forward, then they watch as the water builds closer to the shore, growing into a huge wave that throws the kayak into the air. Although their own boat is facing towards the shore, they feel the water rumbling beneath them as it spins the boat the other way, dragging it in the direction of where the kayak toppled.

"Fuck," says Pete, his eyes widening.

Without any warning at all a wall of water has built behind them at the beach. It's at least ten metres high, stretching the entire length of the bay.

Their driver reacts quickly, putting the boat into full throttle.

"We need to get out to sea," Steve shouts, but the engine whines unsuccessfully against the drag.

"Fuck it," says Pete, "let's get the hell out..."

Suctioned into the bottom of the wave, his voice is drowned as they choke and gasp for oxygen. Steve tries to protect his head with his hands, bringing his limbs close to his chest. If he gets hit by something, it's all over. But he surfaces and gasps a lungful of air, before being yanked back under again. He knows not to fight the current, but panic almost overrides good sense. *Float. Relax.* Bobbing back to the surface, he recognises the approach of another monster wave. He follows Pete, who dives straight into it, ducking down as low as possible so as not be picked up and thrown about. Thank God they're far from the coral garden or they'd be ripped to shreds. Up again. He's taken in water, and feels his body heave as he vomits. Steve tries to float, but already feels weak. He can't see their driver, but Pete is a few metres away. He's holding onto something, one of the waterskis. It's buoyant, but only partially so. Then Steve sees one of the life jackets. He's exhausted, but knows this is as good a chance as he is going to get. He lunges for it. Paddling. Reaching. Grasping the wet jacket with the tips of his fingers. Closer. *Got it!* One arm in. The other. He clips himself in, feeling immediately safer.

He won't drown. Not now. He'll just bob here until someone comes to rescue them. The water isn't cold. And they promised they'd only be two hours. Laura will call someone. The thought of this calms him. He'll bob here. In the water. And wait for the rescue. He just needs to breathe. And wait.

09h59

They laugh at first on the wave. The speed of the kayak as they catapult towards the beach. Tom leans forward, encouraging. Pushing.

"There's something wrong," Kelly says.

"We're just catching a wave, babe. This is surfing Thai-style."

He's giddy with adrenaline. *You only live once.*

When the kayak lifts, he's almost too high on velocity to notice.

"Tom!" shouts Kelly.

They gather momentum. Tom's not even sure which way he's facing. The kayak thuds back down. Under the water, he ducks to avoid a falling oar. Tom focuses on holding his breath. He remembers the times he's removed his regulator to help a student with a damaged O-ring. Rising to the service, buddy-breathing. *No panicking.* He can't see Kelly. She's flung under the water somewhere here with him in this giant whirling washing machine. And they're right over a rocky outcrop. He crunches. She'd better be doing the same. He doubts it though. Kelly's always been crap in a crisis. But this time if she wants to live, she'd better pull herself together. Tom feels the water surging again. *No panicking, dude. That's the only way to get through this. Chill, kick back. And wait for this to be over.*

10h15

When the second wave hits, Jay is still up on the roof. He watches, helpless, as corrugated iron sheets roar through the narrow footpath below them, slicing and deadly. The screaming is unbearable. It seems to him that though some may have survived the first wave, they are defenseless against the drag of the ocean. The rushing water creates a fog denser than the mists of a cascading waterfall, and the smell enveloping them is fishy, salty, bloody. Below him, the man cushioned by the mattress is unconscious. If the water gets any higher, he will drown.

Jay doesn't want to look any more, but he finds he can't stop. People succumb one after the other. First their waists. Their chests. Then up to their necks. Jay can only imagine the horror of the dirty black water washing into their lungs. They will never survive it.

As the wave sluices out again, Jay wonders what to do. He needs to find Kerese, but the Internet café down the pathway is buried under the rubble. If she didn't leave even minutes before, he can't think how she could still be alive. And what if there's another wave? The French girl pukes loudly. She gags on her own vomit, leaving a sticky mess just near him.

They can't stay out here. It can't be more than ten o'clock, and it will only get hotter. Jay lifts himself up to slide to the edge of the roof. Looks down. There's a balcony just below them, and he could jump, or edge his way there. If the Canadian helps him …

"We need to get down," he says.

The man nods. His face has turned grey.

"I'll help you first," he says.

"Jay," Jay offers, as they grip each other for the second time.

"Liam," the man returns.

Jay dangles precariously. They move as slowly as they can, trying not upset the balance of the flimsy roof. It seems too high to drop straight down, so he hooks his toes into the side of the building, mustering all his rock-climbing strength. Some plaster showers down as he grips his way along the wall. There's a flimsy cane chair below him. He wonders if it will hold his weight, but he sees little alternative. Bracing himself, he lets himself fall. His feet land squarely on the chair, but it doesn't give in. Jay looks up. Liam is holding his girlfriend, her eyes widening as she realises she will have to follow him down.

"I'll catch you," says Jay, holding out his arms.

She hesitates. Her face is already raw and pink from the sun. Liam offers her his hand. She grips him tightly, too afraid to move. He coaxes her, and when she hurls herself onto Jay, she knocks him off balance. They tumble, landing solidly on the veranda.

"*Pardon*," the woman says, then giggles.

The nervous laughter triggers all of them, but the sound of their voices seems unnatural and completely inappropriate. In all of less than an hour, Jay has heard this stranger pee, seen her puke, and felt her breasts pressed against him. He doesn't even know her name.

"Pascale," she says, extending her hand to shake it.

"Jay," he says, taking her hand in his, but feeling strange for their politeness.

Liam is close to the edge. He's sturdier than Jay, and probably a great deal heavier. Jay has no intention of having his new companion landing on him too. He gestures for Liam to wait. Using the back of the chair, he crashes open the balcony door, then pulls a mattress outside for Liam. The man nods, jumping safely down. One level lower, they look over the balcony to the destruction wreaked by the waves.

"*C'est tout,*" Pascale says.

She's right. Between the trapped bodies and crumbling walls, the water is receding. Jay watches with sick horror as a pram floats towards the ocean, a trail of baseball caps and suitcases following behind.

This is the reality of it.

Jay walks into the hotel bedroom, overcome. Numb. Like Pascale, he feels slightly nauseous. He collapses on the bed, trying to pull himself together. The emotional overload has immobilised him. He hears the banging on the door to the corridor only distantly. Liam moves past him, pulling the door open.

"Do you guys know first aid?"

The man is carrying the limp body of a young woman. She's naked from the waist up and the wound in her abdomen is deep and wide enough to fit a fist.

Jay stands up.

"I'm a doctor," he says, almost uncertainly.

"Thank God," the man blurts. "Save her Doc, please. You've got to help me stop this blood."

Chapter 5

May 5, 2004 – Wednesday

For once in her stupid life, Ruby's finally given me somethin' I can actually use. A journal with a pretty cover, and a pen and everythin'. Because Lordamighty I need *something* to keep me occupied in this FUCKIN' hospital. So it's true then. Cuss words do actually look dirtier on the page. And I'm not making excuses for myself. I have a *lot* to be cussing about.

Broken femur. Broken tibia.

Broken, aching heart.

Anton. You bastard. You unforgivable bastard. I'm stuck here in this institution and I wasn't even awake to go to your funeral. Full military honors. So damn what? I am so angry at you. You weren't supposed to die; you promised me. You did. 'I'm going to come back to you.' That's what you always said. But not this time…

I can just see everyone's faces. Shame, shame, poor her. A widow at twenty-three. That's just no way to be. They'll whisper amongst themselves. That's her. Poor dear. Poor darlin'. Bring me meatloaf and pumpkin pie and try to feed my feelings away.

Forget that.

I can't believe you Anton. I can't believe them. Ruby even cried here for me. Not the tears we used to laughed about, though. Those crocodile tears, when yet another boyfriend left her. These ones looked almost realistic. So she does love me. Just a bit. And I think she kinda loved you too. Taken a long time to get to that point. And you're not even here to see it. You'd never believe me if I told you. Well, I'm tellin' you now. That'll give you something to laugh about. Wherever you are.

And so where am I? The bell rings constantly. Nurses skittering like mice through the white corridors. And nobody quite looking me in the eye. They're wondering how much I know. How much I remember. Crazy thing is, I remember everything, that's for certain. The helicopter spinning around and around, and all of us terrified. But now you're gone, I'm just a half-person lying in this ward. The sheets are stiff and impersonal, not like the linen on our bed at home. The flower pictures shoved in old-fashioned frames, lopsided on the slightly yellowed walls. Of course I *know* you're dead. I'm not blind. I can see it in their shifty looks. I'm not deaf either. I can hear the mutterings in the corridors. And Ruby's voice carries. You know how she is.

—I just want you to keep this under wraps. She's not strong enough yet to deal with it.

Of course, the moment your mama stepped in, I knew it was true. Her eyes red and swollen as strawberries. For the first time I've ever seen, her carriage slumped. She brought me flowers. A magazine I'd never read. And she tried to talk to me. She took my hand in hers, patted me. So she's also got a heart.

—There, there, Sugah, we're all goin' to have to get through this.

She wore one of those dumbass pink suits again. Pink from head to toe, like cotton candy. Pearls at her ears. Her neck. And I remembered her disapproval the first time we met. I was wearing tight jeans and a black leather jacket with tassels. I thought she'd just faint. Every time she put her fork in her dainty little mouth, she would look at me. A freak dropping in to destroy her prim-and-proper life. Her thoughts were so obvious as though projected onto the walls in giant letters. *What's happened to you, Anton? And where is that nice young Lillian from church you used to step out with?*

I'm lying here doing a lot of remembering. The first time I saw you. You were gorgeous; you know what they say about a man in uniform. But it was more than that, really. And I'm not easily taken in. I wasn't even supposed to be back-up that night. Ruby dragged me in. To sing in the background while she strutted up and down the stage in sequined hat and trousers too tight for someone half her age. The rest of you were knocking back shooters and catcallin'. You were the only one who looked a little serious. But you were different, even then. You looked straight at me, and I felt like I was being seen for the first time.

And who is going to see me now?

Your mama warbled on. Trying to fill the space between us. She was as uncomfortable as I was, that much was obvious. But she was doing what was right. What was *appropriate*. But even as she perched there on my bed like a sparrow about to take off, I had this feeling she was saying goodbye. Final signoff. Over and out. So she talked and she talked. And I was so tired. I wanted her to go so it could all be over and done with.

It was only when she was leaving the room that she came out with it. Her real reason for coming.

—Did Anton ever tell you about his brother Benjamin? He's not dead you know, despite what everybody says.

But that's just it, Ant. That's all she said. And I'm lying here wondering how on earth you could keep a secret like that from me. Ben, the shadow from your past. Unless you didn't know what she's suggesting you did. Or something so terrible happened, that your respectable Southern family had to close ranks. To protect someone. You? Ben? Was Ben in trouble? Did you fight? You hardly ever mentioned him to me. And paging through albums, you glossed past the photos with the two of you in cowboy boots and toy pistols. Sharing a bath. Standing on the lawn, his head marginally above yours. Now that I recall, you moved those pages quicker than the others. Were you wary, or just sad like I used to think?

I know now I need to get out of this bed. She asked me if I wanted anything from our apartment. That is, your mama did before she left for good. Or was that just a ruse to get in there and find out for herself just how much I know? The point is, I don't know anything. And I just can't believe you didn't tell me. I told her Ruby had the keys. And Ruby was treating me just fine. But thank you, Ma'am. It was very kind of you to come by. That was the last of her. Your mother. No chicken pot pie for when I finally get home. Now *that* I can almost guarantee.

June 8, 2004 – Tuesday

So I got out today. Ruby fetched me in Jimmy's pickup. She told me he was asleep on the couch, his shoes kicked off with the football game on. He stank of beer and a late night and God help her if she hasn't found herself another loser to take up more than his fair share of space on this good earth. She rambled like she usually does. Then her eyes clouded over and she slipped into her love-is-blind daze. She told me how he first saw her outside Milly's on the corner of Market and King, under an umbrella. Bought her coffee—not the newfangled Italian stuff—and a huge slice of chocolate fudge cherry cake. And they waited for the rain to stop.

It's a pity she doesn't remember even the slightest bit about my father. Or so she claims. I've always suspected she knows a lot more about him that she has ever admitted to.

And what about you, Ant, what did you know about Ben?

Thinking that I can never ask you what I need to ask, I've tried not to cry, but I'm just no damn good at that. I've cried every day, and my tears don't seem to dry up. Susannah an'nem came to see me yesterday. They dropped off a copy of Elisabeth Kübler-Ross's *On Death and Dying*. I don't trust a word of it. You'd better believe it, I'm angry. Anyone would be. But bargaining? There's nothing to bargain about. You're gone. I'm all alone and nothing'll make me feel better about it.

Ruby wanted to take me home to stay with her.

—Yeah Ruby, I've really got a mind to spend my first day out with Jimmy and his dog breath.

And she told me rightly there was no need to be so rude. Jimmy, he'd had a night of it, and that was all.

So we went to our apartment. I'm telling you I was that scared. The grass was as high as cotton, tangled with weeds. The magnolia tree smelling sweet and light. It was hotter than two Julys in August. Springtime playing summer. And my leg was wet with sweat—all bandaged up. My hands were blistered up from the crutches like I'd been working the fields. I wrapped them with padding in the hospital, but it just didn't seem to help.

Ruby went inside first. I made her. She chatted to me, but even I could tell how nervous she was. Bringing your daughter back to a shattered home can't be anybody's idea of fun.

It was exactly as we left it. Except for the coffee cups on the wooden counter next to the sink. Someone—Ruby I suppose—had cleaned these, stacking them on the rack to dry. The sugar you spilled as we were on our way out. Well, that was gone too. So maybe it wasn't exactly the same.

A lot can happen in three weeks. You can learn the basics of a new language. You can fall pregnant and not yet know about it. You can become a widow and miss your husband's funeral.

I choked back my tears. Ruby stood back once we were inside. So unlike her. Perhaps time is even softening my unmotherly mother. I hobbled up the stairs. Ruby tried to help, but I backed away from her. Not wanting to be touched. Past the photo gallery you and I'd spent hours piecing together. Remember how impatient I was? And you wanted every frame lined up, perfect. We compromised. I went out to get pizza. And when I came back with that pepperoni feast you were grinnin'. So proud. And we ate our dinner on the stairs under the black and whites, blinking like stars. Even thinking about it makes me smile.

I almost lost my balance two stairs from the top. Ruby stood behind, waiting to catch me if I fell. You would have done that for me, Ant, and now you can't.

I didn't want to be watched when I went into our bedroom.

—Please, Ruby, can you let me go this part alone?

She nodded, retreated down to the kitchen to feed Mishka. I could hear her mewing, imagined her rubbing her long, white fur against Ruby until she sneezed. She hates that darn cat.

I walked into our room. Your shoes were still next the bed, exactly in line. Polished jet black. My slippers sticking out from where I'd half-shut the wardrobe door. Giant clawed feet that made me laugh. Once. Before I grew up. All your shirts lined up. Pressed and pristine. Your jackets neatly buttoned. Your trousers hanging in perfect rows. And then your fun clothes, your jeans, and T-shirts. That bomber jacket I bought you with fake fur round the collar. The one you never wore.

The bed was made. Uncreased on your side. Sloppy on mine. Novels towering like mini skyscrapers next to the window where I'd abandoned them. And I lowered myself onto where your body once curled around mine like a newly formed shell. And don't tell me I can't remember how it was. Your skin against mine, the way your hand would wander, exploring. Tentative. Hot lips. Hot sweat.

I lay there, uncovered, in the hot afternoon. My body arched around your pillow. It still smelt of you. What happens when you're all washed away and all that's left is me?

Ruby moved around the kitchen. Puttered in the lounge, the TV down low. And for once her presence reassured me. And yet I couldn't move. I lay there for hours, or minutes. The time didn't matter. I don't even know what I was thinking. Everythin' and nothin'.

And when she tapped on the door, I didn't hear her at first.

—You gotta eat somethin' honey.

I wasn't hungry. But I ate the Frogmore stew she'd reheated from the freezer. It filled our room with the scents of shrimp and sausage. Corn. And garlic. I spooned the hot liquid into my mouth, tasting nothing.

—You don't have to stay, Ruby.

Actually, now that she was here in the room with me I desperately wanted to be alone. To trace my hand against your rain jacket. Sit immobile in front of the TV. I wanted to climb in the bath and drink red wine and drown in my sadness. But she filled your space with chitchat and suggestions.

—And we could visit that plantation you used to like. Take a picnic.

A picnic—Ruby? If I hadn't felt so very awful I would have laughed. And then, the subtle glance at her watch gave me all the ammunition I needed.

—Go home, Rubes. I need to be by myself.
—Honey, I can stay all night if you want me to.

God help me.

She let herself out. When the door clicked behind her, she trotted down the path, raising her hand to wave, where I stood at the window. I was alone. Completely alone. But I needed to wallow in it. This unbearable misery. It was only when I was finally drifting off to sleep that I thought about Ben, and how you never ever spoke to me about why your family left Atlanta so suddenly.

Chapter 6

June 17, 2004 – Thursday

When her maid led me to where your mama was sitting in the manicured garden out back, she pretended to be surprised to see me.

—Well, hello Sugah. And how are you getting along?

It's not as if, since her visit six weeks ago, she'd even been in touch. Why would she be? In the two years you and I were married, we only spoke once on the telephone. When you were awarded that medal, you know the one I mean, and I could tell her for the first time that your career prospects were safely intact.

I hadn't yet managed to totally ruin them for you. Even if I wasn't from a military family praising the army like an unholy idol. Sorry, Ant, this is the first time I can actually say what I feel about the whole sorry institution, and I know it meant everything to you. Maybe more than I did, but that's just more of my self-pity speaking. Since you left me, I don't really know any more what direction I'm going in. It's all so confusing. You were my compass. My routine. And I don't mean that in a bad way, but then if you were alive, you would know that. I never did have to explain anything to you.

But when it came to Eleanor, I didn't know what to say to her.
She put her arms around me, her perfume wafted around me,
sweet and cloying.

—Come inside, dear. William is out. He will be so sad to have
missed you.

I doubted that.

—Maya! Maya! Where have you disappeared to?

Your mama's voice echoed in the hollow hallway, bouncing on
the once terribly fashionable faux marble. I could hear Maya's
feet on the wooden staircase as she made her way to the
mistress's voice.

—Yes'm?
—Run along for me, and get us a pot of tea. Ceylon. Unless
you want iced tea, Sugah? No? And, Maya, bring us some of
those pecan cookies you baked yesterday.

Maya looked at me, a sympathy-smile locking us. She was
always good to us, remember? Letting us sneak past her room,
and leaving the back door unlocked so we could slip out again
so you could walk me home. Covered in you, inside and out.

—Hello Maya, I said.
—Hiya, girl. You takin' good care of yourself now?

I nodded.

—I'm tryin'.

Eleanor led me into the formal living room. I'd dressed for the occasion. You would have been so proud. I'd put on a summer dress (no cleavage or shoulders exposed) and the presentable pair of dress shoes that you made me buy for Sally-Anne's weddin'. My, doesn't that seem a long time ago?

And it had been so long since we were last in her house that it felt as though I was seeing it for the first time.

The teal silk curtains were tied back. Great big swathes of material, looped and twisted and framing the windows overlooking the Charleston Harbour. I always thought the view would have spoken for itself, especially when it's a clear day and you can see Fort Sumter. But your mama always liked to impose herself on her environment. All the couches—Eleanor would have called them settees—were draped in luxurious materials from India. I always wondered what the furniture underneath looks like. Did you ever see it? They've collected a few books since we last visited. The only empty shelf, the one on the top left, is filled now. But the contents look just as tired and dusty as the rest of the books. Mine may not be in the best condition, but at least I read them.

Eleanor switched on the lamp in the corner. The red shade danced pink light onto the parquet floors.

—Sit … Please.

The second word came as an afterthought. Your mama gestured to the armchair opposite where she always sits. It's shorter than her chair, and so even though I'm so much taller than she is, she towered over me. I shifted.

—So, Sugah, how are you?
—I miss him.

I told her this honestly. I miss you every day, every moment. It's been the longest six weeks of my life and I still haven't had the heart to go through your things. I walk around them, pretending the toothbrush next to mine is actually being used.

—Why, of *course* you do.

Eleanor nodded. Perhaps this was one of the few times we actually understood each other. But I don't think her longing can be more acute than mine. We didn't see her much, did we, Ant? Not after the drama she made at our wedding. It makes me cringe just thinking about it. I glanced towards the portrait of your great-grandfather, and remembered his reputation for emotionless interactions. I wondered what he would have said if he'd been sitting in there with us. I locked eyes with him, his gaze penetratin' but devoid of any sympathy.

Maya walked in the room. She was carrying the tea tray, beautifully laid out. There was even a rose plucked from the garden and displayed in a short vase. The silver teapot was cloaked in a cosy resembling a miniature Charleston house. Silver teaspoons, floral-dabbed plates. The cookies thick as slices of bread.

—Thank you, Maya.

I murmured this. Eleanor said nothing. I've always thought that she would prefer it if Maya were completely invisible. Leaning forward, she poured the tea with the genteel courtesy she reserved for guests. That's always what I was, wasn't I? An unwelcome one at that. I could hear the sound of classical music coming from the library. Chopin. Tchaikovsky. Who knows? I never could tell the difference.

Your mama handed me the teacup, gesturing for me to help myself to the biscuits. I was too nervous to eat, but I took one anyway. She sat back, her ankles neatly crossed. She spoke without any further preamble.

—To understand Ben, she said, you have to understand Anton.

I thought this was a remarkably stupid thing to say. Of course I understood you. I married you, didn't I? But I kept my mouth shut. It just wasn't the time to argue, or interrupt for that matter.

So she continued:

—Anton was the perfect child. He could count to twenty by the age of two, recognize the alphabet and read by the age of three. Nothing complicated, of course. We knew he was a bright child from the start. He was everything his older brother was not. He slept through the night from nine weeks. Ben still woke me all through the night when he was four. Anton was comfortable with everybody. He was an attractive little boy, and people responded to him. He expected people to like him and so they did. His smile was so open. It lit up his whole face right into his eyes. And that never changed. He wasn't afraid. Not of anything. And unlike many people, he adored Ben. Ben was his older brother, he could do no wrong. Which, as their mother, I knew wasn't in the least bit true.

—Ben must be the only child I have ever known who had to be removed from his first kindergarten. He was vindictive. Angry. He couldn't concentrate, or focus on anything for longer than a few minutes. When one of the boys at the kindergarten refused to let him use a puzzle, he locked him in the toilets, having bitten him first until he bled. I saw the teeth marks along the

69

child's arm. His skin was raw. It was horrifying. I couldn't understand where the anger came from. William had no patience for the tantrums. His only response was to send Ben to his room. He told him to come out again, when and only when he was able to behave. Ben wouldn't come out. Eventually, hours later, I would pull him out. Usually he would have occupied himself with something that would only rile William even more. Once he drew over all the walls in his room with felt-tip pen. Another time, he hacked at his sheets with a pair of scissors—I didn't know where he got them from. I loved him regardless.

Eleanor looked at me, as though challenging me to defy this. I said nothin'. She went on.

—The only person who evoked a positive response in Ben was Anton. Anton mimicked Ben. But it was also as though their natural roles had been reversed, transforming Ben from the older son to the younger one. Once, Anton got into a fight at school. He'd seen Ben being teased during recess. The usual things ... Ben was a terrible student. Nowadays I suppose he would have been diagnosed with attention-deficit disorder, then he was just 'dumber than a box full of owl poop'. I can remember some of the insults even now. Kids can be mean. And Ben had a harder time of it than most. But Anton wouldn't stand for it. He came home with a split lip and a black eye. And William gave him the belting of his life. But it didn't stop him. He loved Ben. And Ben loved him. They were inseparable. If I think about it, Anton was the only real friend that Ben had.

I wondered how you could have told me so little about Ben if what your mama said was true. In all the time we knew each other, you might have mentioned Ben twice and only in passing. I never wondered about it before, but now that Eleanor had started speaking, I felt as though something of you had been missing the whole time we were married. Did this explain the empty silences when you told me you were 'resting'? Or the times when you disappeared into the study, seemingly transfixed in front of the computer, when the screen was completely blank?

Eleanor's pallor changed. Her face took on a more crimson sheen, and she leant forward as though to make the story go faster. To speed things up.

—Anton was an exceptional student. William favored him, almost from the start. It was difficult not to. Sometimes I even had to check myself, make sure I was giving Ben the attention and love he needed. After class, I sat with him, trying to help him with his studies. So that even if he wasn't the top student, he might just scrape through. He failed one year. It broke his heart. And mine. William was incensed. Humiliated, as though Ben was doing this just to embarrass him. Ben told me he wasn't going to go back. But his father sorted that out with the strap. No more conversation. He went back.

—I'm not sure when the gambling started. Funny enough, the only thing Ben seemed to be good at was cards. It was the only game when he was able to concentrate long enough to finish up. At the beginning, I let him win. So did Anton. We never talked about it, but we both knew it was something that Ben needed. To be good at something. But then I realized that after a time, he was winning all on his own. We used to bet with matches. Poker. It isn't a ladies' game, I know, but he liked it and I didn't have much else to do with him. His face would flush with pleasure. A trace of a smile emerging as he pulled his winnings towards him. He'd grown tall by then. Taller than

William even. By eighteen, he was a man, physically. But such a little boy inside. Always trying to prove his worth, and never succeeding.

—William ignored him. Mostly. He addressed Anton, calling him into his workshop or getting him to help service the hunting rifles. The pistols. So he hardly noticed Ben's absences. If I'm honest, his disappearances for most of the day relieved us. The house was lighter. Happier. And when Ben came home, he seemed content. Well, more so than he had ever been.

—Anton was doing exceptionally well. Captain of the football team. Excelling academically. He was aiming for West Point. Just like his father. He'd already completed the PreCandidate Questionnaire, and Senator Allen had agreed to nominate him. And there was little chance he wouldn't be accepted. Family connections and brilliant in his own right. His candidate file was open, and he was ready to sit the SATs. We were so proud of him. He had a lovely girlfriend, Peggy. She was beautiful, leggy, blonde. A cheerleader, and from the right side of town. She'd have made him the perfect wife.

Unlike me? I looked at Eleanor. You'd never mentioned Peggy and I wondered why she felt the need to. Hurting me now when you're gone is so pointless. But old habits die hard. Yet, your mama seemed so engrossed in her tale, I thought that for once, Peggy was just part of the detail and not just another way to upset me.

—Ben didn't have a girlfriend. But Peg was kind to him. Talked to him gently. She organized a double date for them once with one of her friends. I don't know what happened, but after that, she barely spoke to him again. Nothing beyond 'hello' or 'pass me the salt, please'. She couldn't look him in the eye. Mealtimes were excruciating. But she kept coming round, and she and Anton were as tight as ever. Stuck together Siamese twins. They were a beautiful couple. Everybody said so. Homecoming king and queen.

—Ben finished school, but only just. He was mixed with the wrong sort of crowd. Drinking. Smoking. I could smell it on him. Told him almost every day to clean himself up before his father got home or God help him, he would kill him. Ben came to church with us. But not willingly. He'd take the Lord Jesus' name in vain, mostly just to upset us.

—Then the trouble really started. Things started going missing from the house. An emerald ring I'd inherited from my grandma, some silver candlesticks. We sacked the help. Anna swore it wasn't her, but William said who else could it have been? I had my suspicions. Paid her a bit extra when William's back was turned. Told her to go quietly. She cried at the back door. Her grandbabies. Her grandbabies. I turned away. She'd been with us for fifteen years.

—Nothing changed. New help. More things missing. William took the boys hunting. Ben shot a deer. For once, he'd done something his father was happy with. We ate deer jerky. Pot roast. The men went into the woods a few more times. Peggy visited me, while they were out camping. We embroidered together. Passed the time. She was waiting to tell me something, I could tell. But she never did.

—The thieving stopped awhile. Ben had this job at the filling station. Was paying his own way. No girlfriends though that I knew of. Anton was keeping fit, practicing for the Candidate Fitness Assessment—basketball throw, running, pull-ups ... He was in perfect condition. It was the last hurdle in the application.

—Of course, he got in. Were we proud when the letter came! We celebrated at the Côte d'Or. The boys, Peggy and us. Anton and Peg were a bit shifty with each other. She must have been upset he was going to go away. The letter put a barrier between them. I think that was the beginning. Of the end of them, I mean. Peggy stopped coming around.

Thank the Lord, I thought, not sure I would stand much more of this passionate flame whose name I'd never heard mentioned before. *Why didn't you tell me, Ant?*

—It happened a few weeks before Anton was leaving. I don't know everything about it. Except what William told me. The boys went to him first. They were hysterical. Blood on both of them. William called me then. Urgent. He ordered the boys to strip in front of me. Sent me to wash off the clothes. 'Not the help, Eleanor, you! And not later. Now. NOW!'

—I took the clothes into my bathroom, where the servants wouldn't notice. Soaked the clothes. Scrubbed them. It took hours, or it felt like it. But I got them clean. The boys showered. One after the other. They were shivering. Terrified.

—William paced up and down the passage. I could hear his footsteps even from the kitchen. Shouting.

—They left the house. William said they'd be back. He was stiff as a rod. His eyes blazing. Ben and Anton wouldn't look at me. The Lincoln roared out the driveway. I heard another car. Thought it was Ben's old Ford. I didn't think then why they needed two cars, but I've wondered about it recently.

—And when the washing was done I couldn't eat anything.
But I kept aside the food the cook had made. Gone for hours
that night, they were sure to be hungry. But by midnight, they
weren't back. No phone calls, either. Not that a call would
have been as easy to make as it is now. I drank coffee. Tried to
read. Picked up my needlepoint and put it down. I wanted to
go out to look for them, but seeing as I had no idea where they
had gone, there didn't seem much point. And in the dark?

—I waited until a small sliver of moon had risen in the night
sky. No word, until after midnight when I heard the sound of
William's car in the drive. And sirens behind it.

—I brushed my hair. Lipstick. I don't know why I'm telling
you that, Sugah, but it just seemed important at the time. I
knew, just knew, that something awful had happened.

—William unlocked the door. He hollered for me before he'd
even stepped inside. The troopers behind him, with their hats at
their chests. And I looked behind him, wanting to see which of
my sons was going to come through that door. Hating myself
for hoping …

Eleanor didn't finish that sentence. The admission must have
been hard enough to start, never mind complete.

—Anton walked in alone. He was filthy, covered in something.
Ash or dirt. His face was streaked where the tears had soaked
through the grime. I walked to him, my arms outstretched and
he cried. I hadn't seen him cry, not in years. And there he was
against me, smelling of flames and heartache. I didn't need to
ask about Ben. It was clear enough from everybody's faces he
wasn't coming home.

—William made me sit down in the drawing room. The troopers stood to the side, respectful, silent. I can still see their expressions. Pitying me. Pitying us. And William told me what had happened. How Ben had set his car alight just near Oakland Cemetery, you know, in Grant Park?

I *didn't* know. I've never been to Atlanta and you never wanted to go back. Not ever.

—It was complicated. He'd gotten in with the wrong crowd. Stolen some of our valuables to place higher *and* higher bets, and pay off his debts. But he was completely hooked. On the gambling. Sure, but also on the adrenaline of high stakes. Well, that is my belief. And not just on cards, either. He was deep in it. The horses. Indebted to some bookie who called in his goons. Anton heard what had happened. Got all protective. Went with Ben to sort things out. That was earlier in the afternoon. They were in a terrible fight. Knocked this individual unconscious. Thought they'd killed him. That's when they came to fetch William. Turns out when they arrived there, the man was gone. They spent the whole day looking for him. William was going to pay him off, sort things out. That is, until he found out how much Ben actually owed. He would have wiped us out completely. All our savings. We'd have been left with nothing. *Nothing.*

—And William, who never showed much emotion, hit Ben. He punched him, knocking him down. Anton tried to pull them away. William released him. Eventually. Anton told me *that*, not William. Because, of course, I would blame him for what happened next. By then, Ben was bruised but it didn't solve anything, not the debts, not the danger to the family. He was stupid, stupid.

—Neither William, nor Anton, expected it. Ben grabbed the keys for the Lincoln, tossing them into the shrubs, then darted for his car. The next time they saw his Ford, he was in it, burnt beyond recognition. They found him first. Then the troopers arrived. Someone called about the smoke. But by the time everyone got there, it was too late; they couldn't get Ben out. And what a terrible way it must have been to die ...

I looked at your mama, seeing her softness for the first time. Her eyes were swollen, and I found myself crying too, for you. For the day that everything changed. But then she continued.

—It was all an utter lie. Fabrication. I didn't know it then. I didn't know it when we packed our bags and headed out of Atlanta back to Charleston. I lost my first-born son that June, and I didn't get how I was going to deal with it. The funeral was unspeakable. William stiff-lipped and rigid. Anton inconsolable. Ben didn't have many friends, but we did and they were there in droves. It was overwhelming in an undeniably awful way. I needed to be alone. You'll understand how *that* feels. Wallowing in grief is something you need to do by yourself.

I nodded. But she hadn't answered why she knew Ben was still alive. And that was why I was there, wasn't it? I waited for her to go on.

—After Anton's—and your—helicopter crash, said Eleanor, I needed to remember my children. My boys. Twelve years and I still mourned Ben, but the pain of two deaths, well, that just can't be described. I found the boxes of photographs I'd never had the heart to look at again. There were just so many of them, and what I'd put in the albums had been enough. Before. But this time, I needed to soak in everything. Remember. I spent hours going through the boxes.

—I wouldn't have noticed the postcard, except that it was an image of Saint Christopher. I'd never seen it before. Well, I didn't remember it, anyway. I'll show it to you.

Standing up, she moved to the cabinet near the door. She opened it, digging into a shoebox on the top shelf. Having looked at it so recently, I would have thought she'd have found it easily, but she moved things around. Shuffled the contents like a deck of cards. Like Ben might have. Once. And just as she extracted it and began to walk back to where I sat, we both heard the front door bang open. Without the slightest hesitation, Eleanor increased her pace, then slipped the card down the side pocket of my purse. She sat back down, straightened her pencil skirt, then picked up the teapot.

—More tea?
—Yes, please.

We heard him before he even stepped into the drawing room. I'd always found William, Bill, a little intimidating. His silver hair and dark skin like thick leather. His thick ox-like neck. The way he barked orders, and expected his house to run like a military operation. I dreaded serving him a meal, or arriving a minute late. The aftershock just wasn't worth it. I looked at your mama, and for the first time ever, a look of complicity passed between us. He walked in.

—William, darlin'. Guess who's come to visit?

Eleanor stood up, calling for Maya to bring some fresh tea. It was obvious Bill had no idea what to say to me, but I think it was more because of you bein' gone than because of our relationship. We hadn't gotten on too badly, your pa and I, despite his gruffness. Nonetheless, his eyebrow raised quizzically at your mama did not escape me. He walked over to me to hug me, making the physical exchange as brief as possible. All that touchy-feely stuff wasn't ever Bill's speciality. Good thing he had two boys.

Had?

Bill stepped away from me, walking to the scotch, to pour himself a finger, or three.

—You gettin' along alright?
—I'm trying to.
—Good, good.

Bill nodded, then turned to Eleanor.

—You remembered the cocktail party this evenin'?
—Of course.
—I have to eat somethin' before we go, honey. I'm hungry enough to eat the south end of a north-bound skunk.
—William, *please.*
—She's *family*, Eleanor. Ain't washin' out my mouth for family.

I smiled.

Maya came in with a fresh pot.

—Tea, darlin'?

Eleanor stood up to pour.

—Nah. It's been hotter'n a goat's butt in a pepper patch. Can't drink tea. Maya, bring me some more of 'em cookies. And make me a sandwich. Fried chicken and mayo. And cut up some tomato on the side.

Maya nodded, taking our crumb-strewn plates with her. It was clear that Bill had settled in. There was nothing and everything left to be said between your mama and me. I leant over, picking up my purse from the coffee table.

—I best be going then. Thank you so much for the tea.

Bill stood up.

—I'll walk you out to your car, young lady.

Eleanor shifted.

—William, dear, why don't you relax? I'll show her out.
—I'm up, honey. It's no trouble at all.

He opened the front door, flinging it so hard it banged against the wall. I slipped into the driver's seat, placing my purse next to my feet. Bill leant his head in through the wound-down window.

—You take care of yourself, now. And if you need anything fixed, you call me, you hear? I'm no good at words, but I'm better with my hands.
—I know it. Goodbye Bill.

I smiled at your pa. I still had this feelin' I couldn't quite believe him but I wanted to give him the benefit of the doubt.

But as I drove off the frustration began to set in. We had unfinished business, Eleanor and I. And when I looked at the postcard she'd slipped in my purse, it raised a lot more questions than it even began to answer.

Chapter 7

June 21, 2004 - Monday

We met today in a busy bar right on the tourist route. I like it there. Since you've been gone, I've changed a lot of things. Our old haunts make me sad. I can't bear to go in them anymore and see the looks of pity. I didn't used to be a *widow*, and the title doesn't fit me well. I don't wear black. I wear cut-off jeans that somehow make my legs look shorter. Crop tops. Slip-on sandals from India with lots of sequins and beads. I've been painting my toenails different colors, and I am thinking of changing my hair. Your mama might even like what I've chosen.

Eleanor sat down. And for once she was the person who was out of place. Her baby blue twinset—how can she even wear something like that in this weather?—clung to her. Her hair, set that morning at the beauty shop in her usual rollers and lacquered down firmly, was unaffected by the wind. Your mama's eyes darted around the room, fixing on the jukebox, and the fishnets, with plastic fish and cheap-looking starfish. The crab pots and murals of mermaids. Until I saw the place through her eyes, I hadn't even noticed its dinginess. Perhaps I was being unkind to choose that spot. I hadn't meant to be. Being alone can teach you how strong you are, and what you long for. It also teaches compassion. Now that I don't have you to anchor me, I have to keep remindin' myself why I need to stay here in Charleston. That bar made me happy, but looking at your poor mama holding herself back from calling for a damp cloth changed the mood.

—Shall we go somewhere else, Eleanor?
—I'm sorry, Sugah, it's just been some time since I've been in a place like this. It's quite ... educational.
—Let's take a walk, I suggested.

Remember how you used to tell me about the walks with your mama? Pointing out the centerpieces of gardens close to the sidewalk, how she'd dart in when no one was looking and help herself to slips? No wonder her garden was a riot of blooms.

This time, we headed for the Battery, walking past a display of sweetgrass ornaments and baskets on Meeting Street. Catching my eye, the black woman handed me a leaflet on the history of the craft. We stepped past the rows of mansions, hammers colliding and electric saws shrieking. Signs up on windows announced upcoming renovations. Ruby was always a bit disparaging about Eleanor's protectiveness of Charleston's landscape, never to her face, or yours for that matter. The 'hysterical historicals', she called her and her group of cronies from the Preservation Society of Charleston. Harsh, but accurate.

It was always easy to walk and talk with you. Now my leg is a bit stiff, but at least I'm free of them crutches. Eleanor, however, seemed distant. I wanted to know about Ben. To know more about you. And Bill—why did your mama slip the card in my purse and change the subject when he came home? Did he even know about her suspicions?

—A storm's brewin', I told your mama.

She studied the sky.

—It'll be a relief, she said, after all this hot weather.
—I'm near 'bout ready for a bit of a cooler spell.

You know me. I never talk about the weather. I hardly notice
it. I'll go outside when it's pourin' cats and dogs and dance in
the rain. But I didn't want to force the issue. Eleanor was
biding her time and I just had to be patient. She spoke in her
own time.

—Bill, she said, wants me to let things alone. He tells me
there's no point. Ben is dead and buried, and if I insist on
believing my overactive imagination, he still may as well be.
—Then what about the postcard?
—A prank. 'Don't believe everything they say, Mama.' What
does that mean? I've no proof it was Ben who sent it anyway.
—Well, how did it get into the box?

Eleanor looked at me, her gaze penetrating.

—That's what I keep asking myself. If William thought it
wasn't it important, why didn't he throw it away?
—Anton? I asked.
—I don't know.

Your mama turned to me, grasping my hands in hers with a
ferociousness I'd never seen before. Her thumbs dug into my
palms.

—I need to know what Anton told you.

I looked her in the eye, thinking of you. Of your silences. Your untouchable melancholy on birthdays or the holidays.

—He didn't tell me anything about Ben. It wasn't a subject I was ever allowed to broach.
William tells me I'm just fanciful. Clinging at straws. But these days he won't meet my eye when I try to talk to him about it. I've been married to the man for near on forty years, and you think I can't tell that he's hiding something?

We were an unlikely pair, your mama and I. I wondered in the hospital why she mentioned Ben, but then studying her, I realized she couldn't speak to anyone else. What if we discovered something heinous, something horrible? She had to keep it close to her chest. And why did she think she could trust me? Because I loved you. Love you. And despite all her protestations about how unsuitable I really was as your wife, as a co-conspirator, well … And I *knew* you. Better than she ever did. For the first time, ever, your mama needed *me*. Perhaps she felt if she handled me well enough, I might actually tell her what I knew.

In some ways, I have to admit that I was offended. This is the first time she's ever reached out to me. She didn't after the miscarriage. She let that wash over as if didn't matter. And at least for her there weren't nothin' more to bind us together then. And now, it seems the situation has changed. Eleanor needed somethin', someone to cling to. Me.

—You think he's lyin'?

I ask this straight out. Straightforward. She looks at me, patting her hair. As if it could get mussed with all that spray and all in it.

—Lying is a strong word.
—Well, is he?

Eleanor doesn't hesitate this time.

—Yes, I think he is.

We stopped outside a beautiful Greek Revival style house—
and I only knew this definition from Eleanor. Columns and
pediments and imposing symmetry. Your mama was
perspiring, a triangle sheen across her nose and forehead.

—I need to sit, she said, and you must too.

So we found a bench, donated in memory of Cheryl-Lee
DuBose, died age 27. *Missed and loved*—like you.

I wondered what kind of games your mama was playing with
me. Don't get me wrong, Ant, she did seem different. Less
confident. Warmer. But I have to say I didn't quite trust her. It
just came out. Somehow I couldn't help it. It just blurted out.

—What d'ya need from me, Eleanor?

She started.

—How do you know I need anything, Sugah?

I looked away from her turquoise gaze. Even in my newfound
confidence, she was stronger, in charge. Like the time I tried to
cook dinner and I burnt the rice and she didn't need to say
anything to make me cry. But I made myself meet her stare.

—I'm not simple.

—No, Eleanor admitted. You're far from it. And it seems I may have underestimated you before.

It was the closest thing I would ever get to an apology. And I have to say, Ant, that I clung to it.

—Then let's get to the point, then, shall we? I said.

June 24, 2004 – Thursday

So I went to your grave today, Ant. I don't know how long I'm goin' to be gone. But it might be quite a while. I've rented out the apartment. Eleanor helped me. Friends of friends—army connections, you'd approve if you were here. And your mama's takin' Mishka. It's not as if Ruby would have her, is it now?

And I finally went through your things. I gave your hunting rifle to your pa. I don't need to keep that around. And your clothes made a precious pile outside the door of the Salvation Army charity shop. I drove up and dropped the boxes off; didn't even turn off the ignition. I didn't want to look at what I had done. Left you in boxes neatly packed but overflowin' outside in a hot wind.

And I'm peeling away the *secret* Anton. Bit by bit. And even though I'm reluctant to pull out your skeletons, I feel as though I can't help myself.

Why didn't you tell me about the postcards? Your mama's wasn't the only one, was it? And much as I have never really gotten on with Eleanor, I can't believe you and Bill could've been hiding something as big as this. What happened that day that you couldn't even tell your own mother?

Toronto. Calgary. Vancouver. Banff. Montreal. There they were, these postcards fanned out on our bed, arranged by the dates on the envelopes. Erratic. Years pass between them. Or months. Weeks. Looking at them, a moment flashed in my mind. You scooping up the mail, almost furtively slipping an envelope in your pocket. So this is where it went? And how did Ben know to send them here? If it actually was Ben? Your mama is convinced that it was.

Then she offered me the money to go—it's my money, she told me. And I get to choose what to do with it. It seemed to me anyway this wasn't about the money. It was about the answers. She wasn't going to leave Charleston. How could she? Your pa denied everything already, and wasn't about to let her go on some goose chase around the world searching for a son he assured her was long dead.

—You have a passport still, Sugah? Just in case?
—In my maiden name.
—That will be fine. It's still you.

And wouldn't she just have like to have kept it that way, but I guess it was too later to bother now. We talked then about where I should try first.

—You need to go back to Atlanta.

I looked at Eleanor. She was sitting in our apartment, a gin and tonic in her beautifully manicured hand. It wasn't like her to drink in the middle of the day, but then your mama wasn't quite the woman she used to be.

Her suggestion made sense. Start the search in the heart of the mystery.

—You'll need to speak to the men who found the car. Check the police records.
—If Ben is alive, Eleanor, then there was a reason he ran away. If we get the cops involved…

She tapped her nails against the glass.

—You're right, she told me. Then what do you suggest?

A vision flashed through my mind of meetin' the girl you would've married if you hadn't married me. I have to tell you, Ant, that my stomach churned at the thought of it. It wasn't that I was insecure—and even if I was it was a little late for that now. It just made me uncomfortable digging into the life you had never told me about. I wasn't so sure I wanted to know more about that other Anton since you'd obviously made so much effort to keep him away from me. But I said it anyways.

—I'll have to see Peggy.

Eleanor's face crumpled, her confusion evident.

—If something happened that night, I explained, who would have been Anton's most likely confidante?
—They weren't talking to each other by then, Eleanor reminded me.
—But why, Eleanor? I said. You told me they would have gotten married. So what really happened around that time to change that?

Chapter 8

26 December 2004. Sunday. 11h02.

Most of Jay's cancer patients died slowly. It was a gnawing, constant process, life draining away at an almost leisurely pace. He hadn't thought of it then, but now he does. Pascale sits outside on the balcony, stripping bandages from bedsheets. And she can't tear them fast enough. Not that there's all that much time for him to think. Thank God. Outside, in the passage, Liam topples a maid's cart. Jay hears the crash of bottles falling. Shampoo. Liquid soap. He's looking for bottles of alcohol from the minibar stocks.

Another man walks into the room; he's wearing nothing but a drenched swimming costume. It's ripped badly, and his legs and arms are a riot of bloody cuts. Under his left eye is a deep incision, sliced almost as though surgically. Jay recognises him, from another time and place.

"Hey," he says gruffly.

"I'm sorry," answers Jay, elbow deep in entrails and shattered bones. "I should remember your name, but I don't."

"Steve from the boat."

"You here to help?"

"Helicopters are landing on the beach, we need to carry the worst injured outta here. There're a few army blokes. Some stretchers on their way. But I thought if someone could help me, we could carry them on a door."

Liam walks into the room, his shirt held out like a basket filled with Johnny Walker, tequila, rum. He dumps them on the floor.

"There's more," he says.

"We need to get her out here first. Can you help Steve carry her?" says Jay.

"You look like hell," Liam comments. "Sure you're up to it?"

"I can't find my wife and son," Steve answers, as if that is an answer.

And in a strange kind of way it is.

"Pass me that sheet," Jay instructs, nodding at Liam, "we'll need to cover her. Protect her from the flies."

The people keep coming. Somebody from the hotel – a manager? – moves Jay to a bigger room.

"There's another wave coming at one o'clock," the man says. "We need to get the injured out, and everybody else needs to climb up the hill."

Jay grunts as he pours brandy over a Thai man's leg. The skin is sloughed off from the ankle to the knee. His girlfriend, wife, retches each time she looks at him.

Steve and Liam come in again with the door.

"Is he next?" Steve asks, then looks over at the woman. "Better get her out of here too before she chunders all over the floor."

"They won't take her out with him," Liam comments, "no room on the heli."

Jay sees Steve touch his face.

"She's in the way here, mate. The sooner she's out from under Jay's feet, the better. Let her follow us at least."

"Steve?" Jay says.

"Yeah?"

"I'll need to sew your face together when you get back."

Steve shrugs.

"Ta mate, but I think you've got bigger fish to fry. Let's not waste the sewing kits on this ugly mug."

When the next patient is carried in, Jay feels the bile rise in his throat. Last time he saw Rikke, she was walking away from the boat, her flippers in her left hand and her towel flung over her shoulder. Now her friend Margot is trying to hold Rikke's neck together; she's lost half her throat.

"Jesus," Jay says.

Margot doesn't seem to recognise him. Her eyes are glazed with shock, as though she is standing in front of a loaded gun that she knows is about to go off.

"We tried to climb up the stairs into the gym," she explains. "We got up the stairs, even managed to close the door behind us. When the water came in, it was like being in a blender."

"Pascale!" Jay yells, and she brings him some more strips of sheets.

"The water went right through, pushing against the windows until they exploded. We were lifted by the current. It moved so fast. I held my breath. God and I felt I was drowning. I *was* drowning."

"Are you hurt?" Jay asks as he tries to staunch the blood.

"I hit my head. We were being dragged through the room with the bloody Stairmaster, the bicycles, a shitload of glass. It was so friggin' dark I didn't know which way was up. I think I passed out for a few minutes. But I could hear Rikke screaming. She's going to die, isn't she? Is she going to die?"

"I don't know," says Jay, "but we need to get her to Krabi. They're moving people from there to Sarat Tani where the hospital is."

Margot sits next to the bed, holding Rikke's hand. Rikke groans. Jay can hear her muttering, but he doesn't understand her. He's patched her as much as he is able.

"Do you know her blood type?" he asks Margot.

"O positive."

"Well, let's be thankful for small mercies. Write it on her arm with this pen. Here, as big as you can. And also her name. In case you get separated. And keep those bandages tight against the wound, if you can."

Liam walks back to fetch Rikke. He's accompanied by some paramedics who seem to have been airlifted in from Krabi. Liam's face is the colour of beetroot. He's been up and down in the scorching sun with no sunscreen and even the back of his neck looks scalded.

"They're expecting another wave at two o'clock," Liam repeats a new variation on the rumours. "We need to move faster."

"What's it like out there?" Jay asks.

"You don't want to know. Steve and I have got some people to throw mattresses over the debris, to make a path to the choppers. I walked past where the swimming pool was. One of the cabanas has collapsed, and you can see someone trapped underneath it. There's just no way he could have survived it."

"Where's Steve?"

"Lost him outside somewhere. They're putting all the bodies together in the shade. You can't believe the smell. It's like some sick tropical morgue. There are kids in that pile. I'm telling you man, you don't want to know."

Liam walks to Pascale, taking her into his arms. He kisses her as though trying to prove to himself they're both still alive.

Jay wonders if his mobile phone is still working. With their room on the second floor, some of his stuff might still be okay. Maybe he can find Kerese if she's called him. And then there are his medical supplies. The little bag of tricks that no self-respecting doctor would travel without. If he could get to it …

"You think you guys could hold the fort? I need to get my medical bag from my room."

"Your room," Liam almost laughs, "you think it will still be standing?"

"It was on a slope higher up, and I don't think the meds we've got are good enough. At least I've got some decent antiseptic creams, antibiotics and sterile bandage kits. If another patient like Rikke comes through, they're stuffed."

"Nice," says Liam. "So what do we do with everybody while you're gone?"

"Plug their wounds, and try to get them out of here as soon as you can."

11h31

Jay does his best to wash the blood off. Ironically, the water in the hotel is disconnected, so he's forced to use a puddle downstairs and a towel he's extracted from one of the rooms. But despite this, his skin is streaked. He must look some sort of horror story. At first he doesn't know how to orientate himself.

A man passes him.

"You better get to safety, dude, then next wave's gonna hit at half past one."

Jay nods. He only realises now how terrified he actually is. And maybe this is just a fool's errand. Crossing the sandy isthmus the width of a few football fields at its narrowest point and only ten feet above water level is well and good – just as long as another wave doesn't come. If it does, he's history, washed away like the screaming mass he's witnessed from the roof.

95

He stands there. Hesitates. Then he notices as a boy of about sixteen rifles through some of the bags and suitcases that have been washed from some of the bungalows. He's holding some binoculars, a camera, and what seems to be a handful of passports.

"What the–" he mutters, his anger dominating his uncertainty.

Grabbing the boy by the scruff of the neck, he lifts him up, and shakes him hard.

"You little fucker," he says. "Give me those things."

The boy drops the camera. Jay watches it fall lens-first into the sand. The boy yells hard, kicking viciously out at Jay. With no real idea what to do with him now he's caught him, Jay grabs the documents and the equipment then lets the boy go. But now he's got them, what to do with them? He can't leave them here. He looks down, then notices a dive bag. It's already stashed with the boy's loot. Cash, and wallets. A few books. Passports and diving cameras. The odd piece of jewellery. Even a small laptop. It's soaked right through, and Jay tosses it aside. He'll take the bag with him, then try find someone in authority to give it to. If he doesn't that little bastard will come back and take it. It's clear he's spent enough time assembling it.

Jay flaps through the passports. God only knows where the boy found them. They're a hodgepodge of nationalities and couldn't have come from just one place. Jay's struck by a bout of nausea. It has never helped him to think of his patients as people when he's in surgery – although of course this is usually unavoidable. But now as he looks down on the official identities of people who may well be floating somewhere out there in the Andaman Sea, the reality of the disaster is sickening. He needs to get back to the hotel and quickly, but not without his medical supplies.

The pathways between the toppled bungalows are difficult, if not almost impossible, to navigate, especially with bare feet. He and Kerese weren't even away long enough for his soles to toughen up from his shoed, indoor existence. A few days of unforgettable paradise and this is what they are left with. They? He doesn't even know where Kerese is. Or if she's still alive.

Compared to the roar of the waves only hours before, what is left of Tonsai is eerie. Silent. Jay estimates that having only walked two hundred metres, he has already seen twenty dead bodies. Most of them are caught under rubble, their limbs just visible. The others have bled to death from their injuries. A little further, he can hear a man calling. All his clothes have been ripped completely from his body by the water, and he's sitting under a tree as though incapable of moving. The only thing he is wearing is a pair of trainers.

"Can I help you?" Jay says, feeling stupid even saying it.

"My daughter's under there," the man says. "We need to get her out. I've already tried to lift the poles, but I can't do it on my own. I was afraid if I moved, I wouldn't find this place again."

"Under here?" says Jay doubtfully.

The man nods. Jay puts the bag down, bending his knees as much as he can so he can take the weight when he straightens. They heave, the naked man grunting like a tennis player. Nothing. They lift the next pole. Nothing. And the next …

Jay can feel the sweat pouring down his back, running down the cleft between his buttocks. He needs to rest after the seventh pole, but the man is undeterred.

"One more," he says to Jay. "Just one more. Please?"

Jay nods, too tired to answer. And this time, as the pole rolls away, he can hear something. Tapping. Tapping.

"It's Debbie," the man says. "We've got to keep at it."

And the sound gives them new energy. They lift the sheet of corrugated iron, using some discarded clothing to protect their hands from the white-hot sizzle of the metal. The tapping fades for a bit, making them work faster.

"We can't lose her," the man says.

Jay sees the little figure first. The building has collapsed around her, and she's underneath a wooden table. One of the legs has given way, but the rest of it has formed a strange sort of shelter in the mayhem. Her one foot, however, is sticking out, caught between shards of wood.

"Daddy!" the girl cries.

"Hello, honey, just don't move. We're going to move these last things to get you out."

Little by little, they move the debris.

"Don't lift her out until I've taken a look at her," says Jay, "I'm a doctor."

But one glance at her foot tells him all he needs to know.

"The helicopters are taking off on the beach. She needs to go on one of them, or she may lose this foot."

He digs in the dive bag, remembering a multi-coloured beach towel he saw in it.

"Can you carry her on your own? I was on my way to get more medical supplies."

The man nods.

"You can use this towel, if you like."

The man stares at him blankly.

"If you want to cover up," Jay explains.

A flash of understanding.

"Oh right, I'd forgotten all about that. Cheers."

As Jay walks on he hears the man calling behind him.

"You saved my daughter, Doctor, I won't forget it."

12h04

He's got to do this quickly. If the next wave is coming, he'll need to get up into the hills with everybody else. Patting his pockets, he remembers that it was Kerese who locked the room, not him. So much for security though. He puts his full weight against the door and it flies open on the first shove. The calm inside the room is uncanny. Even the shattered glass from this morning – was it only this morning? – has been cleared. Fresh soap has replaced the mangled bar that was in the shower. The bed is made. It's almost tempting enough to lie on, and fall asleep. It makes him realise how exhausted he is.

Opening up Kerese's Burberry bag, he shoves in everything he can think of. The medical kit. Clothes for her. Some tampons. A few things for him. Their passports. Flight tickets. Suntan lotion. Insect repellent. He finds himself a pair of sandals and slips them on.

Then Jay empties the contents of their minibar. The booze: 5 bottles of Singha Thai beer; vodka; gin; rum and a few cans of Coke and lemonade. Then the snacks: mixed nuts; a few packets of crisps and a Toblerone.

He looks at the dive bag, then unpacks the contents into his case so he only has to carry that. This time, he's more selective about what he's going to lug with him. He tosses the soggy novels and leaky binoculars. But he keeps the camera in the underwater casing, the official documentation, the wallets.

In the pocket of the dive bag, he finds what looks like a notebook of some kind. It's enclosed in what seems to be at least five sealable plastic bags.

It must be important to somebody, he thinks, *and if it's survived all this, maybe I can give it back.*

12h11

While Jay is walking down the hill back into the wreckage of Tonsai Village, groups of people are going the other way.

"Are you frickin' touched?" a man calls, "there's a wave coming."

Jay thinks about joining them in their climb, but remembers the people bleeding and desperate in the hotel bedroom. He lugs Kerese's suitcase along with him, feeling it bump against his legs. From his slightly elevated viewpoint, he can see how the tsunami must have launched itself up the beach from both sides. He shivers. At least two hundred bungalows must have been swept away and hotels with more than a few storeys have collapsed, as though sliced at the knees. In the harbour, ravaged boats float like driftwood.

The irony is the sunshine. The sky is as blue as it was that morning, dotted only by the helicopters, hovering like dragonflies over a pond on a hot day. As they land, he can see men dressed in military gear jumping out with stretchers, and when the injured are loaded up, they are left behind.

Surely they wouldn't leave them if there was another wave coming?

He doesn't reach the hotel. Steve, Liam and Pascale are walking in a tired cluster when he bumps into them. He looks at himself in their expressions, realising his attempts at cleaning himself have not being very successful.

"We have to get up the hill," Liam says to him. "There's already a group of injured people there. They've set up a basic hospital, or that's what I've heard. You got your bag I see."

Jay nods.

"Any news about Laura and Finn?" Jay asks, suddenly remembering Steve's family's names.

"None. But I'm hoping ..."

Jay knew what he was hoping. If Kerese had survived the wave that was the most likely place she would be, too.

12h20

Crossing over the level expanse of flattened village takes longer than Jay anticipated. They only realise after a few minutes that they are going the wrong way when two Thai kids rush up to them, pulling them through a narrow passage.

"You come. You come."

They brave the bamboo-covered incline, the kids dancing in front of them. The still air is suffused with the high-pitched shrieking of cicadas. Jay slaps off a mosquito, his arm reddening with his own drawn blood. His leg hurts. Though he hasn't studied it in too much detail, he knows it's just a surface cut, but like everybody else, he's bruised. Steve's story distracts him on the toughest bits.

"I was out at sea when the wave hit," Steve tells him. "We were supposed to be skiing. God, we were lifted up on a swell."

"Were you out there alone?"

"I don't know what happened to Pete and the driver. I used to surf when I was an anklebiter, but Christ, when that wave hit the mainland it was out of control. I took in a lot of water."

"But you got out?"

"I had a lifejacket. It wasn't exactly a great match for the waves though. It was almost like being high. Choked with water. Euphoric. You know? I puked my lungs out. But I felt okay. I grabbed onto some tree, like a monkey. I wasn't coming down, that's for sure. Not 'til that black muck subsided. And when I started looking for my family, I realised it was pretty hopeless."

"Chaotic."

"Yes."

Steve's expression darkened. Jay thought about Nina. How many of the islands had been hit? Was hers one of them too? Had he maybe just lost his brother and his sister in the space of a month? And Kerese. He'd tried not to focus on the Internet café as they walked past it. What was left of it. Shattered screens and keyboards lurking in gloomy puddles. Wires, tables and dislocated chairs.

He's followed Steve's lead near the supermarket, picking up any food items that might still be edible. His shorts pockets are filled with damp packets of peanuts and instant noodles. How they are going to cook them he has no idea, but the weight of them is oddly comforting.

The kids have vanished into the forest. They come out with an old man. He shuffles rather than walks, gesturing to them. Jay follows first.

Sitting near a ramshackle hut that on any other time would have seemed close to collapse, but now seems welcoming, is a group of disheveled tourists. The old man beckons them to join as a giant pot of rice is passed round the group.

Jay's stomach grumbles. He hadn't realised how hungry he is, but even as he notices this, his eyes scan the tousled crowd for Kerese.

"I'm starved," says Steve, noticing the food, but Jay can see his eyes darting from stranger to stranger, searching.

Even though they have been separated by continents, there isn't much difference between him and Steve.

Liam walks forward, his hand in Pascale's.

"Let's eat something, y'all. We've still got some walking to do."

12h48

Nobody has seen Kerese. Or at least, nobody remembers doing so. But a South African couple mentions a little boy being carried in his mother's arms all the way from Tonsai.

"She wouldn't let him go," the man said. "I offered to carry him for her, but it was almost as if she was glued to him. We got separated somehow. I guess we were walking a little faster than she was."

This news is too much for Steve.

"I need to keep going. If it's Laura, I've got to find her," he says to Jay, as he stands up.

Jay stands too, then bends to pick up the suitcase.

"I'll come with you," he offers and as they take the pathway again, they meet a man carrying a walkie-talkie.

"Another wave. One o'clock," the man tells them. "Move . Move. Fastly. Wave. She coming."

Steve indicates where the other people are.

"You'd better warn those people," he says.

"I tell them, you go. Fastly. No stop."

12h53

It's an exodus of the disgruntled, the distraught, the devastated. A woman in front of them is wearing a pair of silk pajamas. Jay can see the sweat trickling in dark rings under her arms and down her back. Another woman is wearing a g-string, and a t-shirt that doesn't do much to hide her state of undress. Every few steps, she pulls the shirt down, her embarrassment almost tangible. Jay thinks about giving her one of Kerese's pairs of shorts, but wonders if this gesture will make her feel even more self-conscious.

When they arrive at the makeshift camp, there are about two hundred people already settling themselves. To the one side, the injured are lying in the shade. They've been carried up the hill on blankets, doors or wooden planks – anything available.

Jay needs to find Kerese.

He walks with Steve from group to group. Some people are huddled protectively. Some are sullen.

Nobody tells them anything that can help. A man shakes his cellphone, as if that will improve the reception.

"We just don't know *anything*," he says. "And I want to get the fuck off this island. I can't leave here fast enough."

"Yes, I saw a little boy. Little redhead," says a woman, then registers Steve's expression. "Not yours then?"

"The water was coming out her ears," another says. "Her ears! She was dead, of course."

"And that wailing. So high-pitched. I can't get the sound of it out of my head."

Jay wants to block out the stories. But he can't because everybody has one. *Where were you when ...* and like everybody who's lost somebody, he's searching.

But when they find Pete's wife Susan, it's too much for Jay. He watches Steve clinging onto her, the tears coursing down their faces as they speak.

"Oh my God, you're safe, you're safe! Where're Laura and Finn?"

"Where is Pete?"

Susan steps away from Steve, shielding her face from an onslaught.

"She had him, Steve. She had him."

"Had him?"

"I saw her scoop him up. I was running away from the beach. Laura ran towards it. She reached him, but she had nothing to hold onto. The wave knocked Finn out of her arms. She followed after him, I think."

"They're gone?"

"I don't know for sure. I'm sorry Stevie, but I think so."

Steve sinks to the ground. His arms are tight across his chest as he topples onto his side. He moans, rocking against himself. Jay watches Susan slide down he thinks to comfort him. *Slap!* Her hand across Steve's face.

"Where is Pete, damn it? I need to know what happened to my husband. This isn't just about you!"

Steve grimaces, catching her hand in his.

"You're right," he says, "but I can't tell you. The last time I saw Pete was before the wave hit from the bay."

Susan takes her hand away, cradling her face.

"I'm so sorry," she says, "I'm so sorry I just did that."

Steve says nothing. His body is limp in their own circle of grief.

"He was my friend too," says Steve. "So this *is* about me."

Jay steps away. He can't listen any longer and finds a rock where he can sit by himself. And every step away from the crowd, he pushes through a wall of grief and shock.

It's Liam still wet with sweat from the upward trudge who focuses Jay back on practicalities.

"What are you doing, Jay? If you can't find your girlfriend, you can't stand here wallowing."

"I wasn't wallowing."

"You got the medical kit?"

"Yes."

"Then get your ass over to those people. Right now, they need you. The time will pass quicker if you're busy."

18h35

Even as the sun sets, the heat is unbearable. Jay looks across at Liam, who is holding a woman's hand. Nobody knows who she is, but Liam switches from French to English hoping for some recognition. Pascale fans the flies away. Jay notices now in the twilight how pretty she is, her bobbed hair and rich red lips reminding him of Snow White.

Yet this is no fairytale. They've shared his insect repellent, but it's almost already finished, and the welts line up along Jay's exposed arms and legs.

He checks one of their patient's bandages. The blood has stopped seeping through the wound, but his lower leg has taken on a greenish tinge that worries Jay. With nothing more than his last few doses of antibiotics and pain suppressants, there isn't much he can do about it.

Stragglers come up the hill all afternoon. There was no wave at one. Or two. Or three. That doesn't make Jay feel any better though. He doesn't notice when the girl from Tyt's gets to the camp, but now he finds her standing in front of him. She's fashioned garlic bread out of a stale loaf and a blowtorch and offers him some off a fork.

"So you're a doctor," she says.

"That's right."

"It's gonna be a long night, you call me over if you need some help," she says.

Jay looks at her, taking in the ringlets that have come loose around her face, and the patch of red like a ripped plaster off her nose.

"You know anything about medicine?" he asks.

"No," she answers, "but I know more than I need to about pain."

23h13

In the darkness the camp has settled. Liam has passed a list of survivors around, not knowing yet how they will pass this on to worried family. A few people have managed to light fires, but mostly the night has penetrated. Most people have made make-shift mattresses out of banana leaves. But even these don't help on the hard ground, and the thick stems stick into their backs. Jay has given almost everything he owns away, keeping only one outfit for Kerese and a change of clothes for himself. He's saving the batteries in his torch, flicking it on only every fifteen minutes or so, to check his patients are still breathing. And in these circumstances, he's not even sure he can help much if they aren't. Jay is exhausted, but he doesn't think he can or should sleep. He stands up, walking to the edge of the clearing for a pee, but he's mindful of the snakes everyone has warned him about.

Jay walks back to his belongings. Digging in Kerese's case for his last bag of peanuts, his hands touch on the notebook taken off the young thief. Momentarily distracted, he unwraps it, looking inside the cover for a name or address with his torch.

Nothing.

His eyes scan the first few lines of text. It's so large, flamboyant and bold, that he can't help being drawn to it.

For once in her stupid life, life, Ruby's finally given me somethin' useful.

And then he can't stop himself. *It's not right, is it, stealing someone's memories like this?* But the journal keeps him company until the first rays filter through over the horizon, his batteries dying at first light.

Chapter 9
June 30, 2004 – Wednesday

I went through your school yearbook. You were mighty fine to look at even then. Not sure about the haircut, Ant, but I guess your mama had her hand in that. Peggy didn't fall out no ugly tree neither. Pretty in a debutante, pom-pom sort of a way. I'm not jealous looking at her like this. Twelve years can do a thing on a girl's figure, but all that depends. You know? It what'nt that difficult to find her, anyways. Eleanor gave me her mama's phone number, and I just called lookin' for her. She's left Atlanta. Lives somewhere in San Francisco. Married rich to some shipping billionaire and her house is streets away from Danielle Steel's mansion. Streets! Panoramic views of the Golden Gate Bridge, Alcatraz, San Francisco Bay and all that. You would have sworn listening to her that her daughter had married Mister Trump himself.

My first time flying scheduled and I needed a shot of something to keep me calm. The man next to me tried to make conversation, but I was concentratin' on blocking out the engine noise. Reminded me too much of that day in the chopper when we spun out of control. I was glad at first to be sitting next to the aisle. Stretch my legs out. But when the plane started to land, I couldn't help myself, I remembered what it felt like looking down on the world from a dizzy, incredible height. I tried to look over the man's shoulder, and he offered me a look for little bit of somethin' extra. That's how he said it.

—Sure, I told him, you can carry my suitcase to my taxi if you like.

He looked at me funny, like I were dumber 'n a sack of wet mice. Strange, he disappeared the moment we landed and didn't look back. It's sure nice to laugh a little, Anton. I just wish I was laughing with you.

I scoped out the house a few hours after I checked into the Holiday Inn on Fisherman's Wharf. I have to tell you I was excited. I walked from the hotel to Pier 39, and near jumped out of my skin when those sea lions barked as they hauled themselves out from the docks to the water. They smell a bit funny. Like dead fish and sea salt, but they're kinda cute. But you probably don't even want to hear about that. Not when Peggy is sitting up in her fancy house surrounded by celebs taking in the temperate micro-climate (I read about it on the plane) and young professionals walking their dogs or catching a weekend tan at Lafayette Park.

She didn't come to the door. Not that I even got there without an explanation or two. (I lied.) I had to get past two security guards. I bet they were packing some nasty pieces, but they were casual enough with me. I guess I don't look all that threatening. I'm still a bit of a hobbler after the accident. Anyways, it was the housekeeper who let me in, once I walked up that long, steep drive. Her accent was heavy Mexican, rich and promising as chocolate.

She smiled at me. A gap between her front teeth. Like
Madonna. She lead me outside to the patio, offered me some
lemonade. And I needed it. Dehydration from that flight and
all.

He came out first. Peggy's husband, that is. Dark, and
sandpaperish. A mop of black hair, tinged with grey. A beaky
nose and ears that I swear weren't the same size. Not even
close. Beige-and-white striped pants (would he call them
trousers?), and a white embroidered silk shirt with some sort
of Indian motif. Then some thonged sandals that pretended to
be casual, but looked like they'd cost half our apartment.

I had the time to notice all this because Peggy didn't arrive for
at least ten minutes. Somethin' about this man made me shift.
His gaze was just a bit too direct. Too, well, penetrating.

—You've come to visit my wife, he said to me.

I nodded. Something told me not to say too much. If you had
a secret, so did Peggy, and I wasn't about to ruin things before
they even began.

—You're from Atlanta?

I was glad then for her mother's chatter.

—No, Charleston, I said honestly, but I did a brief stint at
UCLA when Peggy was there too. Not sure she'll even
remember me. It was a few years back.

He nodded, temporarily satisfied, then indicated my empty
glass.

113

—Would you like another drink?
—Thank you.
—Maria! he shouted.

She scuttled back with a fresh jug, but replaced my glass with a fresh one. I watched her pour. So my first impression of Peggy came from close up. I didn't even hear her footsteps. At first I thought I was imagining things. She looked nervous, tentative. Not quite the prom-queen confidence I was expecting. But this reaction was a temporary one. She came forward, flingin' her arms around me, as though we were long-lost buddies, which in this scenario I suppose we were.

—Amanda, she said to me, her eyes locking with mine.

I didn't correct her.

—Peg, I said.

She took me in. My hipsters and floaty pink top. The denim jacket over my arm. My ankle boots in soft cerise suede. Walking over to her husband, she linked arms with him, her movement determined, plotted. Then she spoke again.

—It's so good to see you again! How are Megan and Alison?

Who the heck were they?

—Great, I said. Same as always.
—And Alison's little boy? He must be about two now?
—Thereabouts, I answered, cute as a button.
—Darlin', she said, turning to her husband, I'd love a spritzer. And you know how Maria always messes those up. Would

you like one Amanda? I see you're on the lemonade, but let's celebrate old times!
—Sure, why not?

As soon as he stepped away, Peggy's expression changed.

—I knew this would happen. One day. Why didn't she come herself?
—Eleanor?

She nodded.

—She can't leave Bill, he's already reinin' her in.

Peg twisted her finger into her hair, making a haphazard ponytail.

—So where do you fit in then?
—I'm Anton's widow.
—Widow?

Peg looked ready to gag. She held at her chest as though trying to keep it from exploding. Lowering herself into one of the porch's wicker chairs, she looked at me with an expression that made my heart pound.

—How did it happen?
—Helicopter accident.
—You were with him? she asked, indicating my leg.

I guess I wasn't hiding my limp all that well.

—Yeah.

—I still miss him, you know, but there were just too many secrets. I couldn't cope with all of that. And especially as it was all my fault. Or at least I started it. He's really dead? My God! I just thought, maybe one day …

I didn't want to hear her fantasies about my husband.

—He loved me, I said, stopping her. He loved me.
—And once he loved me. We would've gotten married. It was all planned out. Spring wedding. Peaches and cream. We made a beautiful couple.

I felt myself moving towards the door leading inside. Why was I doing this, Anton? Listening to Peg with her lovestruck fantasies and expectations? As I walked to the door, I saw Peg's husband striding towards me, the spritzers held aloft and a quizzical expression on his face.

—Leaving already? he asked me.
—Do you have a restroom I could use? I returned.
—Straight back into the hallway and to the left. Maria can show you.

I washed my face off with cold water. The conversation was making me sweat. I was a fish out of water in this fancy-schmancy house. Gold taps. Marble. Thick folds of material draping the windows. And Peg in her designer dress and *Sex and the City* shoes. The dark mysterious husband whose name I realized I didn't yet know. I flushed, daring myself to go back out. And I have to tell you Ant, I considered just leaving. Did I really want to find out all of your secrets? My life just seemed to be crumbling away and my memory of you with it.

But I went back.

—Please sit, Amanda, Peg said. Christos will give you your drink once you're settled.

I sipped the spritzer. I never quite got the point of them. You know me, swiggin' back the cocktails, and wine never really was my thing.

—What did you study together? Christos asked.
—Psych, that's why I know you so well, darlin'.

I was glad she hadn't given me the chance to answer. I would've guessed English lit or social studies of some sort. Or maybe Shopping 101. Oops. Catty. But what was I doing there anyhow?

Peg took center stage, boring both Christos and me into a numb silence. I learned everything there is to know about: the Thysen Bornomisa (however you spell it) in Madrid; endless weddings of people I didn't know, an update on her mother's irritable bowel syndrome; growing roses in poor soil …

Christos yawned openly, I stifled my own open mouth with my hand. Eventually, Christos stood up.

—Well, I see you ladies have a lot to catch up on.
—You won't stay? Peg purred.

But he'd had just as much as he could handle.

—Lovely to meet you, he said, kissing me European-style on both cheeks. How long are you here in San Fran?
—A few days, maybe.

—Well we're having a barbecue on Friday. I'm certain Peggy would love you to come.
—Oh yes!

Peg flushed pure pink.

—Now, that sounds about the nicest offer I've had all day, thank you, I said.
—Goodbye then, he nodded at us.

We sat silently, listening to the heavy footsteps retreating up the stairs. And in the strangest instant, Peg's face straightened, her dizzy, glazed look focused and her neatly crossed ankles separated.

—Sorry, she said, standing up as she pulled me by the hand. He normally takes less time to fold. Now come along quickly, let's go into the garden where he won't be able to hear us.

Chapter 10

27 December 2004. Monday. 05h03.

When the first helicopters start landing, people stir. Jay
tries to massage his neck, his fingers barely penetrating.
Who is she? he thinks. *Is she still alive?* Occupied all night
with the woman in the journal, he's been able to transport
himself away from this nightmare. But as light begins to
sparkle, reality hits once more.

There's a couple with twin baby girls, who walk to
other parents trying to beg a bit of formula. An argument
breaks out.

"We've got two babies to feed, and you've only got
one, surely you can spare something …"

"I'm sorry, but I don't know how long we're going
to be up here. If it were your tin you would do the same."

"Actually, I don't think you can presume to tell me
what I would do, you don't even know me."

"Yes, that's right. So why would I put my child in
danger for a complete stranger?"

"They're just little babies."

"I'm sorry."

Jay tunes out, checking the patients. Surprisingly,
the man's leg doesn't look any worse, but he needs to be
taken to the choppers.

"Liam! Liam!"

Liam walks over.

"He needs to go?"

Jay nods.

"Okay, I'll get someone to help me."

They don't mention the threat of another wave. Nobody knows whether their walk down to the beach through the flatland will put them in danger or not.

Steve's pacing, as he has been the whole night. He's walked higher up the hill, and shakes a cell phone with the determination of a golden retriever. Jay doesn't know where he got it, but he's set on getting a message out. His face is set, grim, like the impenetrable Ao Ling rock face. Susan is curled up in a ball. Her eyes are swollen, the streaks of last night's tears ingrained with dust. A mosquito bite reddens on her cheek.

Jay digs in his suitcase, extracting a bit of sunscreen. He rubs it onto his patient's face. Who knows how long he'll stay on the beach before they can take him.

"You didn't ask me to help you," says the girl from Tyt's.

"No. You burn easily?" Jay asks, handing her the cream.

She pours a dab into her cupped hand, rubbing it into her face.

"Thanks. Becky," she says.

"Jay. You live here on Koh Phi Phi Don?"

"For a while. I'm kinda homeless."

"Well, if you weren't before you are now," says Jay surveying the scene below them.

His weak attempt at humour makes them both laugh.

"Where were you?" she asks.

"When it happened? Tonsai. You?"

"On my way to Tyt's. I took the most awesome photo of the wave comin'."

"Did you?"

"Pity I don't know where it is."

Liam walks over to where they are sitting. His hair is a little long at the fringe and falls into his eyes.

"There're not too many heroes here," he says gruffly.

"No takers?"

"Not until we know something more, they're just too scared of the waves. Fuck it, man, *I'm* too scared of the waves."

"I'll do it," says Becky. "I'm pretty strong."

Liam looks at Becky.

Even to Jay, his expression is obvious. *A woman?*

"Liam, is it? I'm all you've got. Take it or leave it."

Pascale sits near Jay under a tree. She says little, but Jay can see her teeth biting into her lips as she watches Liam and Becky's unsteady descent. Jay admires her – she didn't even try to stop him. She's brave, but silently so. Pascale stands up to brush a fly away from one of the women's faces.

"We'll need get them all down," she says. "They cannot rest here in this hot."

"Let's wait for Liam and Becky to get back. They'll have heard something at least."

She nods.

Steve comes down from the hill, his body flopping like the airless tsunami fish.

"I need to get out of here. Have you guys got any news yet?"

Jay shakes his head.

"We argued again on Christmas," Steve confides. "Ever since Finn we argued all the time."

Jay leans forward. He's not unused to sickbed intimacies, but usually it is something distant to him. Flat characters in tragic decline. This time, Steve is talking about Laura. And little Finn.

"She always put Finn first. No sex for months. It was impossible with him constantly in the bed. And she didn't want to, anyway. She'd shut down. This trip was supposed to give us a chance. Sue said she'd take Finn for a night or two. Imagine it. Fixing things so you can shag your own wife?"

Jay can't imagine it. He's never had any limitations on his freedom that he hasn't set himself. Not like that. And he doesn't really know what to say.

"You don't need to say anything," Steve says, studying Jay's face. "What could you say? Beautiful girlfriend. Great job. It just isn't your world."

Jays feels his hackles rise.

"I work in a cancer unit, Steve. I watch people die for a living. And as for my beautiful girlfriend, I haven't seen her since the wave hit. You're not the only person suffering."

Steve flinches.

"I'm sorry mate. You're right of course. I just feel so out of control."

"Then help us get some of these injured off the hill. Someone is looking for them. And we can only hope the people we care about are being looked after by somebody else."

Steve stands up, marches over to a huddle of tourists.

"Eleven volunteers. That's all we need. You want these people to die up here?"

The group tries to look away, gazes misting into the distances.

"Even if you don't look at me, you know you can hear me. No-one is getting off the island until the injured have been airlifted. So the sooner you get off your asses, the quicker we get out of here too."

"What about the waves?"

"What about them? It's been almost twenty-four hours. We have to go down some time."

10h00

Not everyone is prepared to move. People waiting for official word decide to stay up the hill, slapping away flies and mosquitoes, eating instant noodles or nothing at all. But as Becky and Liam stagger up the hill announcing news, the crowd gathers around them.

"Some of the cell phone signals are back up," says Liam.

"The tsunami was triggered by an earthquake off the Indonesian coast. An 8.5 on the Richter Scale," Becky adds.

"What about more waves?" someone asks.

Becky shrugs, then wipes a trail of sweat from her face.

"We don't know much else."

Jay moves away, he's going to help with the last of the patients. If climbing the hill was difficult with the suitcase, now it's almost impossible. Balanced at the side of the door that he is carrying, the case squashes his fingers, making him wince. Jay trips on the undergrowth, his foot catching on a root.

"Let me carry the case, at least," says Becky.

"You've done your bit," Jay says, "better stay in safety up here until we know more."

"What can I say?" asks Becky, "I sure love my adrenaline."

Liam stops.

"My hands are burning," he says, moving to put down his side of the door.

Jay halts, bending to right the door.

"Thank God this is the last person," he comments.

As they move downhill, Jay watches a man digging under the debris. What is left of a small wooden bungalow is ripped open. Even the corrugated iron is shredded in two. *Imagine that going through a body,* he thinks. Everywhere they go, people are salvaging their belongings. They pass the souvenir shops, soggy postcards showing the Koh Phi Phi of only two days ago. Restaurants – where plastic chairs lie legless and bent and hotels disgorged of mattresses, which now line the trickiest paths.

Another helicopter is landing nearby. A crowd has gathered on the beach – a boat approaches, and people push and shove to get to the front of where the pier used to be.

"Oh my Lord," says Becky.

She's stopped short, her pale face flushed, her mouth agape. Jay sees where she is pointing. The military have piled all the bodies together in a macabre pile.

But she must have seen this earlier?

Becky drops Jay's suitcase, running towards the corpses. She touches a face. Then turns away quickly to vomit. Then Jay recognises him too. Deng from Tyt's Climbing Shop – his guide up Tonsai Tower. What is left of his finely sculpted torso is a horrifying jaggedness, red and raw.

Jay indicates to Liam to stop. Lowering the door quickly, he moves to Becky. She's crunched up and shaking. Putting his arms around her, he wipes her face with his hand. He feels her weight sink into him, and she is wordless, shuddering.

"Come," Jay says, "we need to get you away from here. Help us get her onto the chopper."

Becky nods, then stands.

"We'll need to tell someone who he is, so they can tell his family."

Liam pulls a marker pen from his pocket. *God only knows why he's carrying that around*, thinks Jay, watching as Becky writes his name on his arm.

A group of soldiers surrounds them, pointing out the girl on the door.

"She not dead?"

Jay nods.

"What her name?"

"We don't know."

They lift her effortlessly, a doctor walking with them as he checks her pulse. The transfer is quick and the helicopter takes off again in minutes. Watching the propellers whirl, Jay is relieved to have passed on the responsibility. Maybe it's time now to change his focus. Jay thinks about Kerese, wondering if she's lying somewhere in this pile in the shade of the banana palms, her body battered and bruised as Deng's. He glances across at the bodies, walking closer to look.

Liam tried to pull him away.

"If she's in there, you don't want to see her," he says.

"If she's in there, I need to see her," Jay corrects.

He's heart beats in his ears, his breathing quickens. But nobody but Deng is familiar.

126

"What now?" says Jay. "Do we go back up the hill?"

"You made it," he hears behind him. "But where's your chick?"

It's Tom. He's carrying two scuba tanks. One grasped firmly in each hand.

Tom shrugs, noticing the direction of Jay's eyes.

"I've got to keep busy, dude," he says. "Kelly's floating somewhere out there. Switching off my mind."

"She's dead?"

"Well, I'm not dead and I was out there too. How the fuck do I know?"

Jay flinches.

"You haven't seen Kerese? And what's the news from Nina's boat?" he asks.

"Jay. Mate. I haven't seen anybody really. Except a pile of corpses. Maybe you should walk up to the Phi Phi apartments. It's a refugee camp. Stray tourists clogging up the rooms."

"You haven't been up there yourself?" asks Jay.

"Everything I own is stuck under the debris. Shit man. I was guarding my stuff."

10h23

Jay is relieved as they climb uphill. The further above sea level they are, the safer it feels. Now that all the wounded are on their way to hospitals, he can worry about himself. And Kerese. He finds that Becky is walking with him.

"You're not going back up?" he asks.

"What, and be stuck up there with them whingers?" she says, rubbing her leg.

Jay looks at her. Her bounce has dissipated having seen Deng, but her face is resolute. Resigned.

Liam has left them to find Pascale. They can see his blue-and-white T-shirt standing out between the bursts of bamboo as he moves.

When they get to the hotel, they find the whole pool area, lobby and pathway outside has become a makeshift dormitory. People's bags are pushed together or being used as seating or head rests. Although it's still day, and fairly early, some people are fast asleep, their clothes over their heads to shade them.

"I need to use the restroom," Becky says.

"Bring your own bucket," answers someone who overhears her, and she and Jay won't know why until they see the state of the toilets.

"Lot people," says a Thai, shrugging. "Pipes broken. You carry from swimming pool. You like drink beer, maybe? "

Perhaps that is why everyone is so listless, passing the day in the heat in an alcoholic stupor. The idea is actually quite attractive, but Kerese ... where the hell is she?

"You got a photo?" asks Becky.

He nods, pulling his wallet out of his shorts.

"Pretty."

Jay looks at Becky. Her red curls are tied up on her head like a giant pineapple. And her face is streaked with grime, but her eyes are incredible.

"Which way you want me to go?" she asks.

He smiles.

"You're going to find her?" he asks.

"No harm in tryin'. Don't disappear now. We'll meet back here. Half an hour?"

"Sure. I'll do this level. You go upstairs."

Jay walks through the lobby. He can hear the sounds of vehicles pulling into the street. He peers out the main entrance. People being led towards the shore.

"Where are they going?" he asks a receptionist.

"Inland. There are some hotels to put them up until we can get these people home. They're linking up with some boats somewhere."

The woman looks at him. She's not a Thai, but he can't place her accent. Gesturing towards the pool area where some people are still clumped, "I didn't see you here last night."

"I was up in the hills," he answers.

"A lot of people there too?"

"A few hundred."

She nods, then looks at the Burberry suitcase.

"A terrible thing. You looking for someone?"

"My girlfriend. Blonde. Tanned. Quite tall. British."

The woman shrugs.

"A lot of tall blondes," she says. "Maybe she's already left on a boat?"

"I hope so, that would mean she's alive."

The receptionist considers him.

"There was an American last night. Beefy. Biker-type. He was passing a piece of paper around for people to write their names on. He's staying in one of the rooms. Number three. Maybe you should speak to him?"

In the end, he and Becky go to the room together. The man is nowhere to be found, but the room has been left wide open and a couple is asleep on the bed. Wary of waking them, Becky and Jay step back.

"Now what?" Becky says, her hands on her hips.

"I've no idea."

The woman downstairs considers them, as they emerge once again.

"The generator's working," she says, "and there's fresh coffee. How about a cup, while you think what to do next?"

10h59

Becky hands Jay the sugar.

"You look like you need a little," she says.

He dips the teaspoon in, stirring quickly.

"I'm looking for her, and I don't think I love her anymore."

He didn't realise that admission was coming until it popped out.

Becky considers him.

"Of course you're lookin' for her. It's only right.
And when you find her, you can sort everythin' out."

Jay nods.

"This is such a mess. I'm not sure yet if I should be
grieving. Can you even grieve a girlfriend you're not sure
you love?"

"Quit thinking like that. You'll find her."

They decide to wait. If the biker-guy is coming
back, at least they have someone to speak to. And although
they are shaded by a large banyan tree, the heat envelopes
them.

"I'm goin' in," Becky says.

She stands, her pale body almost luminescent in the
sunshine. Stripping off her T-shirt and shorts, she wears a
light pink bra edged with lace and a pair of matching
knickers. Unlike the practical side of her he has already
recognised, her panties are flimsy and fanciful, forming a
neat edge around her bottom. Without her shorts, her legs
seem even longer, and though pallid, are taut and muscled.
One of her calves has the trail of a faint scar, attesting to her
recklessness. Seemingly unaware of his scrutiny, Becky is
unselfconscious as she walks to the water. She untwists her
hair, then dives into the pool in a swift slice.

When she comes to the surface, she is laughing.

"Come on," she calls, "We'll feel better after a
swim."

And Jay strips off too, dive-bombing close to her.
The water is lukewarm, but compared to the outside
temperature it feels refreshing. They circle each other like

sharks, not touching. Becky's bra is almost completely see-though now, but he finds he is distanced from this. His observation is almost clinical – something that amazes him.

Jay doesn't hear the man at first.

"You looking for someone?" he asks.

His expression says it all. This isn't the time for frivolity. Not now after all that has happened. Jay stops, pulling himself out the pool as soon as he reaches the edge. The water washes down him, leaving a puddle at his feet. Walking towards the American, he catches the towel hurled at him.

"I've just pulled ten bodies out of the water," the man says. "Even after such a short time, the corpses are green, bloated. I'm not really sure even a loved one would recognise them."

Jay nods, not really sure how to react.

"We were waiting for you. We didn't know where else to look," he says, after a slight hesitation.

The man's expression tightens. His moustache and beard are only just longer than a prickle, yet form a dark outline around the man's pursed lips. He doesn't have to say anything. Jay can already feel his disapproval and is at a loss to get him on his side.

But suddenly the man relaxes. He holds out his hand.

"Sorry pal, it's been a trying morning. I'm Nick."

"Jay."

"Kate at the desk said you're looking for your girlfriend."

"I think she was still emailing down the road when the wave hit. I'm hoping she managed to make it up here."

Nick takes out a piece of paper. It seems to be torn out a journal and is uneven on the edges.

"I didn't get everybody's names," Nick says. "So if her name isn't here it doesn't mean she wasn't."

Jay's stomach tightens as he takes the list. Each person has obviously written their own name, as the handwriting changes all the way down. He follows the words with his finger.

Eventually, he hands the paper back. His expression is blank.

"Nothing?" says Nick.

"No."

Becky has climbed out the water. As she puts on her T-shirt, her wet bra makes patterns through the material.

"It doesn't mean anythin', Jay," she says.

"It means she wasn't here."

Nick touches his shoulder, his massive hand dwarfing Jay.

"I told you, I didn't meet everybody. It was a dog show here. Heck, I was sharing with two couples. And three kids. I don't even remember one of the kid's names. Dylan? Damian? Dexter?"

Jay nods.

Nick continues, "I heard there's another boat heading to Phuket, you know. The British Embassy has set up some sort of crisis centre there – in Phuket Town. That had better be your next port of call."

Jay looks at Becky.

"What do you think?" he asks her.

"It's either there or Krabi. At least in Phuket you're closer to an airport to get out of here."

"If that's what I want."

"If that's what you want."

"And what about you?" Jay asks. "What are you going to do?"

"I'll find Deng's family first. If I can. Then there's someone else I need to speak to. If I can find him. Now's as good a time as any, right?"

Jay wonders at his instant disappointment.

"A boyfriend?"

"Oh no," Becky says. "This relationship is much more complicated than that."

Chapter 11
July 2, 2004 - Friday

There I was—standing outside her house, a bottle of wine in my hand. White. Of course white. How else does the love of your life make her precious spritzers? And I'm sure she has enough club soda to fill a bath. Wine too, probably. But I had to bring something, didn't I?
So Peggy was pregnant. Something like that isn't that hard to understand. It happened to us, didn't it Anton? But then of course we were married, and I couldn't even keep the baby for five months, never mind forty weeks. You were cut up about it. Real cut up. I was so darned touched. Pity I didn't know this wasn't a world of firsts for you.

Her garden was beautiful. Not quite as beautiful as the Homecoming Queen herself, but it looks like your Peg has green fingers. I wonder if you ever knew that. She didn't ask me my real name. Not immediately, anyways. Too strung up by her own past to want to identify the person in the present bringing it back to her.

—You don't look his type, Peggy said.
—You mean I don't look like you? I returned. Might it be so hard for you to realize that Anton may not have been quite the same person you claim to have known so well?
—A changed man? Peggy replied, her laughter coming out in a snort.

—He married me, didn't he?
—Well that certainly does show something.

I reached for one of her roses, plucking off the dusty petals
one by one and lifting them onto the air. She flinched, her
desire to restrain my hand written in her eyes.

—Do you think I want to be here? I asked her. The first time I
ever heard your name was a few weeks after Anton died. I
knew nothin' about you.

Peg's face remained unchanged.

—You know what that means, Peggy? Anton never
mentioned you. Never. Not once.

I didn't know what was happening to me. Faced by her
perfection I was becoming some sort of spiteful she-cat,
sinking my claws in. But all she did was smile.

—So you're chasing after Anton's secrets. Not very becoming,
is it?
—I'm tryin' to filter out the lies.
—Sweetheart. You're going to find there are a lot of them.
Like …
—Yes?

She laughed.

—Not so fast, honey. I want to know how Eleanor fits in here.
—She asked me to come.
—So you said. Eleanor and I were always a good match,
that's why I could play her so well. And actually if you can
get past her superiority complex, she's not a bad person. But

her motives—well you'll have to enlighten me; I feel I am at a slight disadvantage.

—You're at a disadvantage? Peg. I'm the go-between and the only people who know what this is really all about, are dead, incapacitated, protecting something or missin'.

—Missing? Peg mused.

—You know as well as I do that Benjamin is alive.

—Dearest Ben, Peg replied. It was quite a funeral. I felt perfectly horrible for it. Poor Eleanor was distraught.

—Peggy, she lost her son.

—I know that. But I'd lost just as much by then. My lover. My best friend. My soul mate. My child.

Peggy's face clouded. She hadn't mentioned the baby before. I looked at her and found my hands were shaking. I tucked them together behind my back, willing them to still themselves.

—Your child? I repeated numbly. *What in the Sam Hill did she mean?*

But she seemed lost to me—her gaze headed somewhere to Alcatraz. And even when she looked at me again it was like I had a whole head of simple. *How,* her glance said, *would you even begin to understand?*

—It was a terrible time, she continued, truly terrible. And to think how it all began.

—And how was that?

—When I first met Anton, I was besotted with him. His parents had just been stationed in Atlanta. An army brat—but a good-looking one. Those gorgeous blue eyes—well they just about drowned me.

—And Ben? I asked quickly.

137

I didn't want to be hearing no accolades to your blue eyes.
Seems to me, Anton, I couldn't see properly into them
anyhow.

—They didn't look a bit alike. Anton was angular and
contrasts. Ben, well, Ben was a bit of an oaf really. A
swimmer—with enormous feet and hands. His shirts were
always untucked. His hair uncombed. But when he smiled,
you could say his whole face lit up like a new day. He had
some special charisma, Ben did. But he was restless. Up to no
good, most of the time. Trying to get Daddy to notice him.
—So you chose Anton.
—It wasn't a choice, she said to me, and I could see her trying
to place my name, I liked Anton from the start. And he
expected me to, have no doubt about that. It was like it was
predestined.

Predestined? How quaint. How ... nauseatin'.

—He came up to me in Math class. Sauntered over, really.
'You wanna go for ice cream, later?' he said to me, 'I hear the
pralines and chocolate flavor is especially nice down at
Angela's.'
—So you went.
—You *are* in a hurry. No, I asked him first if he might like to
know my name. That's when he smiled at me. 'I already
know it,' he said. 'You're Peggy Lott Gibson. And I'm
Anton.' 'So how do you know I like ice cream?' I asked.
'Peggy Lott Gibson,' he replied, looking me straight in the
eye, 'everybody likes ice cream.'

So this is what Eleanor was putting me through. Reliving a
courtship that ended for reasons unknown but that should

have lasted forever, if Peggy is to be believed. It puts *my*
Anton and me to shame. We didn't do no dates for ice cream
and couple up at the pictures. Not like you and Peggy ... You
weren't any sort of sweet-talking thing for me our first night
neither. Seems we had a few too many beers at that bar near
your base where I was singin', you tearful and distraught.
Two shakes of a sheep's tail, and we were bumpin' and
grindin' in the back of your car like a couple of teenagers. It
was shameful, unbridled. You drove me home, while I tried to
pull up my knickers. Straighten myself out before Ruby saw
me again. But she knew the moment I walked through the
door. And I didn't rightly care—as long as I could see you
again.

—We were a couple after that, Peg told me. All sweet and
innocent. I told my beau Patrick we were over. It wasn't a
hardship. I was tiring of him. And Anton was a football hero.
—Status?

Peg shrugged.

—So what? I would've liked him anyway. It was just another
advantage to hanging with him.

I almost laughed. Peg, in her Prada and Manolo Blahniks,
didn't *hang*. She occupied, annexed. Even I could see that.

—We got along so well. And Eleanor and Bill, they
worshipped me.

Well, you'd certainly like to think that, I'm sure.

Peggy looked at me.

139

—Seems to me, Anton was doing a bit of stirring when he married you. You're not exactly Eleanor's cup of tea.

I blanched.

—That may be true, I said, but she's trustin' me with her secrets. Would she have done the same for you?
—Honey, she and I shopped together. For camisoles and brassieres once. She bought me gifts because she felt like it.

Touching at her top, she stroked along the hem.

—Eleanor's a material girl, she said pointedly, and she'd always choose silk over denim …

I didn't bother to take her inference. The sooner I got out of there the better.

—Well, what happened? I asked.
—Ben happened, that's what, Peggy said. Anton was just so … good. The first time he touched my breasts, I had to open my top for him. And even then he was hesitant. He had me home before curfew. My parents loved him.

I bit my lip.

—Sure Ben wasn't what any parent would have wanted for their daughter. But he was exciting.
—You slept with him?
—I slept with Anton, but I was getting to that.

I flinched.

—You want to walk a bit, *Mrs. Heyward*, she offered, my married name twisting ironically in her pouting posh mouth.
—Sure.
—And maybe, you're just the tiniest bit thirsty?

She was goading me and I wasn't going to fall for it.

—Why don't you just finish the story up?

Peggy smiled.

—I've been waiting twelve years to tell this story, she said. Surely you can wait a few minutes?
—Lemonade, I said shortly.
—Coming right up.

As she tottered back up the path, I looked up towards the house. Christos was standing at the window. I could see him moving back to his desk as soon as he realized I'd seen him. Obviously thinking twice about it, he stood back at the window and waved half-heartedly. I waved back.

I didn't hear Peggy coming behind me. Not until she was standing near 'bout on the back of my heels. Looking up towards her husband's study, she made a drinking motion towards her lips. He shook his head, retreating inside the room.

—He *is* curious, said Peg.
—He probably has reason to be.

Peggy laughed again, her voice tinkling like ice in a glass.

—Now you sound like my mother.

—Ben? I asked.

—Ben, she repeated. He was Benjamin to me. It made him grow up a few years. But before Benjamin, there was always Anton.

I waited.

—When I was fifteen, Anton was a year older or so, we competed together in a competition in Nashville. I sang mostly, although I was passable on the harmonica. I had a sweet voice—a bit like Dolly Parton. Anton played the guitar.

You played the guitar?

—We really were beautiful together, although he was much more talented than I was. We made it right through to the finals. Got to sing on the stage of the Ole Opry, just like some of the real country legends.

—Must've been a high, I said, prompting her, knowing where this was going to play itself out.

—It was more than that. It gave Anton just that extra bit of confidence. Well, he was amazing that night. And I knew we were in love.

I wondered how necessary this was to Peggy's—and your— story. Or was she enjoyin' my discomfort? I wasn't entirely sure. A glimmer of a smile appeared at the corner of Peg's mouth. But for once the expression had nothing to do with me. I used to have those smiles thinking about you too, Anton, but now I'm wondering if I ever knew you at all.

—Eleanor might have told you a little about Benjamin. God knows how he even stayed in school. He flunked out one year—ended up in the same grade as Anton. It didn't go down

too well. Especially not with Bill. If Bill and Benjamin had a bad relationship before, now it was fraught with bad feeling.
—And Eleanor?
—She was a mother first and foremost. But I always thought she was a little afraid of Bill. She couldn't quite keep the peace.

I had the same feeling about Eleanor, but I didn't say anything.

—So Benjamin experimented a little. Dope mostly. Some Ecstasy. Coke once or twice. Actually he tired of all that quickly; it bored him. He was always easily bored. Part of the reason he didn't quite fit that family. Too predictable.
—And Anton?
—He was horrified. I, on the other hand, was fascinated. Once, Bill and Eleanor were out. Anton was late back from football practice. Benjamin and I smoked a few joints together. We were pretty high by the time Anton came home. He was furious with me. Nothing much happened, but we were down to our underpants. Some strange version of strip poker he invented: I wasn't very good at it. Of course, I didn't know then that Benjamin was gambling professionally at that point.
—He planned to get you naked?
—And he almost did.
—What did Anton do?
—They argued. But Benjamin was so high by then, he just laughed. It was always so difficult to believe that Benjamin was older than Anton.
—That's what Eleanor said.
—We agree once again. Anyway, it was a small thing. But not to Anton. He was actually quite a shy boy in a braggart's body. Benjamin, on the other hand, didn't care about

anything. Or so it seemed. I don't think I've ever met someone quite so relaxed. Funnily enough, Anton never blamed me at all. He was just so angry with his brother.

—Eleanor said you went out on a double date once. After that you and Ben hardly said one word to the other.

—A double date? Peggy mused. I don't recall that, although perhaps that's what we might have told her. Benjamin wasn't exactly the dating type—especially not something as trite as a double date!

—Then what were you doin'?

—Honey, you *are* impatient.

—Eleanor said the weekend the boys went camping, you sat with her sewin'. She was sure you needed to tell her somethin'.

Peg sipped her spritzer.

—I thought about telling her, then. She's right, but we were right in the middle of it all. What was she going to do about it?

—What about the missing jewelry?

Peggy looked at me, unable to mask her surprise.

—She told you about that? My heavens, you have formed a tight little friendship!

I felt myself moving away from Peg. It was voluntary and involuntary. I detested her arrogance, and I wanted to get away from her. Her company was cloying.

—If you go now, Peg said, her voice barely raised above a whisper, I won't see you again.

—Do you think this is easy for me? I asked.

144

—I very much doubt that, Peg replied. Actually, I admire
your courage.
—And I don't much like your condescending to me. I may not
be *educated* with a mansion and a shipping magnate husband,
but I loved Anton. I miss him every day.

See what you've gone and done, Anton? I was cryin' there in
front of the Prom Queen and I didn't so much as have a
tissue. What was I goin' to do, wipe away the snot on my
arm?
Peg's expression softened. She reached out to pat my
shoulder, but drew her hand away before it reached me.

—It was Anton's idea to take the jewelry, she said. It was the
only way we could get the cash.
—The cash for what?

Peg's eyes darkened.

—You want me to tell you or don't you? We took little bits. It
was easy enough, although once Eleanor cottoned on, she
started to be more careful. Locking things. Changing hiding
places. Bill fired the help, but I rather suspect Eleanor knew it
wasn't Anna.
—She thought it was Ben.
—Of course she did, and that's what Anton suspected she'd
think. It was a little bit of revenge for the poker. Besides, we
were desperate and we didn't want her to call the cops. You
think Anton would have stolen if he didn't absolutely have to?
—Why didn't he just borrow the money? Bill favored him
after all?
—Oh, I can see it now. 'Peg is knocked up, Daddy. She's
needs an abortion, and we need some cash. Any chance you
can give us a few thousand?'

—You needed an abortion?

—*We* needed an abortion. We decided to pawn the stuff. Get enough money through Benjamin's poker to get it back. That part was his idea. But that only came later.

—Except somethin' went wrong.

—Something? Everything! I almost bled to death on the butcher's block. No little whippersnappers running around here. Any guesses why not?

—I'm sorry.

—Honey, by the time we managed to get that baby out, it had little hands and feet. Teeny tiny toes, teeny tiny fingers.

I thought about our baby, Anton. That heartbeat, the curve of a spine. All gone. No wonder you couldn't take it. Cryin' for the baby we were never goin' to have.

—I don't understand, though. If you had the money, then why?

I watched Peg straighten, her hands at her dress, smoothing out the creases. Ever so slightly, she shook her head.

—So you'll come, Amanda? she said brightly, on Friday for the barbecue? Christos could send a car to fetch you.

—Of course I could, Christos said, his voice at my back like a knife.

I shifted into gear.

—Oh don't trouble yourself, I said, I'll make my own way, I don't rightly know when I'll be back from my sightseein'.

—You sure? he asked.

—Absolutely! Six o'clockish?

—Divine, Peggy said, slipping her arm around her husband.

So that's why I'm here again, Anton. Courtin' your ex. And this here bottle of wine is a good one—something French. Why not, after all? Eleanor is payin'.

But I am payin' just a little bit too. Don't you think?

Chapter 12

27 December 2004. Monday. 15h02.

Like everybody else, Jay has to fight his way onto a boat. Some of the corpses under the trees have been removed, but more are being piled up. Jay stands in the sun. A film of perspiration coats his face, and his T-shirt sticks to his back. He is peeling a little at his neck, and the flaked skin makes him itch. Buffeted by people desperate to leave the island, he is glad for his height. He is tall enough to disconnect from the anxiety around him. When Pascale taps on his back, he almost doesn't notice. Liam is behind her, cradling her protectively.

Jay finds he is happy to see them. But not in the 'I-met-you-once' sense – somehow the connection is bigger than that. Gripping Liam's hand in a firm shake, he remembers the strength of this man pulling him up as a wave hit again.

"Hey," Jay says, "you made it back down again."

"What can I say," says Liam, "I needed something other than noodles to eat. I'm hoping to get a Big Mac in Phuket Town."

Jay laughs.

"Besides," Liam adds, "Pascale and I are getting married, aren't we, honey? Nothing like a near-death experience to give you some perspective. I need to get my gal a ring."

"Wow," said Jay, not really sure how to react.

"We have to take something positive out of this, eh?" says Liam.

He waves his hand in the direction of the trees.

"You're right, of course," says Jay, "good news is what we all need."

"You have not found your girlfriend?" asks Pascale.

Her voice has a lilting quality he hadn't noticed before; she almost sounds like she is singing.

"No," he says.

"You'll find her," says Liam reassuringly.

But as he stands there with his arm around his fiancée, Jay feels his temper rise. *How can he say that? So many people have lost somebody, why should he be one of them?*

"You're probably right," he says, biting on his lip.

Assailed by the smell of mortality, Jay tries to distract his senses. He studies Liam more carefully. The Canadian is as tall as he is, but sturdier. His belly is slightly rounded under his T-shirt – the approach of a middle-aged spread. Yet he can't even be thirty. Around his eyes are creases of laughter, worry lines almost imperceptible. If it weren't for his sheer bulk, Liam's physical appearance wouldn't have been all that noteworthy. Although his eyelashes are almost giraffe-like, thick and incredibly long.

And his eyes are unusual – rounded, and flecked with an interesting mixture of brown and blue. Women probably loved them.

"You okay?" Liam said.

"Was I staring?" asked Jay, knowing that he was. "Sorry, I was trying to meditate myself from the stench."

Pascale has been pushed forward against him. He can feel her body against him, and he sinks into the human contact. He has tried to block it out, but now that he is heading to Phuket, he is mostly likely to find out the truth about Nina too. The destroyed dive shop wouldn't have been any good in making contact with the boat, but he wonders if someone in Phuket will have better luck. He has no idea whether Nina was safer where she was, but he has nothing left but hope.

Jay lurches as the boat moves forward. He can hear the cries of people being left behind.

"They have to keep going," says Liam, "those people will sink the boat. It's overloaded as it is."

Jay hears the splash of people falling into the water. He doesn't want to turn, see the desperation on their faces as they realise they are still stuck on Koh Phi Phi. Wet. Hungry. Bereaved. He's not really sure how he got on this boat, but he knows that he needs to be here. He should have stayed in Snowdonia like he wanted to, but now he feels part of something he can't yet quite explain.

One of the crew indicates for them to try sit. Their boat is probably for about 35 people, so at least fifteen are sitting on the floor. The irony strikes Jay the moment the boat starts to move. They're on the water now, and it's almost completely flat – how could it possibly have caused so much destruction?

He looks at Pascale. She's biting into her red lips with such force that when she releases the tension as they begin to move, her incisors have indented her mouth. He watches Liam take her hand, murmur something to reassure her. Jay wonders if they will leave as soon as they have managed to secure new passports. Unlike him, they don't have much more than what they carried up onto the roof, but they also don't have anybody to look for. Wouldn't he just leave, if he were them?

They arrive an hour later at a makeshift pier.

"I thought we were heading towards Patong Beach," Liam mutters.

"Patong Beach too very bad," one of the crew members replies, "cars, motorbikes, peoples into the sea. People escape in tall hotels for more than ten hours. Run. Run. Some not so lucky."

Instead they are at what looks like a fishing village. There are nets hung out for repair, but boats are stacked to the side, clearing a path for rescue vehicles. What may once have been a fish farm has been devastated. Jay watches the faces of curious children who peer from their corrugated iron and wooden shanties. *Did they lose people too?*

The boat's engine sputters. Clearly they are being transported over mudflats when the tide is out. Jay expects their boat to scrape at any moment. But it doesn't. Instead it lurches forward, the crew peering over the edge, shouting instructions. Beyond them, herons tiptoe over some floating debris.

"They come back," the captain says to Jay. "Tsunami, they fly."

As the boat moors, there are officials with clipboards waiting. Some are in uniform; others look like volunteers. They wear name badges and have set up tables. Flags fly overhead: the Stars and Stripes, Union Jack, Tricolore and various others he doesn't know the names of.

He's never been particularly patriotic, but this time even the suggestion of home catches in his throat. He separates from Pascale and Liam, moving towards the table.

16h36

Everybody Jay meets seems to be called John. Jon. Jonathan. He doesn't know where these volunteers have surfaced from, but they look at him sympathetically. Blood-stained clothes. Unbrushed hair. Dirt. They scan the photo of Kerese. It's already dog-eared.

"Beautiful girl," John says.

"Beautiful," Jay agrees.

"You'd better get some copies of this. You'll need it all over town. There are walls ..."

"You have no record of her?"

"You have to understand, Jay, is it? Many of the Thai's English isn't great. People are unidentified all over the place. Wrong spellings of names. Incorrect nationalities.

Kerese could be in a hospital somewhere recovering, and she may be tagged as a South African, Kiwi, Canadian or any other nationality you could think of."

Tagged? Jay wonders. *It makes her sound like she's in a body bag.* He shivers.

"I'm not trying to be unhelpful," John says, "I just want you to be realistic. Finding your girlfriend may not be a quick process. Won't be a quick process."

"And what about Nina?"

"That's going to be a little harder. If you don't even have a photo ..."

"She was diving in the Similans."

"Yes," the man answered. Patiently.

And Jay remembers he already told him that. Twice. He doesn't know what to do. He's in unfamiliar territory. Nina would have been so much better at this than he is. God, Jay doesn't tend to change his favourite *restaurant* and here he is in Phuket where he doesn't even know where to buy water. *I'm so thirsty*, he thinks. *When did I last drink something?*

"What do I do?" he wonders aloud.

A crowd has gathered behind him, its anxiety buffeting him forward. He begins to lift the bag away, to make way for the woman behind him.

"I found some passports," he says suddenly. "In Tonsai Village. A boy had collected them from the rubble."

John's eyebrows rise.

"I don't know what I should do with them."

"British?" John asks.

"Some. Not all."

"I'll make sure they get to the right authorities," John says, then takes them from him.

Jay is rooted in place. He can feel John's hand at his shoulder. Careful. But authoritative.

"I'm sorry, chap, but there are a lot of people to talk to."

John gestures behind Jay; people are shifting. Uneasy.

"What do I do?" Jay says again. "What do I do?"

"Get yourself to City Hall, the records are better there. They'll find you somewhere to stay. Maybe you'll get some news."

How?

Jay begins to walk. His feet are leaden. Shoulders weighted. He hadn't realised how tired he is. He drags Kerese's suitcase behind him, and even empty it feels too heavy for him. The sweat clings under his arms; his face is coated. Mucky. Clogged.

"You look as though you need some help," Liam says, taking the suitcase.

"Let *us* help you," adds Pascale.

"I'm so tired," Jay says, looking at them both. "So tired."

"It's going to be fine," Liam says with his usual optimism. "I'd bet on it."

Chapter 13

July 2, 2004 - Friday

It was kinda snazzy for a barbecue. Cocktails on trays—
mojitos and martinis—I had to stop myself downin' the lot I
was that nervous. Christos came up to me, lookin' me up and
down. I didn't like that expression. Like he was gulpin' me in
and leaving nothing for the imagination.

—Amanda, he said, welcome!
—Christos.
—You girls had a nice little chat?
—It was good to catch up.
—Have you had some canapés?

Canapés? I guess he meant those little bites of food bein'
circulated by those penguins. Smoked salmon, caviar ... what
happened to an old-fashioned chilli dog?

—I'm a-fixin' to.
—Try the tequila shrimp skewers, they're delicious.

I've never met an Amanda I actually liked. And there I was
trying to be one. Fitting into Peggy's world—I even wore a
dress, and *heels*. I was giving it a go. As Ruby always said, if
you can't run with the big dogs, stay under the porch.

—It's a beautiful evening. You must enjoy the views.
—We bought the place for the views. Peg wanted it, and I give her what she wants.

I didn't doubt it.

—It's strange, Amanda, he said, coming closer. Peggy never told me about you before.
—Oh, I never was the star she was. I kinda paled in her shadow.
—That, he said, his finger down my cheek, I find hard to believe.

Glory, Anton. I was bein' set upon by her pervy husband. And where do you think Peggy was? Working the crowd like some superstar. You think she'd even noticed me?

I stepped back. Sharply.

—Well, I'm sure you don't want to spend all your time with me, Christos, you have just a heap of guests to chat to. I'll introduce myself. And I better get to those appetisers before all the best ones are gone.

He nodded, looking towards where Peg had emerged between the topiaries.

—You enjoy your evening, he told me.

And just to prove I was goin' to, I knocked back a mojito, taking a second with my other hand.

—Don't you worry about me, I told him. I'll just drink myself interesting.

You know me, I'm not all that bad at social functions. Ruby saw to that when she dumped me in the front table at dingy bars when she was singing. All those lechers comin' up to me, wanting to chat and a little bit more. I soon learned to send them on their way. That was why you were so special, Anton, you didn't make me feel like that. So I knew I could do this, Amanda working Peggy's hoity-toity crowd. Lord help me, these folks all think that just having a few bucks makes 'em special.

What was that first clown's name? Graham. (You know, like the crackers.) That Billy Ray was windier than a bag of assholes, as your pa used to say. I just let him talk. And talk. Didn't get a word in edgeways. I had my eye on Peg, waitin' for her to acknowledge me. But she didn't even look up to where I was standing.

That Graham believed himself something fascinatin', it sure was obvious. I thought I would never get away, until this woman comes up to me.

—Amanda?

I looked at her. That girl was so skinny she probably had to dance around in the shower to get wet. She was taller than me, and that's sayin' something.

—Yes?
—I'm a great friend of Peg's. She thought you might like me to give you a tour of the house.

I could sense Peggy watching, even though her eyes were focused on her companion. Her head was tilted and as she sipped her cocktail, she nodded ever so slightly.

—Why not?
—I'm Uma, she said, Peg and I went to school together.

She linked her arm with mine, and drew me upwards towards the house. As we stepped onto the porch, I could feel the tension between us. Uma waved vaguely at Christos, then, her grip tightening, led me into the library.

—I just don't understand why you have to be here, Uma said once she'd checked we were alone. Peg has enough to worry about what with that psycho husband of hers. If he finds out about the abortion, he'll divorce her. He doesn't like lies.
—Who does?
—Sometimes lies are necessary to get what you want. From what Peg tells me about you, you were happy enough to live with lies yourself until your husband died.

I felt ice cold, Anton, like you'd just walked over my grave.

—I didn't know anything about them until he was gone, I replied.
—Sure. Your husband was such a perfect specimen that he let his own mother believe her eldest son is dead.
—What the hell do you know about this?
—Enough, she said. Enough.
—Well, I'm here aren't I, and either Peg is goin' to talk to me or she isn't. And what's up with that husband of hers anyways? Seems to me he's got Peg under a lock and key.

We walked into the entrance hall. She flat-out ignored my question. What a surprise.

—It's a Modigliani she says, pointing at a statue. Christos bought it for Peg for her birthday.

Whatever.

—Lucky Peg, I said, but my sarcasm was obviously a little hidden.
—Yes, Uma replied. He loves her, in his own way. And despite what Christos says, Peg isn't having an affair. She doesn't want to break another trust.

Whose trust has she already broken, Anton? Maybe you know just a little somethin' about that?

I followed Uma down the corridor. I could feel the martini circulating my belly like a catfish caught in a puddle when the rains are done. And maybe, just maybe, it was mixing with a little bit of my fretting. We climbed a flight of stairs. She waved at the paintings as she passed them.

—Mondrian, Magritte, Manet—we call them the three Ms.

Ugly. And the colors didn't even match. Fire the decorator, Peg.

I looked out the window from the next floor. Peggy's mother wasn't joking about the views, now that was what I call impressive. We used to do a bit of swimming, didn't we? But we never had a view like that, not even on vacation.

Uma led me into a guest room. Not a piece of furniture out of place. Lace and prettified like some museum. She opened the wardrobe. It creaked, then spilled open, smelling of mothballs and lavender. Digging underneath a pile of runners and tablecloths, she extracted a shoebox. The lid was out of shape, as though water had spilled on it.

—You're not to take anything, Uma said.

She opened a drawer, extracting a pen and a notepad.

—Here, she said. And there's a photocopier two doors down to the left. You need me to show you how to work it?

I shook my head. As Uma turned to leave, she stole a final glance.

—You must understand, she said, that Peggy really is a good person. Things just went a little awry.

With that I was alone again, the door shut quietly behind her.

Chapter 14

27 December 2004. Sunday. 17h32.

It's Pascale's idea, but he can't even fathom why he didn't think of it first. Jay needs to phone his mother. Who knows what she may be thinking. He can't even believe he hasn't been in touch yet.

Pascale and Liam hover outside the Internet café, giving him some privacy. But the grief and shock is tangible even in here.

The man at the terminal cries into the phone.

"I was holding her, Amy, I was, but I just couldn't hang on."

Jay shivers, but masters a medical distance he is used to adopting with frantic family members.

"Mum. There's no point in your coming too. What about Dad – what if he turns for the worse? And anyway, if Nina makes contact you need to be there to answer the phone."

His mother is crying.

"I can't cope, Jay. Nina? Thank God you're okay. That wave. Daniel. Oh my God."

Her sentences are jumbled. Connected – but not in any logical order. She talks and chatters in a puzzle. A gridlock of meaning that frightens Jay. He should have contacted her sooner.

"I need a photo, Mum. Of Nina. A good one. And you need to email me her distinguishing characteristics. In case I forget something. Is the dragon tattoo on her back or her shoulder?"

He can hear his mother sobbing.

"Mum," he says, "Mum. I need you to send it to my webmail. Have you got my address? Can you get someone to help you? What about Sara?"

His mother gulps, then replies, "Sara's still on holiday."

"Then what about your neighbour. Owen?"

Silence.

"Mum, you need to help me. I have to put Nina's photo up. In case someone has found her. Seen her."

"Right," she replies, calmer. "I'll speak to him. How will I contact you?"

"I'm going to charge my mobile. It's dead now. But it'll be working tomorrow. Email me, Mum. Please. Within the hour."

"Okay," she says, "okay."

Jay phones Kerese's parents next. It takes him a few goes to get through, but when he does Kerese's mother must have been standing right there. The phone only rings once.

She's calmer. More measured.

"I've booked a flight, Jay. I'll be in Phuket by the thirtieth."

Jay considers telling her he is taking care of this, but doesn't. Instead he repeats his mobile number.

"For when you arrive," he says.

"Right."

She rings off briskly. Businesslike.

Jay steps outside. Without the aircon, he begins to sweat almost immediately. Liam and Pascale are drinking fruit shakes in the restaurant opposite. No. 13. Lucky number 13? Jay looks up towards the clouds building. They'll have an afternoon squall and all those people queuing outside City Hall will get drenched. Some entrepreneurial Thai will probably be selling plastic ponchos – or knowing the kindness of these people – giving them away.

"*Ça va?*" Pascale asks him.

"Yes," he replies, "I think I'm okay."

Liam waves to a waitress.

"What you having?" he says. "You'll need to build some strength."

Jay nods.

"It's going to be a long night," he replies.

18h45

"Still nothing?" Liam says, stifling a yawn.

"You don't have to stay with me," says Jay, almost defensively.

Pascale pats his shoulder.

"It is necessary to wait for our passports," she says

"We don't have anywhere to be, either," says Liam.

Jay stirs listlessly. This coffee tastes terrible but at least it has a good dose of caffeine. He tastes, then adds another spoon of sugar.

"So where do you come from, Pascale?" he says.

"Quebec, you know, in Canada."

"Is that where you guys met?"

"No," says Liam, "We met in Peru, on the Inca Trail. We were in the same group going over the mountain. God, did it rain that day. We hadn't even left and our packs were almost drenched through."

"Good climbing?" Jay asked, not that he knew much about the Andes or South America for that matter.

"Not climbing so much as hiking," said Liam, "I'd just flown in, so you can imagine how I battled with the altitude. I'd acclimatised for a few days, drinking coca tea, but clearly not long enough."

"You got ill?"

"Well actually, when I first saw Pascale, she was shouting at the guide. She'd organised a porter who hadn't arrived, and they were telling her she was going to have to carry all her belongings herself. So, I offered to help her ..."

Pascale began to laugh.

"Except that it turned out she was tougher than I was. By the second day I was vomiting, and not coping well at all. But it was a bit late to turn back. The guides shared our stuff between them, and Pascale virtually pushed me up the mountain."

Pascale pulled a photo out of her wallet, which had been zipped in her shorts when the wave hit.

"*Nous voilà,*" she said, pointing at two bedraggled looking individuals sitting on a rock wall.

"That's at the end of the hike, at Macchu Picchu," added Liam. "Never in my life have I been more pleased to see civilisation, even an ancient one! And of course my manly prowess was so impressive that Pascale fell head over heels in love with me, which was an added bonus."

Pascale laughed, punching Liam lightly in the shoulder.

"Once we'd hooked up, we travelled a bit together," continued Liam. "Pascale's been working on my French so that when we move back to Quebec, she and her family can talk rapidly without my missing ninety percent of the conversation!"

"Your French sounds pretty good to me," says Jay.

"It is," agreed Pascale.

"Pillow talk," says Liam, with a wink, "works wonders!"

"But didn't you have to learn French at school?"

"Not in the US, I did a bit of Spanish. But all my French I learnt in Canada."

Jay looked at his watch.

"Let me check again," he said, distractedly.

He stood up, knocking his chair over in a swift movement. One of the restaurateurs hurtled over, retrieving it, then smiled unreservedly at him.

"No problem, no problem."

"Back in a moment," Jay said.

19h10

The Internet café's lights had just been turned on. Most of the fittings were paper bubbles. Underneath them, dim electric globes. A fridge stacked with Pepsi and various unrecognisable soft drinks whirred near the doorway. Logging into a computer, Jay begins to download his mail. This time a message is coming through.

    Finally.

To: Jay
CC:

Subject: Nina

Hi Jay

I don't know if this is going to be good enough, but it's the best I can do. Owen scanned a few photos from when Nina was last home. They're not all that flattering. Is this the last photo we are going to have of her? I'm also attaching one of Neen from her birthday picnic at Cannizaro. I know it's a year old, but it captures her beautifully. Please let me know you get these. Owen and Michelle are cooking me dinner tonight. Thank God. I need the distraction. HAVE YOU EATEN??? Please look after yourself. And

keep me updated. Even in the MIDDLE of the
night. I'll be awake, worrying anyway.

Love, Mum.

Jay replies quickly, then prints out the photos. The older
one is definitely better. And anyway, he thinks, Nina
would kill him if he plastered that really dreadful pic over
half the hospitals and walls in Phuket. It wasn't long before
Jay had recruited an assembly line of willing helpers once
people realised what he was trying to do.

"It's flee, we print. Many, many."

Jay considers his first attempt, wondering if he should add a Union Jack, then sketches one in on the corner of each page. He hadn't realised his hand-writing was as poor as it appeared. Not until he saw it in huge black felt-tip pen and wasn't sure if even he could it read it all that well.

"So you weren't lying about being a doctor," said Liam, taking the pen out of his hand. "You mind if I give this a go for you?"

21h03

By the time they leave the Internet café, they have at least two hundred posters. They had to adjust the machine to the different women's colouring, but both photos are clear now. Nina, her head thrown back, giggling. Her cropped hair framing her face, the dark eyeliner bringing out her eyes. Kerese, serene. Her hair perfect, make-up layered and unblemished. The rise of her breasts visible under the buttoned-up white blouse.

Pascale reminds him to buy some Sellotape – how else will he put these faces alongside the others that are unclaimed or unfound? He'll start at the main hospitals at Phuket, drop off a photo of Nina at City Hall in the morning. But now he is tired. They've found a guest house far away from the beach. *No charge. You sleep here, my fliends.* Jay needs to sink away into dreamlessness. He's numb. Solid as a statue. His limbs, his lids feel too heavy. Tomorrow, he will search. But he can't do anything more tonight. He thinks of his night-time vigils next to Daniel's bed, wondering if Nina or Kerese are waiting for him to come. But he won't find them now. He can't.

He'll slip between his sponsored sheets and escape from the chaos. What happened to his measured life? His sense of duty? His strength under pressure?

Too tired, he thinks, *exhausted.*

When he sinks into bed, he closes his eyes, and in seconds, his body is washing out to sea on a black and murky wave.

Chapter 15
July 2, 2004 – Friday

So I sat there on the bed while the sounds of Maroon 5's *She Will Be Loved* wafted up muted, but recognizable. Anton, you would've hated that darned song. It plays so often you would think the radio stations were stuck on repeat. Remember how we used to dig around in old record stores and find those tunes that everybody had forgotten about? I listen to a bit of country now—our songs make me sad. And who am I supposed to share them with?

At first I couldn't get settled. I kept expectin' Christos to barge in, demand to know who I really am, then chuck me forthwith from the house. But as I opened the box and began to read, I found that I was getting drawn in. The clippings didn't seem to be arranged in any particular order. But the first, taken from the June 14, 1980 *Atlanta Journal*, told me the sequence of events as I'd already begun to understand them.

```
Atlanta Journal
June 14, 1980
MYSTERY OF COLONEL'S SON BURNT ALIVE!

In the early hours of this morning, the body
of Benjamin Heyward (21), the son of highly
decorated US Army Colonel William Heyward,
was discovered in a burnt-out 1967 Ford
Falcon in Grant Park, close to Oakland
Cemetery. Colonel Heyward, who is the
```

garrison commander for Fort McPherson and Fort Gillem in the Atlanta metropolitan area, has not offered any public comment, but it is understood that the family is in shock.

Says Detective Sharpe, who has been assigned to the case, "Part of the investigation is to determine how this fire started and to discover whether foul play is involved. At the moment, all indications are pointing to a suicide. Additionally, traces of fuel have been identified. However, an analysis of the forensics will assist in determining these answers."

Atlanta firefighters reached the scene around midnight and had the blaze under control within an hour. It appears that the fire followed an argument between the Colonel and his son, although Eleanor Heyward, the victim's mother, has requested that some privacy be given to the family.

Sharpe confirms that the car was found by Colonel Heyward, who was accompanied by Benjamin's younger brother Anton. They were able to identify the body, so no post mortem will be required. Says a close friend of the family who wishes to remain anonymous, "Benjamin was always a bit of a loose cannon. As far I know, his academic record was poor and his addiction to gambling a secret not very well kept by his peers."

At the time of the fire, Benjamin was
working at the Costco Gas Station off
Piedmont and Orange. His employer, Stan
Colicchio, has expressed his deep sorrow on
being informed of the news. "Benjamin was a
good boy, a little lost, but he'd a kind
heart. He was one of my hardest workers.
Can't say I believe he'd have killed
himself. He had too much to live for."

Benjamin's younger brother Anton is well
known in Atlanta circles for his sporting
and academic accomplishments. He has
expressed his feelings of devastation at the
loss of his elder brother, and will be
treated by a trauma and grief counselor to
recover from the dreadful discovery.

The details of Benjamin's memorial service
are yet to be confirmed, although the
Heywards frequently attend the Sacred Heart
on Spring Avenue. A press conference is
scheduled for tomorrow when more information
on the tragedy becomes available.

I thought a little about this one, noting two new names I
hadn't heard spoken before. Detective Sharpe and Stan
Colicchio. I wondered if I would be able to find either of
them? And what, I wondered was Stan referring to—did Ben
have something—someone?—he was unlikely to have left
behind?

The next clipping was written after the memorial service.

Atlanta Star

MY HEART'S IN THE HIGHLANDS
June 18, 1980

A somber looking Colonel William Heyward bid
his farewells to his eldest son today at the
Sacred Heart Church at 10am. Colonel
Heyward, the bearer of a Medal of Honor,
Silver Star and the Purple Heart attended
the ceremony in full military regalia, and
was accompanied by his wife Eleanor (of the
Charleston Hammonds) and only remaining son,
Anton. Attended by more than one hundred
people, the service highlighted the tragic
and early loss of life of a young man yet to
find himself, but who now will never be able
to.

Only 21, Benjamin Alistair Heyward was found
burnt beyond recognition in his car near
Oakland Cemetery; the discovery made after a
frantic search for him by his father and
brother, following a family incident.

Col. Heyward paid tribute to his son by
reading from the poem "My Heart is in the
Highlands" by Robert Burns, which begins: *My
heart's in the Highlands, my heart is not
here, /My heart's in the Highlands a-chasing
the deer - A-chasing the wild deer, and
following the roe …/.*

Says Benjamin's closest friend Ian Colbert,
"I used to think not many people really

173

understood Benjamin, but the poem was just
so right. Ben's recent success hunting was
one of his happiest moments, I know we were
only friends for two years, but I *got* him.
Coming to terms with his passing is
incredibly hard."
The investigation continues, but suicide is
the likely verdict.

I thought Eleanor said Benjamin had no friends? Who was
Ian and how did he fit in anyways? I flipped through the obits.
They didn't seem to reveal all that much, although I noted one
from the Lott Gibsons, just after your family's tribute—such
as it was. What was that anyhow? A son dies, and he gets two
lines?

Heyward, Benjamin Alistair (1959 to 1980). Gone so soon
and so tragically. Missed by his father William, mother
Eleanor and brother Anton.

Heyward, Benjamin (1959 to 1980). A great friend to the Lott
Gibson family, particularly to Peggy. Sorely missed.

My stomach was missin' out on that barbecue downstairs.
The hickory smoke and Cajun spices, curling up from near the
rose garden makin' me hungrier by the minute. If I'd known I
was gonna be stuck up here, I would've eaten before I came. I
wondered what they were serving up—potato salad, corn
fritters or whatever they'd call hush puppies here on the West
Coast, pulled pork with a frou frou finishin' sauce … The
photocopier sounded mighty loud to me—whirring its way
over the papers and churning the copies out—the folds from
twelve years back near disappeared.

There was a lot in Peg's box, and I didn't think I was goin' to finish up reading it all there and then. I'd have to pick and choose, then keep the rest of the reading for later. But even as I thought that, Anton, I couldn't help stoppin'—like the way I kept on reading the juicy stories in the newspapers as we were packing up my apartment to move in with you. It drove you near demented, remember? An hour to fill a box of glasses because the stories were so darned fascinating. I probably would've stopped for the suicide snippet then too.

The Constitution
YOUNG SUICIDES—WHAT DO WE KNOW?
July 1, 1980

With the recent confirmation of suicide by investigating officers of the Benjamin Heyward case, the community has some serious thinking to do about what could bring a young man with his whole life before him to such desperate and drastic measures. Says psychologist Wilson Purvis, "There are many factors that would influence a person's decision to take his life. These include: a history of mental illness, social isolation—or being physically isolated—age and unemployment."

On reflection, it does seem that Benjamin Heyward answers very few of these criteria, and certainly Mrs. Eleanor Heyward has mentioned only Benjamin's difficulty with the frequent moves her husband's job required of them as a family. "Benjamin didn't make friends easily," she said.

175

According to Purvis, "Suicide in men peaks in the 20s and again in the 60s and 70s." At 21, Benjamin was in the right age range, but he was employed and had been for more than six months. He was, however, described by his father as having an "addictive personality".

Benjamin's is not the first suicide tragedy this year, or even this week in Atlanta. In late June, Richard Lowry (22) originally from Conyers, was found hanging from his bedroom ceiling. His death was surmised to have taken place under the influence of narcotics or alcohol. He was not known to have any family or personal difficulties at the time of his demise.

Using these two sad events as an example, what measures can we as a community take to prevent similar tragedies occurring? According to Purvis, "General Practitioners need to play a greater role in preventing the suicide of young people. They also need to be trained to detect the early warning signs of suicidal tendencies, especially in men and boys. This, because men are generally more likely to commit suicide than women and are also much less likely to ask for help."

A few exceptions to this generalization exist, for instance, among elderly women in Hungary and in some Asian countries.
-STAFF REPORTER

Surely somebody must've picked up somethin' strange? What about that Detective Sharpe, or whatever his name was? Suicide—no warning? No wonder Eleanor was devastated. I picked through some more of the pieces in the box, emptying it out to the last crumpled note. And it *was* crumpled, Anton, caught underneath the folds of the box and smudged where it had gotten wet. I couldn't help myself. I knew that this time I was pryin' way beyond what was expected of me. I didn't really want to read your note to Peg, but I did it anyway.

I'll do anything for you, my angel. You know that. And if it means I have to hurt my brother, I'll do it. I love you. Passionately. I have from the first moment I saw you.

Anton, for God's sake, what did you do to Ben?

Chapter 16

28 December 2004. Tuesday. 03h02.

He splutters awake, his eyes darting around the darkened
room and he can't think where he is. In a moment, it all
becomes clear again. He won't go back to sleep now.
Sleeping is frightening – a heightened state of helplessness,
like when the wave came. Before, it was necessary, but
now. Now, he can feel his pulse rising, his heart crushing
his chest. Padding out the bed, he knocks his leg on the
bedside table. He grimaces. Steadies himself, then enters
the bathroom. He can't pee immediately. It's almost as if
his whole body has seized up. But then he feels the release,
the liquid swirling into toilet. He flushes it with a plastic
jug he dips from a larger supply of water. The drain stinks,
his throat clogs with the smell of sewers.

He washes his hands. Closes the door again.

What was he ever doing in this place?

Jay reaches down next to the bed, extracting her
journal. The only name he has to go by is Amanda, and
she's right. She's not an Amanda. She's something sweeter.
More innocent. Plucky. Now that's a word he hasn't used
in ... a lifetime. She's a Tracy, or an Ashley or maybe a

Charley. A Hannah. A Mary-Lou. Whoever she is, he finds
that he likes her. The way she creeps around Peg's
mansion, digging into a mystery from which she can't
really benefit. He can see she's thought things through.
Picked up clues in the cuttings. He hasn't worked out her
code, not yet, but everything seems methodical. Green
highlights. Yellow. Pink. Blue. There are hand-drawn
tables, with names and surnames and charts showing how
people link together. Benjamin's name in the middle.
Fanning out to join up with Anton and Eleanor. Bill. Peg.
Detective Sharpe—ret. Moab. *Retired?* Jay wonders. Ian
Colbert—New York (marr.) *Married?* Stan Colicchio—
Savannah (TG). *Thank God? To go?* Then there are other
names, names he doesn't know yet. Borys Jachowicz. Kim
Harrison. Major Patrick Davies (dead). A stack of others
connected by her ballpoint web.

Jay fingers the photo she's glued onto the page after
her mind map. They're kids really. Eighteen, nineteen,
maybe? Their arms around each other. If that's Peg, she
looks a lot like Kerese. Curved and customised. Every part
of her in place. Anton – if that's him – is tall. A looker, but
not his type – ha-ha! And Ben. His hair is dark brown, then
streaked through with peroxide. Shaggy. Like a Saint-
Bernard, his eyes almost covered. He's out of focus though.
Peg is to the right looking at the boys. What are they
doing? Dancing? Singing? Some kind of Mexican wave? It's
a happy photo. Something he would have kept too. And
when was the last time he felt that kind of bubbling-up, all-
consuming happiness?

179

Certainly not tonight. And he can't stay trapped in this room. The smell of the drain seeps under the doorway. And it's not as if he can complain about it, or even wants to. Jay checks his mobile. Answers the messages that have come in since he charged his phone earlier. NO NEWS. WILL LET YOU KNOW. He saves it to draft, then sends it out to everyone. Nothing from Kerese or Nina though. They won't have phones. Will they? Jay scribbles a message onto the back of a brochure from his suitcase – imagine it – a few days ago they were deciding whether or not to go to Phuket for a bit of a shopping spree. Kerese was anyway. And here he is. Not shopping.

I can't sleep. I'm taking some of the posters now. Jay.

He jots down his number, slips the note under their door. Maybe Pascale and Liam will be relieved to be rid of him for a few hours. He's not exactly a bundle of laughs at the moment. At least he can go out without the suitcase banging about his heels. He doesn't even know where he's going. But he's got his ATM card. He'll draw money. Find a tuk-tuk? Walk until he tires himself out?

His feet echo on the stairs. He pats his shorts pocket for the sticky tape.

I can do this.

The outside air hits him like a hairdryer on full throttle. *It did rain didn't it?* Shit, it's hot. And humid. He steps over a puddle. Misses the next one. Feels the squelch of mud – he hopes it's mud – between his toes. There's a roadside stall, a man still selling pineapple pancakes at this time of night. He buys one and a bottle of water. The pancake tastes good. Of grease and fruit all mixed up. The water isn't quite cold, but it doesn't matter. He downs the entire bottle in seamless gulps.

He thought the city would be asleep by now. But it's isn't. In the window of an artist's shop he can see a man hunched over a painting, an easel next to him of the work he is copying. Recreating. The man looks up at him, measured. Nods, then head down. Detailed work, then.

There's an Irish bar down the road on the left. It's not pumping, but it's not empty either. Mostly mixed couples, older looking European men with their Thai women. It's life continuing where the wave hasn't hit. Jay walks on past, feels a tug at his elbow. He jerks himself away, turns to confront his attacker. Her eyes are wide, she steps back in her stiletto-heeled boots. A hand in front of her face. God, is that what he looks like?

"Sorry," he mutters, attempting a smile.

"You like massage?" she asks him, recovering, "I give you happy ending."

If only it were that easy.

03h37

They clamour for the business when they realise he has some. He's not in the mood to negotiate.

"Your best price," he says firmly.

"Where you go?"

"Hospital," Jay says.

"Patong Hospital?"

"All of them."

Jay holds out his posters, their eyes registering what he is holding.

"I go," says one man, "best price. Sure."

Jay doesn't even ask what this is.

05h13

By the first signs of morning, Jay doesn't remember where he has stopped and where he hasn't. The corridors have merged into a never-ending passageway of lined-up beds, and worse, lined-up bodies. The unidentified dead have been photographed, their pictures displayed on notice boards in the hopes of finding who they are and who they belong to. Nearby are the photos of the missing. It's difficult to find space to put one poster up, never mind two. And there is no way he can cover a photo with one of his own. It just wouldn't be right. So it's a painstaking process, shuffling pages bit by bit across the board until a space opens up. And then Kerese or Nina slide in amongst the others. If he goes away, then comes back, he finds it difficult to locate them, even though he put them there.

And he has to look at all the expressionless faces, separated now from beaten, bruised, drowned bodies. Sometimes they are not without emotion; they look shocked, or surprised, or horrified. With each photo he endures, Jay finds himself becoming more and more numbed. There are so many old people on these walls, he realises. As though the young were the only people able to run, or withstand the battering of a merciless sea. Each time he approaches another section of death masks, he repeats his mantra. *Don't let it be them. Don't let it be them. Don't let it be them.* He doesn't recognise anybody – not until he sees the photo of the man they put on the helicopter. The last man he helped. Or didn't help, it seems. The whole thing is sickening.

Each time he leaves the hospital, the tuk-tuk driver is waiting for him.

"Nothing?"

"Nothing," Jay confirms.

"So maybe that's good," says the man. "Not dead, then, light?"

"Right," says Jay, wondering at his logic.

"We go?"

"Yes," answers Jay.

Wherever that means.

06h47

He doesn't know it's his last hospital, but even then he would have remembered it. It's filled with children. Little bodies, wrapped up in sheets, and numbered in bright red pen. He sees a nurse, gently brushing the hair of a little girl until it frames her face. Unlike the adults he has seen, grotesque and tortured, her face is peaceful as though she has just fallen asleep. The nurse cares for her with such tenderness that Jay turns away, feeling like an intruder.

He walks from her to the bigger bodies, his stomach in a tight knot. But as he moves, he hears a familiar voice behind him.

"I need to see if it's him."

Jay turns. It's Steve. His face chalk-white and his hands clenched in front of him. Jay hesitates, then walks back. Putting his arm around the stricken man, he helps him forward.

"I need to see if it's him, mate," Steve repeats. "You'll help me, won't you?"

"Of course."

And then the body is rolled forward slightly, Finn's little face half-exposed but entirely still. His skin is slightly blue, and a cut extends down his left cheek. Jay shivers, the pain etched so deeply into Steve's face that it seems a physical presence.

"My boy. My little boy."

Steve is on the floor, cuddling the little body to him. He rocks back and forth as he keens, his voice drilling into Jay's head. The sounds coming from him are primordial, all-encompassing.

And despite the many times that Jay has had to distance himself from scenes like this, he finds that he is crying.

Chapter 17

July 4, 2004 - Sunday

I took a walk on *the* bridge. My Lord, Anton, what a kicker!
You would've loved it. It was a bit windy and a fog was
comin' in, but never mind that, this was something real
special. It made me forget, just for a moment or two, why I
was here. The Golden Gate Bridge! Beautiful! And looks like
I'll be headin' off to Utah soon. That Detective Sharpe, he's
retired there, you see and he won't speak to me over the
phone. Eleanor is getting impatient—but what can I do? I'm
findin' pieces all over the place, and puzzling them together.

We talked about Utah once, remember? Going to see the
National Parks. Arches and them others. We were gonna
sleep under the stars. Make love by moonlight. Now I'm
meeting some crotchety old man who needs a machine to help
him breathe. Emphysema, that's what his wife says. From all
them ciggies. And diabetes from all them doughnuts from
Dunkin's. 'He's not a well man.' Or so she said.

I'll fly tomorrow. Peg's agreed to run through everything else
she knows. We're meeting at a funky restaurant on the ocean.
She'd better be payin'. Or it'll be on Eleanor's tab—again.

I haven't managed to reach Stan Colicchio yet. He owns a gas
station near Savannah now. Moved around the same time as

your family did … coincidence, Anton? Maybe you'd know something about that. And Ian Colbert, he's a banker in the Big Apple. The rotten apple, you remember that's what you always called it? I haven't spoken to him yet. He's workin' a bit in London, and they won't give out his number, like I'm some creepy stalker or something.

I googled Ian. He's pretty successful. Part-owns a chain of restaurants with a friend of his. Married to a woman from Brazil. She's hot, but she looks a bit young for him, eighteen or so. Second or third marriage; the papers don't seem to agree on that one. The middle woman may have been just a girlfriend but she didn't last all that long anyways. Ian's first wife, Louisa-May, was killed in a hit-and-run. She grew up with him and Benjamin in Atlanta—you might remember her? A pretty girl. Except for her buck teeth.

I read some more of the cuttings. I don't even know how some of them fit in. There's the one on the abortion clinic, which Peg had written over.

MINOR'S ABORTION, MAJOR FOUL-UP

The Femifirst Abortion Clinic is under fire in medical circles today, after an abortion was performed last week on an unnamed minor, without her parents' consent. Says Mrs. Randall*, from Augusta, "My daughter did not undergo any form of pre-abortion counseling, which is, as I understand it, the legal requirement in Georgia."

A representative from the Georgia Department of Human Resources (DHR), Dr Maynard Crooks, agrees this is the case. "Femifirst has ignored two critical abortion restrictions. This casual disregard for this young woman's rights is not only outrageous; it is cavalier and highly unprofessional."

The termination was only discovered after the young girl (15) was found bleeding and unconscious in her bedroom by her grandmother. And it brings to the fore the question: how many of our girls are being allowed to have these operations performed without their parents' knowledge?

The good news, however, is this. Cases like these are almost unheard of. For women in the US, abortion is one of the safest surgical procedures they can undergo. Fewer than 0.5% of women obtaining terminations experience any complications whatsoever. And the risk of death is approximately one-tenth of that associated with giving birth.

Dr Crooks says that in Georgia, abortions are usually performed on women who have risked pregnancy through improper or no use of contraception. He has also noted a decrease in the number of induced abortions performed in Georgia this year since last year over the same period. This after a comparison of the statistics obtained by the Alan Guttmacher Institute surveying abortion providers in Georgia.

Dr Westmoreland from Femifirst categorically denies any wrongdoing, stating that the

```
abortion was performed as requested by the
girl concerned, but that she lied about her
age and identity. A civil case against the
medical facility has nevertheless been
instituted. STAFF REPORTER
*Name changed to protect the family's
privacy.
```

LIAR!!! Peg had written across the text, partly obscuring it. And where the text had smudged, I wondered if she'd shed a few tears over it too.

July 5, 2004 – Monday

I had to drive some of the way to Moab. What a landscape. Desolate. Rock stacks and pinnacles. I don't know the right geological terms for them, but they were real beautiful. It was already dusk when I got in—a pinky haze coating the scenery as though I was lookin' through a pair of tinted sunglasses. John Wayne stayed there once. All those Western movies you used to get a thrill from filmed here in this dusty desert. I knew Detective Sharpe wasn't gonna see me that night, so I drove around. I passed this strange place on the side of the road—some sort of saloon with *real gun totin'*. I didn't have anythin' better to do. Signed myself in right there and then for an evenin' of cowboy entertainment.

Ordered up a cold cider, and watched these men duellin' away over stolen property and unfaithful wives. I sat at some long table, strangers next to me. They looked at me, a girl on my own, and you could see the questions ticking round their brains. But they welcomed me okay. Tourists. Like me I suppose. But it wasn't until I spoke to the owner of the place, all dressed up in a pink Stetson, and tassels, that I learned about the man I was to meet.

—You here to see Chet Sharpe?

She repeated this to me as though I were a little crazy.

—Yes ma'am.
—He's not right in the head, that one. Must be the lack of oxygen. He came to these parts ten years ago. Doctor's orders. Good for the lungs and the asthma.
Sure.
—Well, he wasn't as bad then as he is now, but he sure used to talk to himself. Always muttering in the supermarket. You'd catch him examining the tomatoes as though they were clues for some murder. He covered a lot of murder cases you know. Famous in his day.
—Was he?
—Oh yes. Lots of crime in Atlanta, not like here. Chet's wife, Caryn, well she says he has all the unsolved crimes in some book. Studies them at night. Chet doesn't enjoy nice family photos, spends his time flipping through photos of banged up bodies.
—He won't give up then?
—Not until he's dead, and quite frankly, my dear, that day won't be all that long in coming.

July 6, 2004 – Tuesday

Caryn met me at the door. I'd expected an old lady, white-haired with a walker. She's nothin' like that. She's got Botox written all over her face, and to tell you the truth, she looks good on it. Her hair done up, in one of them French styles, and her boobs perkier than mine. She brought me inside, offering me coffee, as she led me into the conservatory. A lovely room, filled with sunshine. Yellow walls and blue flowers in a tall glass vase. I sat. A little nervous, I gotta tell you, Anton, but she put me right at ease.

—You're not the first person to come all the way to Moab from Chet's past, she said.
—I'm not sure I am from his past, I answered. My husband Anton was, though.
—The Heyward boy?

I nodded.

—Chet always said something wasn't right with that fire, but he was told right from the top to leave it alone.
—Leave what alone?
—The questions.

Caryn poured the coffee. It was hot and bitter. I had to stir a spoonful of sugar to drink it down. She passed me some cookies.

—Walnut and date, she said. But I didn't bake them myself.

I took one. I could see she expected me to. I bit into it, wanting to ask if Chet was comin' through, but she'd already anticipated that.

—Chet's a damaged man, she told me, he's seen a lot of terrible things, and he can't forget them.
—I'm real sorry to bother him. I don't even know if he'll be able to help.
—Darling, he'll help if he can. I'll bring him through, but don't tire him too much. I'll fetch him then leave you two alone for a bit. You just holler if you need anything.

Chet shuffled through the door, lookin' at least twenty years older
than his wife. He was white-haired and the contrast against
his deep tan was almost shocking.

—That Heyward boy is dead?

He said this directly, but it came out as a wheeze. Caryn pulled
the oxygen tank along behind him, settling her husband in a
chair next to the window. *His* chair, I was sure about that. It
was worn right down and the only piece of furniture in the
room that didn't match.

—Yessir.
—Poor little tyke. Carrying secrets around will kill anyone.
—He died in a helicopter accident.
—Whatever, Chet said, it was goin' to happen sooner or later.
Right Caryn?
—Chet, this is the Heyward boy's widow, she reminded him.

He nodded.

—Never liked that William Heyward. He cut my boys off that
night.
—Chet.

Caryn shook her head, warning him.

—Are you here for the truth or not? he asked me, his eyes blazing.
Or do you want me to whisper sweet nothings and send you
on your way?

Chet began to cough, spit flyin' from his mouth and settlin'
around him like landing mosquitoes.

191

—The truth, I said softly.
—See Caryn, this young lady wants the truth. Girl—

He looked at me. I nodded.

—That book on the coffee table. You see it? There next to the
ashtray. You bring it to me.
I stood up, noticing Caryn sidle out the room. Giving it to him, I
watched has he grabbed the mask to breathe, his hands
shaking. The album was dog-eared, with notes scrawled
underneath the photos, and sometimes even on them.

—It was late when I got the call. Twelve? One? Caryn was already
in bed and I was watching some trash on TV. So I got in my
patrol car, went straight to the park. But I could see the flames
long before I was even close. The younger Heyward boy,
Anton was it? Well, he was standing next to his father's car.
In shock. Shivering. I had a blanket in my car, put it around
his shoulders. There was no way I could put out the flames on
my own. You see, I got the feeling—and I still have it—that
Benjamin's car had been burning for quite some time.
—They didn't call straightaways?
—Young lady, he said, pointing at the photo of a burnin' vehicle.
No car burns that badly that fast.
—The fire went out?
—No, a fire truck near blew it away. That body was barbecued
like a fourth-of-July T-bone. The smell of charred flesh. That
Anton puked his lungs out. Of course we knew the car was
Benjamin's. I'd hauled him into the station once or twice for
reckless driving.

Chet coughed again, his hand over his mouth, gesturing to me to give him some more oxygen. As he breathed it in, I waited, not wanting to press him.

—Anton was grubby—dust and soot, and blood on his shoulder. Told me he'd tried to wrench the door open. I didn't believe him, though, no burn marks on his hands or arms. That car would have singed off his hair. And I asked myself, now why hadn't they rescued Benjamin?
—And Bill?
—William Heyward was far too smooth. Hushed up Anton, quick as a flash. Told me he'd called the Chief of Police. And he had. The Chief was there about ten minutes after I was. They shook hands, chatted while I secured the scene, called in the other cars. My partner and I wanted to question the Heywards, file a report, but the Chief told me he'd do it.

I looked at Chet. He was wiping away the beads of sweat on his forehead with a hanky. I passed him a glass of water that Caryn had left on the table for him. He sipped, then continued.

—It was my case, and the next moment, I was being hustled back home, to 'get some rest'. I have to tell you, nobody cares if you rest when you're in the Force. You do the job or you get out. No autopsy on that body. The Chief vetoed it. 'That family has suffered enough.' That's what he told me. Suicide … Chet hissed through his teeth … that boy wasn't a goodie-two shoes, but he wasn't about to top himself either, that I do know.
—So what happened?
—I only found out by accident. Waiting for Caryn at this coffee house. Not my sort of place, but she was late and I was

hungry. I was tucking into a piece of triple chocolate chip, when I heard some voices on the other side of the booth.

Chet hesitated, his chest seizing into another explosion of coughs.

—You all right in there? Caryn called.
—Just a cough, he managed. Just coughing, woman.

I handed Chet the glass again. He downed the rest of the water. Took another gulp of air.

—The Chief had a voice on him. Booming. I'd never heard him whisper. I was about to get up to greet him, when I heard the other voice.
—Bill? I guessed.
—Who else? Something about the whole meeting stopped me in my tracks. I slipped back down into the booth, hoping they wouldn't see me. I don't remember the exact words of that conversation, but the gist of this was this. The Chief knew Benjamin was alive. Not only that; he'd helped William get a passport for him and sneak him over the border into Canada.
—But why? Why would he do that?
—That I didn't ever find out. Because Caryn walked into that damn coffee shop, calling my name. You should have seen how those boys ducked. Nearly didn't sign the check.

Chet laughed, but his hilarity caught him right up in another desperate gasp for oxygen. I held the mouthpiece to his face as he tried to breathe. He righted himself, pattin' me on the shoulder.

—It wasn't so funny the next day, though. The Chief called me into his office. Mentioned a few of my misdemeanors—a gun

I hadn't signed out properly, that sort of thing. Then he told
me how he'd overlooked them—
—He threatened you?
—Not in so many words, but the message was very clear. I was to
hush up or be marched right out my career. My life.
—You let it be? I asked.

Chet shifted, looking a little sheepish.

—Debts, you know. Kid at college, another at school. But even
then I needed to know who Benjamin became. When the
Chief was away in Texas for a meeting, I found what I needed
on his desk.
—And what was that, I asked, leanin' forward.
—A name, Chet said. I got a name.

Chapter 18
28 December 2004. Tuesday. 08h16.

Steve slumps against the headboard. Thank God for the tuk-tuk driver, or Jay would have had to manage him on his own.

"Laura's dead too," Steve mutters.

"You don't know that for sure."

"Yes, I do, I know it here."

Steve taps his heart.

Jay falls onto the bed next to Steve. The mattress sinks under him, sliding him towards where the Kiwi is lying.

"Hey, mate?"

Jay looks over at Steve.

"Yes?" he asks.

"Do you think we could at least push the beds apart?"

08h47

"Jay?"

He stirs. *How long has he been asleep?* Jay opens the door.

196

"Pascale," he says. "Liam."

"You look like shit," says Liam. "And who's been sleeping in your bed?"

Jay gestures towards Steve, then puts a finger to his lips.

"Can we go outside?"

"Is that the Kiwi nutter with the cell phone?" asks Liam, once the door clicks.

"We found his son last night," Jay says, nodding.

"Dead?" asks Liam.

"Yes."

Liam sighs, putting his arm around Pascale.

"*Quelle horreur*," she says. "We leave him here, yes?"

"Where are we going?"

"We have something to show you," Liam says, scratching the stubble on his chin.

"But what about Steve?"

"Leave him, that poor bugger needs to sleep."

08h51

It's raining again. Not enough to drench them, but enough to make the paths next to the roads slippery. Jay follows behind Pascale, while Liam marches in front, like a giant shaggy bear.

"I was up most of the night," he tells Pascale, wishing they would both slow down.

197

"We see your note," Pascale replies, but doesn't even falter.

They seem to be approaching a temple. Garlands are strewn at the base of a golden statue of Buddha. It's incredibly ornate, the gilt alternated by what looks like blue mosaics. Jay watches as a Thai woman sits nearby stringing white and yellow flowers together, attaching them to a red ribbon. Another creates what looks like a bracelet of tiny white blossoms.

"*Phuang malai? Phuang malai?*" the older woman says.

Jay doesn't understand the words but he understands the actions. He takes a garland, placing some baht in the woman's hand. She gestures to him to follow her, then places the flowers next to the others. The woman hands him a stick of incense, lighting it for him. Smoke curls upwards. The lady beams.

"Good spirits," she says and he wonders where she has heard this.

He also hopes that she is right.

Pascale and Liam are waiting where he bought the flowers.

"*Allons-y,*" Pascale says, as she begins to walk again.

She turns a corner. People are milling outside, following the trajectory of a crumbling wall. Jay recognises those expressions. Like him, these people are searching. It seems they are at another wall of remembrance. More photos and desperate messages. And inside the temple, bodies. But Pascale is smiling. She points to a photo lodged between an image of a girl in a diving suit and an elderly man with a bulbous nose. In a polar-neck jumper, his hair wild in a wind, he recognises the picture. It's him.

"You!" says Pascale, unable to hide the triumph in her voice.

Liam smiles.

"Someone is alive and looking for you!" he says.

09h11

Jay is shaking. The poster gives very little away. No contact name. And only the phone number of a hotel. Only Nina could be that scatterbrained. But why then, hasn't she contacted his mother? He thinks about this, considering the options. She lost her phone and she doesn't remember the number? Maybe she's only just got here – she did have a long way to come back from. Or maybe his mother knows by now and has only just found out? Jay scrabbles in his pocket for his phone, realising he's left it behind in the hotel.

"My phone," he says, patting his pockets.

Liam rips the poster off the wall, handing it ceremoniously to Jay.

"Let's get the hell out of here," he says.

09h29

Steve is sitting on edge of the bed. His bushy ginger eyebrows ruffled and his face creased by the pillow.

"It's ironic," he says without greeting Jay, "that I should be a marine biologist and the ocean should take everything I love."

"Steve," Jay says, "you can't give up. Look at this."

Jay shows him the poster.

"See," Steve says, not even hiding his resentment, "I told you you lead a charmed life."

Liam stands at the door.

"Listen you fat fuck," he says without the slightest change of facial expression. "Jay spent most of the night sorting out the paperwork to get your kid home. The least you can do is be happy for him."

Pascale nods.

"Right now, we're all looking for miracles," Liam continues, "and this is our first stab at one."

09h35

Jay has no messages from his mother. Or from Nina. Or Kerese. Pascale has volunteered to stay with Steve and help him look for Laura, so it's just him and Liam who hail down the first tuk-tuk they can find. In a morning of coincidences and hope, it is ironic that the man who stops is the same driver who carted him around Phuket the night before.

"Don't you sleep?" Jay asks him with a laugh.

"Wife drown," the man says. "Keep busy busy."

Jay can't believe his own selfishness. Last night he thought he was the only person suffering. And the man had not even shown his own grief. Jay looks at the man, their eyes meeting. And he knows he doesn't need to say anything more for them to understand each other.

"Where we go?" the driver says.

Jay points at the phone number and Half Moon Hotel.

And the driver, seeing Jay's face across the poster, beams.

"Good news!" he comments. "But I no know that place."

The driver hurtles out the tuk-tuk, leaving it running. He flags down another vehicle, chatting quickly as his hands wave. Another driver arrives. Then another. They confer pointing towards the beach, then away from it, in the direction of the temple. Then the hospital. Finally one of the drivers pulls out a phone, punches in a number, and chatters into the mouthpiece. He waves the paper triumphantly.

"Not far. Quick. Quick."

The tuk-tuk zips into the road, making Jay lurch forward.

"Do you think we'll get there alive?" he asks.

And Liam, who never seems particularly phased about anything, grins.

"Jay. We just survived a tsunami."

09h46

The Half Moon Hotel is nothing remarkable. In fact, it's accessed via a mini-laundromat, the machines whirling washing and suds right in the lobby. Jay approaches a lady folding socks and babygros. Unsure if she speaks English, he shows her the picture, pointing at himself. She takes the paper, looks at him, then beams. Gesturing to him, she indicates for him and Liam to follow. The tuk-tuk driver, anxious not to miss anything, parks his vehicle and comes too.

Behind a reception desk of sorts sits an old man reading a newspaper. Above his head, a television is blaring; images of boats perched in trees are closely followed by others showing lines of corpses wrapped in white plastic and cooling with dry ice creating ghostly steam traces above them. The old man doesn't notice them until the woman taps him lightly on his shoulder. She thrusts the poster in his line of sight, handing him his glasses.

Studying the picture, he makes the connection immediately.

"You come," he says.

The old man takes them upstairs. A cleaner is sweeping the corridors outside a room, the dust collecting in a little pile in the corner of the passage. A film of light catches on the floating particles filtering through the cracked window.

Definitely Nina, thinks Jay, *Kerese wouldn't be caught dead in a place like this.*

He shivers then, realising the possible reality of that thought.

The old man lifts his hand, thumping on the door. It opens almost immediately. A woman is standing there, barefoot and dressed in a pair of cut-off jeans and a T-shirt at least three sizes too big for her. Her face is lacerated, her arms a tracery of new stitches and purple bruises.

But it's not Nina. And neither is it Kerese.

The woman studies him, her head cocked.

"Jay!" she says, embracing him. "Thank God."

Jay wonders if he has forgotten something. Somebody. Her. Not even her voice is familiar.

"I'm sorry," he says a little hesitantly, "Do I know you?"

She looks at him, then laughs.

"I guess not, but Lord it feels like I know you," she replies. "I'm Tracy Knight."

She pulls Jay into the room, shaking hands with Liam, who studies the reunion with a trace of mirth. The tuk-tuk driver comes into the room too, and soon they are all sitting like birds on a wire at the edge of the bed.

"I don't want to seem rude …" Jay says.

Tracy touches a cut on her arm.

"Kerese and I," she says, "I think we're soul mates. One minute we're sittin' next to each other emailing; the next, we're flippin' about in a washer with all the keyboards and wires."

"Kerese is alive?" Jay says.

Tracy laughs.

"Yes! She looks like ten miles of bad road. But she's alive."

Jay's heart pounds.

"Where is she?" he asks.

"In the hospital. We were airlifted out of Koh Phi Phi together. But they needed the beds. And though I look ugly enough to knock buzzards off a gut wagon, I don't need a bed."

10h32

Kerese has been here since Sunday. In fact, she was one of the first people airlifted out. Jay studies her chart, noting the bruising to her ribs, spleen and coccyx. The skin on her left leg has been sloughed off from her knee to her ankle. Her right arm is bruised and tender. She was unconscious for a day, and has drifted in and out of a deep slumber since this morning.

This makes it all the more odd how much Tracy knows about Kerese. Knows about him. There's something about her that is a little penetrating. Sure, she's a journalist. She's travelled. Especially recently from what he can tell. But she seems altogether too interested in them both.

As he sits at the bed, waiting for Kerese to wake, he can't help wishing the woman who found him, would now simply… vanish. But she's stuck there. Patting the bed and smoothing the sheets. Pouring water into Kerese's glass.

And chatting to him. She's giving him a headache. Apart from anything else, she seems to have a proverb or weird saying for every discussion. Liam calls Jay outside the room.

"Do you think she stops talking?" Liam asks, "Because if not, you, my friend, have a serious problem."

"It's not just me?"

"You want me to get rid of her?"

Jay looks at Liam.

"Maybe you could go and buy us some coffee,' he says uncertainly.

"You got it."

For a few minutes, Kerese doesn't stir. Her face, cushioned by a thick pillow, is only just visible. She murmurs softly, her eyes fluttering. Jay strokes her cheek, feeling the tenderness of the times they have spent together. Asleep, she is so vulnerable. Even gentle. It's easy to forget the hard PR exterior, the selfishness, the demands. But then, he's not exactly perfect either.

Jay finds Kerese's hand under the sheets, clasps it to him. Though she's bruised, Kerese's beauty is exceptional. Rare has been the time that he has had to observe her as he is now doing. To think the last time he sat at a bedside like this was for Daniel. Today he feels different. Today he feels a glimmer of hope.

10h59

Jay watches Kerese. Tears stream down her cheeks, as she thrashes in the bed.

"No, no," she says, turning abruptly.

Jay touches her shoulder, shaking her out of her nightmare.

"Wake up."

Her eyes spring open.

"Jay?"

"I'm here."

"Tracy found you?"

"We found each other."

"I hit my head. It hurts. I hurt all over."

"I'm here," Jay says.

"I want to go home," Kerese says. "I can't stand this anymore."

"We will. But not today. Today you are resting."

"I need to call my mother. I don't remember any numbers."

Jay touches her face, his finger tracing her jaw.

"I called her, Kerese. She's flying over."

Kerese nods, her eyelids heavy.

"What's happened to us, Jay?" Kerese says, "What happens next?"

"Shhh," says Jay. "Let's just take this one step at a time."

Chapter 19
July 8, 2004 – Thursday

New York. New York. Eleanor's tour of the US of A isn't all that bad. Chet Sharpe swore that Ian Colbert knew somethin'. So I'm hanging out here until he swoops in from London to tell me what what that is. I've left a message at the bank, but that secretary in her tight skirt and pinstripes wasn't exactly helpful. I'm stayin' near Central Park. My room isn't big enough to swing a cat in, but the view. Wow. What a view. I phoned that Stan Colicchio. His voice is like gravel, but he seems friendly enough.

—Phone me back tomorrow, he told me.

So I will.

But now, Anton, I'm doin' the tourist thing. Well, sort of. I'm sittin' in the New York Library. Went with one of the librarians into the archives. I don't know what I'm lookin' for, but something's got to come up. I've searched on the name Chet gave me. W. Channing. You'd have thought a detective would've got a bit more than that. But at least it's a start.

—And the passport? I asked him.
—American.

So W. Channing is Benjamin Heyward. Your brother. Not, unfortunately, as unusual a surname as I originally supposed.

There's a Walter Channing in Vancouver. A musician—bass guitar to be precise. His band has just released a CD and they're playin' a gig at the Blue Monkey in Gastown. Then Warren Channing is in Dakota. Some sorta horse whisperer. A Wally Channing died recently in Seattle; drowned on a fishing expedition in the Puget Sound. Got knocked off the boat in a freak accident. Hit his head. Didn't come back up for air. Wayne Channing. An accountant and father of three. He was quoted as a member of a school board in New Orleans, but otherwise hasn't much new information to offer me. Anyways. He was born in New Orleans. Far as I can make out he always lived there. Whitman Channing. Linguist. He's a Professor at Yale, but at least twenty years too old to be Ben. Wally Channing. Plumber. He owns his own company in Calgary that specializes in leak detection. I haven't seen photo but he may be a possibility. Wilbert Channing lives in Toronto. Owns a skiing supplies shop—rentals and sales. He was a snowboarding champion in his late teens. Somehow, I don't think he's Ben either.

Of course other names have come up. Will. Walt. William. Wendel. Wesley. But I just don't know where to start. And who's to say anyhow that our W. Channing even made it to the Web? Layin' low, that's exactly what he may have been avoiding.

As I was sitting there at the terminals, a thought crossed my mind. If that body in Ben's car wasn't Ben's, who was he? Did Ben kill somebody? Were you there, Anton? I seemed to be getting more questions than answers. Eleanor, well she sounds distressed on the telephone. How would I have felt being her, knowing that my husband had let me think my first-born son was dead? Mighty angry, I should think.

—It's too cruel, Sugah, she told me. You have to find Ben.

Her voice changed to a whisper and I knew that Bill had come home.

—Why, thanks for calling, she signed off. You let me know what you get there.

July 9, 2004 – Friday

—Who knows you're here?

Ian Colbert was more than a little imposing. He wore a charcoal suit over his broad shoulders, a blue-striped tie, and a scowl. His secretary wouldn't help me, so I waited in reception, hopin' that something would happen. I knew he was back from London, and he had to come to work eventually. I was lucky. One of the receptionists on the Ground Floor greeted him by name. And though he barely acknowledged her, I had my sights on the target. I hovered there until lunchtime. The receptionists looked at me like I was as lost as a goose in a snowstorm, but I didn't move. Not 'til Ian headed out to Starbucks in giant strides across the pavement.

—Eleanor, I told him.
—Poor woman, Ian said, all those lies. I'm not even sure who knows the truth. The whole truth. Except for maybe Bill Heyward and he's not about to tell her, is he now?
—Can you talk to me?

Ian looked about him.

—I can't sit here for longer than ten minutes. I have meetings. You got somewhere to stay?

I nodded.

Ian scribbled down an address.

—Six o'clock. I'll let my wife know. And for God's sake, don't let anyone find out where you're going.

Daniella Colbert opened the door. I've seen her photo in the papers, but usually there she has a lot less clothing on. This time she was dressed in trackpants and a tight top with bling. She wore glasses and no make-up, her hair scrunched up in a ponytail. Sweat glistened on her arms and face. Though her English was accented, she spoke it perfectly.

—Sorry, she said, I lost track of the time. I was working out.

She noticed my glance inside the house.

—Ian's not back yet. Let me get you a drink.

Daniella poured a gin and tonic over some ice. She handed it to me, opening a bottle of mineral water. Gulping the water down, she wiped her face with the back of her hand.

—Thirsty work, she commented. You like exercise?
—I did, I said, indicating my leg.
—Don't favor it too much, Daniella said. That's a classic mistake. Use it and it will remember what it's supposed to do.
—Right.

I wondered how long I was goin' to have to sit there, listening to Daniella's pearls of wisdom. She sat down opposite me in a white leather chair—it looked mighty uncomfortable. Hard as nails, but real pretty.

—You know about Ian's first wife? Daniella asked.
—Louisa-May?
—Ian hasn't got over her death. Sometimes he's a bit distant. Sad. Plotting something.
—Plotting what?
—He never did find out who knocked her over, but he has his suspicions—
—Daniella!

We turned towards the door. Ian looked different already. His tie was off, his jacket over his shoulder, but his brow was creased in a tight furrow. I'd read he was in his mid-thirties but he didn't look it. He looked at least ten years older. Daniella stood up, scuttling to the bar.

—Drink? she said, not waiting for a reply.

The ice tinkled into the crystal glass, then a swirl of scotch. Somethin' expensive I wouldn't wonder. Ian nodded at his wife, taking the drink. He gulped it down in one swift movement, slamming it onto a side table. Silently, Daniella extracted the glass, filling it up again.

—Dan, he said, do you mind if I chat alone to our guest?
—Sure, she replied, I need a shower anyhow. Nice to meet you.

As soon as Daniella's footsteps faded upstairs, Ian sighed.

—You're playing with fire you know, he said.

—How's that?

—William Heyward is a powerful man. Connected in places you wouldn't even imagine.

—I'm lookin' for his son.

—But he isn't. If Ben suddenly comes alive again, William will lose everything. His status. His job. His reputation.

—I don't understand.

—Military men aren't supposed to *lie*. And they're definitely not allowed to conceal a murder.

—A murder?

Ian stood up, walked to the window. The city lights had already begun to sparkle and taxis hooted below in the homebound traffic.

—Ben contacted me about three months after his funeral. He was furtive. Anxious. Dreadfully lonely.

—Where was he?

—Still in Canada. Calgary somewhere. He was working as a mechanic. Ben always had a thing for cars.

—And gamblin'.

—Sure, Ian nodded.

—That's what started this mess, right? I asked.

—It was part of it, but let me tell you this, there was a lot more to the story than a few bad debts. Besides, I could hear in his voice Ben had changed a lot. A new man and all that … even the words he used …

I could hear the shower running upstairs. Daniella had put some music on, something Brazilian. A samba? Cupboards banged. A smell sifted from the kitchen. Meat fryin'; grease and hickory. Ian continued.

—He tried to joke a bit, put on this nasal Canadian pitch. Talked about his new cowboy boots and hat. He was learning to ride. Ben hated the place. Said he wanted to move on.
—But why did he contact you?
—We were pals. He needed cash. Wanted to disappear where his father couldn't find him.
—You lent him some?
—Of course I did. Gave it to him gladly. Let me tell you something; that William Heyward didn't much care for his first-born. Ben was an embarrassment. Not like Anton.
—Did Ben tell you where he was goin'?
—He didn't know yet. Ben wanted to take the first plane out he could and see where he landed.
—He sent Anton postcards, I told him. From all sorts of neat places.

Ian frowned.

—Anton got them too? That's what I can't understand. Those boys couldn't have been more different and yet they were so close. And it wasn't just sibling duty. I never liked Anton myself; there was something about him I didn't trust.

I should have taken offence to that, I suppose, but I didn't. After what I've learned the last few weeks I'm beginning to think Ian saw somethin' in you I was too dumb to notice. And you know how that makes me feel?

—So what happened that night? I prompted.
—I don't know everything. What I do know is that someone got killed that night. And it wasn't Benjamin. Ben was a bit cagey about it.
—Who was he?

—The corpse? I don't know. I'm guessing he may have been a thug out to extract money from Ben. Maybe Ben had got himself too deep in the gambling. I just don't know.
—But you gave Ben the money to disappear?

Ian studied me.

—It's easy for you to judge, he said, you don't know what Bill was capable of.

I leaned forward, my voice unconsciously hushed.

—What *was* he capable of?

Ian moved away from the window and sat opposite me.

—I hadn't heard from Ben for a year or so. Louisa-May and I were newly married. A baby girl soon after. Sophie, he said. Her name was Sophie. She was born premature. Lung conditions. A weak heart. Malfunctioning liver. But she was a beautiful little girl. An angel.
—What happened?
—We spent a lot of cash on the operations. A lot. We were almost wiped out. There were some treatments… but we couldn't afford them. You have to understand what it was like; we were desperate.

I waited, sensing what was about to come.

—Louisa-May found the postcards when she was tidying once. She knew about Ben. And Heyward had money. Eleanor was a *Hammond*, for Christ's sake. Then Ben got in touch again. We knew he was in the Caribbean.
—Where?

214

—St Lucia. So Louisa-May contacted Bill, said she would
expose him if he didn't pay us the money we needed.
—Blackmail?
—I said we were desperate! A few days later, Lou was
walking from Kmart to her car. A truck rolled right over her.
In the parking lot!
—You don't know it was Bill who did that.
—I might not have, if I hadn't got a nasty phone call just after
that. The night Louisa slipped away.
—Oh God.

Ian looked at me. His face tense.

—I told you. This is a dangerous game.
—It doesn't sound like a *game* to me, I said.
—Then you understand where I'm coming from. So I have to
tell you, I don't want to get involved in this. My life is back on
track. Daniella is different than Louisa, but I love her.
—Then why did you see me at all? I asked.
—I owed it to Ben, Ian replied. I owed it to him, but now I'm
done.
—Do you know where he is?
—I haven't heard from him for almost a year.
—Ian, I said, where was he last?
—Bolivia. A little town called Tupiza. He was working there
fixing the 4x4 vehicles that go out across the Atacama Desert.
—Do you think he's still there?
—No idea. I told him not to contact me again.

I decided to go for a walk. A long walk, past the Rockefeller
Center. I felt a bit like a salmon spawning. Everybody else
seemed to be goin' the other way. I bumped against a large
man in too-tight denims and biceps the size of cannons. He
looked at me, grunted, then kept on movin'. I tried to avoid

the heaving mass of bodies, but it wasn't that easy. I thought that maybe I could take in a museum. I needed time to think, to pull myself together.

Was I frightened? A little. William wouldn't hurt *me* I thought. But look what he did to Ben. Heck, Anton. I don't even *know* what he did to Ben. And Ben is his son. What frightens me more is that you *knew* about this, whatever this is, and let it happen. I wondered if I should just give up. Go home. Tell Eleanor to hire a private detective so that I can go on with my life. I'd gone some of the way. He could take it from here. I walked on.

Whatever had made me agree to come here was still with me, though. I needed to know less about Ben and more about you, the man I married. Anton Heyward a figment of my imagination – and yours.

I was goin' northwards, leaving the Theater District, and headin' up along 5th Avenue towards the Upper East Side. I'd read about it on the plane comin' here. All sorts of fancy museums: The Metropolitan, The Frick Collection, Frank Lloyd Wright's Guggenheim. Them pictures in the guidebooks were great, but somehow I ended up at the Whitney. All-American art for an all-American girl.

At first, I trailed around the building, tryin' to concentrate. I couldn't get myself worked up about the American flags piled on top of each other in a painting. And lines of Coca Cola bottles, was that really art? I liked the Georgia O'Keeffe flowers. She was right. People don't stop to notice the little things. Like flowers. Like postcards arriving and being quickly secreted to a box I would only find when you were gone. She made people stop and look. You never did, Anton.

216

I stood in front of an Edward Hopper. I didn't know anythin' about him except for what I read there but the painting spoke to me. It echoed just about everythin' I was feeling about where this journey was taking me. *Early Sunday Morning.* That's was what it was called. All the shop doors closed, the shutters and windows unblinking. Not a soul on the street. I was there in New York, and I was all alone. Empty.

I didn't really know what to do next. Back out. Back off. Back away. But as I moved toward another O'Keeffe and saw a quote by her there, I knew that Ian's warnings were not going to stop me. I wrote it down to remember it: 'I've been absolutely terrified every moment of my life—and I've never let it keep me from doing a single thing I wanted to do.'

I'm scared Anton, I won't deny it. But somebody needs to find out the truth.

Chapter 20

10 January 2005. Monday. 08h11.

Kerese is getting better. She sleeps less, and is starting to move about the room. Her leg, bandaged but not broken, will be scarred. The skin growing back is white against the rest of her tan. But even that memory of sunshine is fading. Kerese's mother sits at her bedside. She reads Maeve Binchy, sighs a lot and mutters about the state of her hotel.

"It smells, Jay," she says. "And the noise – untenable."

She won't eat the local fare and insists on every meal at a pub run by a man from Birmingham. Jay thinks the pub grub tastes dry or stale. And he's getting used to the smell of Thailand. It doesn't disturb him like it did. And when he walks out his hotel, and bumps into the tuk-tuk driver who helped him find Kerese, they greet each other like old friends. Despite what has happened, Jay thinks Nina was right to bring him here. For the first time in a long while, he has started to feel alive. Perhaps being so close to death himself has done this for him, but he thinks it is more than this.

Thailand is vibrant for him in a way that London never was. It excites him. The way you have to bargain for a mere bottle of water. The smiles of Thai children coming from the temple. Families living and working together and volunteering to do the most upsetting things to eradicate the wave from their minds.

They haven't found Nina. It's about a fortnight since the tsunami and Jay is beginning to doubt that they will. He contacts the British Embassy representatives every day. They know him there, and each day they shake their heads, their eyes clouding. Jay has driven to Krabi Town to check the hospitals and morgues there. The bodies there are unrecognisable. So blue and bloated you can't even tell if the victim was European or Asian. Even as a doctor, Jay can't stop himself from retching. If Nina was among these people, he would never be able to tell. He's done the tests, passed on records of his DNA. If nothing else, maybe genetics will bring Nina home.

Kerese's mother knits. He never knew the click-click of needles could unnerve him so much. And Kerese seems oddly passive. Her eyes are glazed as she looks towards the window. And celebrity and fashion mags are discarded next to the bed, untouched. Jay needs to do something. He can't take Mrs McCall's inane chatter much longer; he wonders if Kerese's dad is enjoying the silence.

Jay stands up.

"Kerese," he says, "I'm not helping anybody sitting here."

Kerese looks up, her eyes focusing only momentarily.

"I'm going to ask the hospital if I can help. They need doctors. I'm a doctor. I can't sit here and watch you healing. You'll do that anyway."

Mrs McCall's eyes registers disapproval.

"Charity begins at home," she says.

Jay taps his mobile.

"I'm a call away. You know that."

Kerese rolls onto her side, her back to Jay. Mrs McCall goes back to her knitting and doesn't look up as he leaves the room.

09h14

Detective Superintendent Murray Hovis has been in Phuket a week. Already his face has taken on a haggard look, his jowls drooping like a bulldog's. His balding head is peeling from a day of forgotten sunscreen and his arms are a riot of freckles.

Jay can feel him studying him. Murray's eyes drill into him, as though analysing his potential.

"You up to this, lad?"

"I'm volunteering aren't I?"

"You can't train for this one," Murray says. "Bodies are decomposing in the sun. We've got kids' shoes on the beach, suitcases floating in the ocean and corpses tied together by their limbs to stop them being lost to the water again."

Jay gulps. He thought he'd already seen the worst of it.

"I'm up for it," he says, but even to him his voice sounds uncertain.

"Hey, I'm not going to refuse an offer. I need everyone I can get."

Murray starts to walk. Jay isn't sure if he should follow him, until the Detective turns around.

"Well, lad. Are you coming, or aren't you?"

10h05

They're in Khao Lak. Bodies in the temple reek of death and Murray and Jay cover their noses with masks. Murray is sturdy, and walks slightly bow-legged, but his movements are fast and accurate. He doesn't stop for Jay, who clutches his stomach, trying to imagine better smells. Roses. Fish 'n chips. Coffee brewing. New rain.

"We have to work together," Murray says.

Jay thought that was what he was doing, but Murray means more than that.

"This disaster is beyond any scale we could have imagined. We can't just look for the 8 000 missing Britons. We won't find them unless we go through everybody else."

"Everybody else?"

"There are thousands of bodies here, Jay. Thousands. And that's just Khao Lak. We'll retrieve them and identify them. But it's mammoth. Mammoth! So there's no other way than to start, other than bit by bit."

12h46

Jay thought he'd be working in a hospital. But he's not. He's treading like other volunteers and workers between collapsed houses and corrugated iron, avoiding live wires and stagnant pools. Dogs trail the people as they dig and move debris. Nobody lets them get too close. Some of them are rabid and hungry. The dangers here are both mental and physical. Jay wonders what is worse. His head is pounding, but he knows he is not the only person who feels like this. He's had to treat a few volunteers for heat stroke, and one man from Dorset has slipped, cracking his head open on a rock.

As Jay works, he tries to block out the reality. He thinks about Nina, and Kerese, and the woman from the journal, whose travels are tainted with disappointment and fading hope. Their searches are the same in many ways, but in one aspect they are completely different. She knows Benjamin is alive.

Steve is still looking for Laura. He's taken a room in the same hotel as Jay, and goes from hospital to temple to embassy on a daily basis. Pascale and Liam are still here. Jay doesn't know why they are staying. He thinks if he were them he would have left a long time ago. They could have flown to Bangkok – free on Thai Airways – rushed through their passports, and gone back home to Canada. But they seem strangely attached to Phuket. Sometimes Jay studies them, observing how they fit together, melding into each other as a couple. Pascale softens Liam. The gruffness he exhibits sometimes alone dissolving almost completely. Jay wonders if he and Kerese were ever improved each other like that and knows without much deliberation that they didn't – not even at the beginning. Pascale is quietly competent, visiting some of her fellow Canadians in hospital, helping them where she can. Liam spends hours lifting and moving away the signs of destruction. He's sweeping, fixing, clearing, finalising. He comes back to the hotel, exhausted. But Jay has never heard him complain.

Jay and his team are following what Murray called "the international protocols of the Disaster Victim Identification procedure". They have to take fingerprints, DNA samples and check victims against dental records. Some of the missing had unique medical conditions, which are still traceable in the body after death.

The job seems almost insurmountable. Some bodies have limbs missing, or are so battered, he even finds it hard to identify the sex of the person. It's horrifying and humbling. He got out with a bit of damage to his arm, that's all. Jay could have been lying somewhere in the heat too, decomposing and unclaimed. It spurs him on to keep going.

And while Jay and others wade through the combination of paperwork and medical examinations, Murray and some of the other team members are trying to narrow down the number of actual British tsunami victims. They're making phone calls, cross-referencing, contacting embassies. They're deleting names that are written twice, but are differently spelt. Murray marches outside gripping a fag to his lips. He curses the hoaxers and the fraudsters making this job even more difficult than it needs to be.

"Christ almighty," he says, "they're claiming missing relatives trying to cash in on insurance."

One man even announces his own disappearance, pretending to be his brother. He's too stupid to realise two phone calls will prove he doesn't have a sibling. Never did.

17h04

Jay is exhausted. He walks through the doors of the hotel, the clothes clinging to him seeped in death and sweat. Taking one look at him, the hotel manager raises a hand for him to stop.

"No can take those clothing inside, too velly bad."

Jay doesn't have much else to wear, if anything, but he follows the woman obligingly to a courtyard behind the building.

"You take off. I clean. Shower. Shower."

The woman stands there, her arms crossed against her chest, daring Jay to move inside.

"Can I please have a towel, at least?" he asks.

But the woman doesn't seem to be going anywhere. Reluctantly Jay takes off everything but his scants. The woman laughs.

"Shy boy. I get soap."

She's right though. Jay does need to wash this day off his body, but he doesn't think it will ever be wiped from his head.

Chapter 21
July 10, 2004 - Saturday

The odd thing about it all was that Stan Colicchio phoned *me*.
I was packin' up my belongings, gearing myself for another
journey. Strange, but I'd completely forgotten about him.

—You didn't call me yesterday, he said. I waited all day by
the phone.

I couldn't decide if he was pullin' my leg or dead serious.
Sometimes a phone can hide a meaning that a face-to-face
never can. I cleared my throat, tryin' to think of a good reply,
but he went right on.

—Do yont to hear my side of the story or don't ya?
—Of course I do, I replied, sitting heavily onto the unmade
bed.
—Then you have one funny way of showin' it.
—I'm sorry, I started, I got some news yesterday. It hurt me
real bad.
—So that boy is alive?

I hesitated. Now that I knew about Bill, I wasn't too sure who
to speak to. But Stan from what I gathered from the reports
was on Ben's side. And leavin' this afternoon for La Paz, I
was takin' a risk anyways.

—I think so.
—I knew it!

I heard a hand slap loudly on a surface.

—I knew it! Because that boy weren't no suicidal sissy-boy.
The gamblin' was near 'bout cleared out his system and I'm
sure he'd hooked up with some broad.
—He was seein' someone?
—Well, if that smoochin' and feelin' up round the back of the
gas station said anything, I would think so.
—What did she look like?
—Shapely from behind. I didn't see her face. Ben's lips were
so stuck to hers I couldn't have seen her mug anyway.
—Her hair?
—She was wearing a hat. A pink hat. I remember thinkin' that
kissin' would have been a lot easier with that hat off.
—Did Benjamin know you'd seen them?
—Darn right he did. I told him if he wanted to have sex at my
fillin' station he could do it on his own time.

I wondered how this information could help me. It wasn't that
I didn't know Benjamin was alive.

—Has he been in contact? I asked Stan.
—Not a word. But I sure am glad to know my boy weren't no
coward.
—Do you know if he was in any other trouble?
—Oh them papers were right about the gamblin'. No lies
there. But there was somethin' else going on with that brother
o' his.
—Anton?
—Was that his name? I don't recall no more. Those boys were
as tight as peas in a pod. Always thought that relationship a

bit odd. The young'un was leadin' his older brother by his nose. He said jump …
—Ben said how high?
—Right. You heard it before then.
—Not like that exactly.
—Well, like I said, somethin' came up with Anthony.
—Anton?
—Whatever. He called in at the station. Looked like he was bein' chased by a hive o' bees.
—Was he afraid?
—Afraid? I don't rightly know about that. But he sure was in a hurry.
—What happened?
—Benjamin came to me. Told me his brother was real upset. Said he needed to take off for the afternoon. I weren't happy about that I can tell you. We were busy on the home run. People need gas.
—You let him go?
—I'm not heartless. I could see there was a problem. Don't mean I have to be happy about it.
—Did you ever find out what happened?
—Nope. Ben called in sick a week later. Two days. He didn't sound sick to me but I gave him the benefit of the doubt.
—How long was that before the fire?
—Two or three weeks? We're talking twelve years on, honey. I really ain't that sure.
—Did you see him again with the girl?
—Once, but only from a distance and they were in his car.
—Did you get a better look than before?
—I got a glance. Gotta tell you I was curious.
—Did you know her?
—Atlanta is a big place. And some girls look the same to me.
—Would you recognize her from a photo?
—You got one?

—No.
—Then why in hell's name are you askin' me that?
—I don't know.

Stan's voice softened.

—I tell you what. You find out some more, I'll do a deal with you. Send me the photo. I'll take a look. Then you tell me what happened to Ben.

July 24, 2004 – Sunday

Ben couldn't have chosen a more out of the way place then Tupiza. I got to La Paz via Miami on American Airlines. But that was only the start of it. I've never been to South America before and I got to tell you, I was nervous. And exhausted. So exhausted I could barely lift my feet. Some guy on the plane warned me about a scam happening near the airport. Taxi drivers pick you up, collecting another passenger en route. It's only then that you realize he's fixin' to take all your valuables off you.

—Take a Radio Cab, the stranger told me. You not stopping in La Paz?
—No.
—Pity. It's worth a good look.
—I gotta get straight to the bus station, I replied. I'm on a deadline.
—A deadline to get to Tupiza? he commented. Are you Billy the Kid or something?
—No, I told him, simply. I have friends waitin'. (And what was he talkin' about anyways?)

The bus terminal itself was sophisticated and architecturally sound on the outside, but from the moment I stepped out the cab, I knew this wasn't Charleston. People approach you from all directions, callin' out destinations. Santa Cruz. Coroico. Sucre. Trinidad. Yacuiba. It was mad, Anton, totally mad!

I stood in line behind a group traveling to the silver mines. Potosi. They waved maps and pointed, speaking louder and louder in English, expectin' the poor woman behind the counter to understand better with the volume.

I had my backpack at my feet. I don't know how the darn thing could be so heavy, but it was hurtin' me and I needed a break. A man stopped, takin' me in with a look of panic.

—Somebody's stolen my bags. I'm telling you, man. Don't let go of your belongings.

I put the bag back on, watching the dejected figure headin' for a doorway. If I was nervous before, now I was speedin' up to a panic. I got my ticket. Finally. Then asked the woman where I needed to go.

—*Aca*, she said, wavin' to the left.

The mere fact that I found that bus is a miracle. God only knows if I would ever know how to do it again, but as the bus employee grabbed the paper out my hand, I heaved a sigh of relief. I was almost on the coach. I thought that was the worst of it. In unintelligible Spanish, the man waved at an office and muttered something. I was marched to yet another chaotic office where an official sat countin' money and doin' his utmost to ignore me. Eventually, he looked up, studied my bag, then waved a young boy over to tag it.

—You leave bag.
—I do not leave bag, I replied.

Your problem then, the shrug said, and I realized if I were to
find a seat, I was goin' to have to. Oh Lord, Anton, what was
I lettin' myself in for?

July 26, 2004 – Monday

Two words, Anton. Eighteen. Hours. Eighteen hours on the
coach from hell with no toilet and no way of guessin' when it
was gonna stop. No reading. The lights were out from the
moment we left the terminal and my sleeping bag was soaked
through from a bottle of Coke rolled down the aisle from one
of my neighbors. I tried to sleep through the empañada
vendors selling meat pastries and the ladies callin' out their
wares of sweets and drinks. I tried to sleep through the
pressing urgency of my bladder and the extensive bulk of the
woman next to me as she picked at popcorn, crunching with
her mouth open.

We did finally stop in the middle of the night. I had to pee in a
cement room with three bays watched on by a small boy who
wouldn't leave, despite his mother's calls to him. All through
the night, that darned bus trundled along dirt roads from the
devil himself. My wet sleeping bag didn't stave off the cold. I
was shivering myself into a state of misery. I thought about
Ben, what made him make this journey. What made him
leave Calgary, but even that didn't console me. I needed the
toilet. I needed it real urgent.

One hour to the next stop at Comargo, the driver seemed to
be saying. Anton, you bastard, it took two and a half. I saw

the signs of Tupiza first, when most passengers seemed to be dulled into dreary submission by the jolts from the coach. On the horizon were what resembled Inca temples built into the rock—the entire town surrounded by these magical stone formations. We slipped into a dusty station, welcomed by locals with tiers of ice-cream cones. I bought one. I was hot, sweaty, disappointed and exhausted. I couldn't imagine Eleanor even lookin' at photos of this place, never mind travellin' here.

Another taxi, then a half-built hotel on the outskirts of Tupiza. The taxi driver suggested it. It was probably owned by his sister or mother-in-law or someone like that. But I didn't care. I took off my clothes, washed the journey off in the shower and fell asleep. I wasn't gonna start lookin' for *anybody* in the state I was in right then. But in my dreams I was already lookin'.

Chapter 22
10 January 2005. Monday. 18h31.

"You stink," says Kerese as he leans over to kiss her forehead. "Couldn't you even have taken a shower before you came?"

"I came, didn't I?" says Jay, "And I did take a shower. Two, in fact. You won't believe the misery out there."

"You think I'm enjoying lying here like an invalid, waiting to heal?"

"I didn't say that."

"At least Tracy's been in to see me. She says when this is over I should visit her in Charleston. She says she has a cottage close to the sea. The only thing is, I'm a bit put off by the ocean."

Jay notes he is not invited.

"A tsunami like this won't happen again in our lifetime."

"Well, I may even go. I'm due a bit more leave."

Jay nods, sitting down next to the window.

"Where's your mother?"

"At that pub. She's wasting away."

"There's nothing wrong with a bit of local food."

"Well, she doesn't like it."

Jay finds his temper rising.

"Your mother doesn't like much."

"If you're going to come in here to insult my mother, why don't you just leave?"

Jay shifts.

"Sorry, Kerese," he says, "I had a terrible day."

"Yes, well don't take it out on me. You chose your day. I didn't."

Jay looks at Kerese. She's still beautiful, but she's hard. Like a diamond. He wonders about the girl in the journal. How would she have been in a situation like this? At least, if nothing else, she would have kept a sense of humour. Kerese's seems to have worn thin.

"Did you see anyone else today?" he says, trying to change the subject.

"Oh yes, I'm just brimming with fascinating visitors."

"You know what I mean."

Kerese relents, her face relaxing. She even attempts a slight smile.

"Well, Steve popped in for a moment."

"How is he? I haven't seen him today."

"Well, apart from the fact that his eyebrows need trimming, there doesn't seem to be more news. Finn's body will be transported back to New Zealand. But he's arranged to have it kept in a morgue until he's ready to leave here."

"God," says Jay, "what a shocking choice."

"Laura's dead," says Kerese matter-of-factly. "There's no ways she could be alive after all this time."

"I'm not giving up hope," replies Jay, referring to Nina.

"Hope is finite," says Kerese. "Sometimes I think our lives would be better if we just gave up."

Jay looks at Kerese.

"When did you turn into such a pessimist?"

"Somewhere between being hit on the head by a computer screen, and puking up lungs full of black murky water."

"An experience that you survived," Jay reminded her.

"That's true," Kerese replies, conceding the point.

They sit silently. Jay looks out the window. The sun is almost set, and the sky has taken on an orange glow.

"Aren't the sunsets here magnificent?"

"I'd rather be in London, in a black coat, waiting for the Tube."

Jay sighs.

"Can I get you anything?" Jay asks, wondering when Kerese will take the hint.

How about a change of subject?

"Maybe something to read. Something trashy like a Mills and Boon."

"I'll see what I can do."

Jay moves towards the foot of Kerese's bed to check her charts.

"I won't be surprised if they discharge you soon. You'll have to do some extensive physio on that leg; the muscles have taken a lot of strain."

"I noticed."

Jay wonders if Kerese will think to ask him how he is doing. His sister is missing. He's spent a day identifying corpses and his arm is septic at the cut. But she doesn't.

"You know, Steve said something I forgot to tell you," Kerese says. "Do you remember those girls from the boat – Rikke and Margaret?"

"Margot," Jay corrects.

"Margot, that's right. Well, Rikke's in hospital here still. This hospital actually. In intensive care. They can't move her."

"She's still alive? That's the best news I've heard all day. I treated her," explains Jay, "just after the wave. Her throat had been slit. It was pretty gruesome."

"Well there you go," Kerese says, "Doctor Gifford's lucky patient. You can visit her, if you like. She's just down the corridor."

18h31

But Jay doesn't visit her. He's steeped in death and can't face another conversation. Tracy's perky head round the hospital door was enough to make him stand up and leave. For Christ's sake, does she ever talk at a normal volume and without using those idiotic expressions? She's positively perky. All of the time.

"I'm knackered," Jay says. "Will you ladies be okay?"

"Oh I think we'll manage, bless your pea-pickin' little heart!" says Tracy, sending them both into titters.

Jay finds he doesn't want to go back to the hotel. Instead he walks down one of the side roads, looking for a place to eat. He thinks back to their arrival in Bangkok. Was it only two weeks ago? He was so uncertain then, but now he slots himself into a roadside table, takes the stained plastic menu and orders a meal. Just like Nina did then. He's not disappointed. Though the food is mainly vegetarian, it stays on his lips in a delicious afterburn.

Sipping a beer to douse the flames, he tries not to think about his day. And the more he tries to ignore it, the clearer it becomes. Then Kerese filters into his thoughts. Her selfishness. Her wallowing. He can't find his sister and she barely even mentions her. Jay has tried to be charitable. Kerese is in pain. She doesn't deal well with suffering. He could count the number of times she visited him at work on one hand. Too depressing. Too dreadful. Too much death. She's always been a bit afraid of hospitals. And now she's in one.

Jay stares out to the road. Dogs bite each other, yelping. A man approaches him with watches. Another with T-shirts. *No, I don't want another fucking massage, tuk-tuk or T-shirt,* one declares. Jay shakes his head. *No. No thanks. No.*

He feels another person bumping his back, and turns to send him away.

"Hiya, stranger," says Becky. "Fancy getting pissed?"

The bars away from the water are livening up already, despite the tragedy. Jay likes the practicality of it. Life goes on. People need to earn a living. Becky pulls out a wallet, orders shooters.

"Kamikazes," she says, "I'm buyin'."

"And why is that?" Jay says.

"You look like you were rode hard and put away wet."

"Whatever that means."

"So what happened? Find the girlfriend?"

"She's alive, but in hospital. Lucky. I think she'll be going home soon."

"She'll?" asks Becky.

Jay realises Becky is right. He's already decided he's not going with her.

"My sister's still missing," he says. "I can't leave Thailand 'til I know what happened to her."

Jay waves for another drink.

"But why are *you* in Phuket?" he asks.

"Roundin' up troops. Phi Phi's a mess. We need people. Volunteers."

"You're not going back to the States."

"Can't yet," replies Becky. "I'm planning what to do next."

Jay waits for an explanation but doesn't get one. A pole dancer slips up onto the bar, her body sliding around the metal as her too-tight skirt rides up her little legs.

"She doesn't even look sixteen," he says. "I'm not sure a teenager strutting up there is even sexy. She looks like she needs to go to school."

"And what about her?" says Becky.

"She's *way* beyond school," says Jay, watching a different woman gyrate around her pole with such intensity, he could almost blush. "I think she could teach *me* something."

His expression makes Becky laugh.

"And why am I talking to you about that anyway?" Jay asks.

Becky shrugs then leans over to ring the bell hanging near their heads. The other patrons cheer.

"What does that mean?" Jay says.

"Shooters for the whole bar," said Becky with a straight face. "On you."

21h04

They drink too much, but it's medicinal. How else can he forget? Murray's expecting him at seven tomorrow, and he'll have to do it all again. Kerese didn't ask him one thing about what had happened. But Becky listens to him, her eyes focused on him, her expression serious.

"Maybe this just isn't your deal," she says.

"It's nobody's deal," Jay replies. "Doesn't mean I shouldn't do it."

"It won't bring Nina back."

"Maybe not, but maybe it'll bring somebody else home."

They walk. Something won't settle in Jay and the anxiety sits in his stomach.

"So what are you going to do?" he asks Becky.

"I was happy in Koh Phi Phi. I'm gonna help," she says. "We'll clear away the debris, rebuild. Make it beautiful again. Then I'll climb and suspend myself from a rope over the ocean, make friends with it again."

Jay thinks about the climbing. The magic of it, before the wave. He can't stay here in Phuket, just waiting for news. Murray needs him, sure, but when the bodies have been tagged and tested, mixed and matched, what will be left for him here except the wait?

"When will you go back?" he says, almost tentatively.

"In a week."

Something decides him right then.

"I've got a few things I need to sort out," Jay says, "then maybe I'll go with you."

Chapter 23
August 3, 2004 - Tuesday

Tupiza is a beautiful place in an isolated, middle-of-nowhere
kind of a way. I think you would have liked it, Anton. Last
night's dinner was less than appealing, though. I sat in a
restaurant called Il Bambino, with a TV blaring in the corner
and the walls decorated with calendars of half-nude models;
metal tables with metal chairs and plastic laminate backs;
plastic tablecloths with non-matching, faded placemats, and
little pots of—yes—plastic flowers. The soup was delicious,
hearty quinoa, but the chops, well, they were a sorry excuse
for meat. At least I could chew a bit on the potatoes and add
some spicy chilli stuff to make it all taste a bitty-bit better.

Sittin' there, I could see I was catchin' some attention. For a
tourist town, I had noticed precious-few travelers, but I'd
heard about Bolivia's instability. So many governments and
uprisings some people were just too scared to come here.

Like I had a choice.

A man in the corner studied me intently, his moustache
ticklin' his lips, a beer in front of him gettin' warm. His hair
was a dirty-blond, not entirely Bolivian and I reckoned he was
a stranger here, just like me.

Eventually he came over, introduced himself, offering me a drink.

—Borys Jachowicz, he said. New in town?

I nodded. I knew I was supposed to chat up the locals to find Ben, but really. I needed the energy for it, and I was too darn shell-shocked from the journey to bother.

—Going into the salt? he asked me.

What was this, some kinda Alice in Wonderland guessin' game?

—You know, into the salt pans. Biggest stretches you'll ever see.
—Actually, I said, I'm waitin' for a friend.

He nodded knowingly.

—Would've guessed a pretty girl like you wouldn't travel to these parts alone.

He'd have guessed wrong.

—You been here a long time? I asked.
—Just under a year. Don't know why though. This place is dull enough to turn you into an alcoholic. Freakish little to do, and hot as Hades. When it's not colder than a well-digger's ass.
—Sounds appealin'.
—Actually I like it. Good place to run away from your troubles.
—You got troubles?
—Who doesn't?

—You met a guy here? Name's Channing, I asked.

—Chan? That guy could outsmart any number-cruncher. Remembers a deck of cards in order. You sort it, he remembers.

—That's him, I said, tryin' to hide my excitement. He live about here?

—Moved to Uyuni quite a few months back. Works on the vehicles. It's a full-time job. Sometimes he's out in the desert. A loner. He doesn't like to stay in one place. Probably has troubles too. He a friend of yours?

—Friend of a friend.

—Well you won't find him here, sweetheart. You'll have to hook up with a tour. Who knows if he's still there? He's running from something. Just like the two of us.

August 5, 2004 – Thursday

So I came all the way to this God-forsaken place to leave it almost immediately. The good thing about a tour was that you paid through the nose for it. So if you wanted to pee, they stopped the car and you peed to your heart's content. Sure, you had to squat in the desert behind *tollo* and *paja* grass which barely covered the essentials. But I was gettin' used to that. I was with a group of three other tourists. A French teacher, who spoke English. Her husband, who hardly talked. And an American named Anita who lived in Cancun, Mexico. Our guide, Jesús, had a name he wasn't livin' up to, and Hugo was the chef who couldn't cook.

The further we drove, the drier the landscape became. Our vehicle was clearly in need of Channing's attention, as its first obligatory stop was about an hour after a lunch of *tamales* and beer. As Jesús and Hugo peered into the vehicle's engine, I

watched a family of llama decorated with red and pink ribbon,
all congregatin, waiting for something to happen.

—Filter problem, Anita said. We can walk a little. Enjoy the
scenery.

It was beautiful. In the distance were peaks capped with snow
or ice, but the wind that blew off them made me tingle.
Eventually, another vehicle rescued us and we were mobile
again. From the window, I watched the landscape changing,
the sand taking on the patterning from the winds. Rocks
gradually wore down to boulders, boulders to pebbles, pebbles
to sand.

We reached the hamlet of San Antonio just before dusk. The
four of us were sharing a cement dormitory, with windows
patched up with plastic and sticky tape. Even then we were
near frozen through. And to think these people were here on
vacation? To pass the time until bed, we ate Hugo's burnt rice
and raw chicken legs. Watery asparagus soup.

I thought about you. And don't think they were the nicest
thoughts, Ant. They weren't.

At Anita's suggestion we played cards. Watched on by Hugo
and Jesús, we flung the cards into suits, the matchstick bets
piling up on the other side of the table. Anita and I shrugged.
We were both useless. The French couple weren't too bad.
And they'd brought a bottle of wine, which they shared. But
soon Jesús and Hugo grew bored, walking outside into the
cold for a cigarette. I could hear their raised voices through
the broken window pane, but didn't understand them.

—What are they sayin'? I asked Anita.

—Not much really. Except that we suck at this. Apparently the only man worth watching at cards was the mechanic who used to work in Uyuni.

Used to work? I sat in my bed with the wind whipping through the unstuck plastic. We'd shared out the blankets between us. Six each, and even with a fleece I was freezin' my ass off. The worry about Benjamin's disappearance was a good way to distract me from the cold, but only temporarily. I still had to live through the night at an altitude that made breathin' almost impossible. I tried to suck up oxygen with my mouth, hopin my face wouldn't solidify. For a while, I kept myself awake with my own breathing.

August 6, 2004 – Friday

I don't want to be blunt about my bodily functions, but this morning I wished to God I were a man. When those bastards I've hired to torture me knocked on the door at three forty-five—yes Anton, in the morning—there were no chance in hell I was going to expose myself to the elements. None whatsoever. We were workin' against the clock to beat the tourists from Chile to the Laguna Colorada. Why? Don't ask me, I only paid to be on this sorry journey. I shifted next to Anita, tryin' to draw some body heat from her in the vehicle. We were too cold to speak. I did notice however, that the heater was another thing, apart from the petrol filter, odometer and speedometer, that didn't work in this tin can on wheels. Benjamin, when I get a hold of you, I can make you one promise, you will have everythin' to answer for.

Three hours in the pitch dark until the sunlight started to filter over the Ututuncu Volcano, turnin' it scarlet. Speechlessly beautiful, I tell ya, but not warm. We stopped in some military town to do star jumps before breakfast. Actually, that was my idea, and good thing too. The gas stove was broken so coffee was long in comin'. Oh for a skinny latte and a fire!

Anita looked at me, the morning steam billowing from my mouth.

—What's with you this morning, kid?
—Cold, I said.
—We're all cold, but you're a whippet on fast forward.

I stopped short, thinkin' my idea through, but not too deeply.

—That mechanic they were talkin' about last night?
—Yes?
—I've come all this way from Charleston to tell him I love him.

Anita's already-red cheeks flushed redder.

—Oh my God! she said dramatically, how romantic!
—Problem is, I continued, he seems to have moved on. And I don't speak a word of Spanish …
—Well, honey, said Anita, I think you're in luck.

So much for Borys Jachowicz (I have his card, so I know I've spelt it right). Seems Ben moved on from Uyuni at least six months back. Neither Jesús or Hugo knew where, but they'd heard he'd been around.

—Don't give up, Anita said, love will find a way.

Jesús and Hugo nodded keenly. Glory. Now I was stuck in a Valentine's cliché, with a team of misfits backin' me up. I didn't talk much on the rest of the journey, I was too wound up. Back to square one, or thereabouts.

We got to the lake near lunchtime. A couple of flamingoes and geese hangin' out, and a fox doing his best to catch them. We headed onto the *hostal*. I couldn't believe Benjamin could have disappeared without a trace. He'd left so many hints to lead me here. Here being yet another cement building, with six rooms alongside each other, with a bathroom—two toilets and an open shower. Along the front of the building was a kinda porch with a roof of yellow plastic. Actually, it warmed the whole area up and I could finally feel my fingers again.

A woman in long Bolivian socks, sandals, skirt and brightly colored shawl was sweepin'. A hopeless task if you ask me. Every tourist that arrived brought another pile of desert in.

—Anita, I said, can you ask her if she knows Channing?

But the woman shook her head, already disinterested and went back to her broom. I bit my lip. Was I about to lose the trail here, after everything I'd been through? Jesús tapped me on the shoulder, jabbered something incomprehensible.

—Come on, said Anita, we're going to the tourist sites. Some volcano or other. Jesús says we can ask the other drivers about Channing.

We drove higher and higher, the altitude clocking up to almost 16,000 feet. From the car we could see a fumarole, but the steam was blown quickly on the high winds, formin' a barrier of vapor. It seemed warm enough inside the car until we had to get out of it. My Lord! Colder than a butcher's freezer.

We stepped beyond the steam curtain to a sulfurous world of bubbling mud pots, boiling water, stretches of colored earth toasted through and steam trails risin' between cracks. Some of the pools were enormous, and deep, bursting with frenzied thrusts of liquid. So I was in hell after all. My heart heaved, and as I battled for breath, I could feel the sharp sting in my ears. I needed a warm hat. I needed a lead. For goodness' sake, Anton, I needed somethin' to work with.

We stopped for lunch at the Laguna Salada. Anita, her woolen blue-striped hat pulled low over her face, led me from vehicle to vehicle. I heard heavy hints about love in every conversation. *Amor. Amor. Amor.* Oh heavens, what in hell's name story have I made up? I stood to the side feelin' about as useful as gooseshit on a pumphandle—excuse the French. The guides and drivers looked at me with truckloads of pity and amusement. Although I endured the humiliation, I could have dug myself into a hole and died.

—I'm really sorry, honey, Anita said, leading me over the frozen ice to the newly tufted grass. Seems your man may have left Bolivia.
—He may? I stuttered.
—Got a big job offer. Met a rich guy on one of the tours.
—But where is he now? Where has he gone?

Anita put her arm around me.

—We'll keep on asking around, okay? He's got to have told someone where he's gone. Love conquers all, right?

Chapter 24
11 January 2005. Tuesday. 12h13.

It's been another morning of bodies and collections. Labelling and packaging. Today isn't nearly as bad as yesterday. Can you get used to devastation like this in just twenty-four hours? Murray walks past. Nods. Moves on. He hasn't the energy for chatter and Jay doesn't blame him.

And then Pascale comes through to Khao Lak. She's asked around looking for Jay.

Pascale is pale, but she doesn't blink as she steps past the bodies to where Jay is writing something on a clipboard. Jay watches her approach, wondering what other than terrible news could bring her out here.

"It's Steve," she says, "I think we have found Laura. We've been trying, Jay, we have. But he simply won't calm down."

By the time they get back to the hotel, Liam's cheek is shredded from Steve's flailing hands. Curled up into a ball, Steve looks completely immovable. Liam touches the mark on his face.

"Don't worry about me," he says, indicating Steve. "The man is a mess."

And as Jay leans down to talk to Steve, he realises not much he can say will reach him.

"How did he find her?" he asks.

"They brought some bodies in from Phi Phi. They were trapped under a collapsed building. But a boat had been pushed against it by the wave. Nobody realised there were people there until they moved the boat."

"It's been a long time. How could he have recognised her?"

Steve shifts, unrolls.

"She's my wife, you wanker," he says. "You think I wouldn't recognise my own wife?"

Jay steps away, his hands up in submission.

"You're right," he says. "Of course you are."

Steve sits up completely, drops his face in his hands. The agony of his grief echoes across the room at high volume.

"He needs to rest," says Liam, looking at Jay. "He won't achieve anything like this."

And when the injection goes in, Steve doesn't even resist.

13h22

Steve's asleep. Finally. Pascale doesn't want to leave him and she doesn't want to eat either.

"*Non merci,*" she said, "I cannot eat now. Not after what I was seeing."

Jay feels a little guilty. He can't help it if he is hungry. He's been up since five, and banging in his head is the hangover Becky left him with. Jay needs grease.

Something to line his stomach. And Liam is always starving. He's a big man with lots of energy to replace.

"We'll bring you something back," Liam promises.

"I don't want anything."

"I know you don't, but you'll be hungry later."

Pascale nods.

"You go. And if Steve awakes?" she says.

"He should be a little groggy, but call me," says Jay, tapping his phone.

Pascale smiles, then picks up a book.

"I'll be here," she says.

Outside, the heat is almost unbearable. Liam and Jay don't walk far – it just seems too much effort.

"What I can't work out," Jay says, "is why you don't leave. I know why I'm here, but you, Liam, you're a bit of a mystery."

"Am I?" says Liam. "And what else are you trying to figure out?"

"What Pascale sees in you," says Jay with a laugh.

"Oh there's no mystery there," Liam says seriously, "Pascale would tell you herself. I'm an animal in bed."

Their meal is quick. Liam wants to get going.

"Laura's body needs to be moved, and we need to contact the Kiwi Embassy."

"I'll come with you," Jay says. "I won't make it back to Khao Lak today."

And even as they pile up the paperwork they will need to take through to Steve, there is something pensive about Liam.

"Before all of this," he says, indicating the queues and the heartache, "had you lost someone close to you?"

"My brother," says Jay. "That's why I came here. To climb and get over it. Now I've lost my sister too and am not really sure which part of me will accept that."

Liam sighs. "Maybe it's too soon to give up."

"Maybe it's too late to have hope."

"And what about Kerese?" Liam asks. "You've found her. Now what?"

"I can't leave Thailand," says Jay, "not yet."

"So what will you do?"

"I'm thinking of going back to Koh Phi Phi. That girl Becky – she's looking for volunteers."

Liam nods, making sense of Jay.

"You'd better speak to Kerese," he says. "I have a feeling, Jay, you made this decision before the tsunami even happened."

17h54

Rikke lies still, the bruises on her face yellowing. Margot turns, studying Jay as he walks in.

"You came," she said. Matter-of-fact.

"Were you expecting me?"

She doesn't answer. Instead she takes her friend's hand, stroking it gently.

"You've prolonged her life, I think," Margot said. "But I don't know what sort of life it will be."

"Her prognosis is fairly good."

"Heck, at least you're honest. Fairly is more realistic than very. Very good. Good. Excellent."

"It takes a while to break bad news," Jay says. "And it's damn hard."

Margot stands up, then moves back to her chair.

"Oh, I'm not blamin' them. How can I? They've kept her alive this long. But she was under the water a long time. No oxygen. I wonder, when she wakes up, who she will be?"

"Are they moving her?"

"Back to Norway? Not yet. Maybe at the end of the week. Her parents have arranged something …"

Jay looks at Margot. On the boat with her fashionable sunglasses and plunging neckline, she was vibrant. Sexy. Alive. It's as if the wave has knocked the life right out of her.

"You need a break," says Jay. "I'll stay with her if you want to rest."

Margot sighs.

"I think I was a little in love with her. Not in *that* way. But she could talk to anybody. I can't stand seeing her like this. Her voice cut right out of her body. And no, I can't have a break. What happens if she wakes up and I'm not here?"

"I'll call you."

"You seem such a kind person," Margot says. "But you also seem to be floating. What do you want? Is life just about everybody else for you?"

"I guess I'm just learning to appreciate it."

"That's the irony about Thailand, isn't it? Even when you're dying here, you're so alive."

Chapter 25
August 6, 2004 – Friday

It was at the hotel made entirely out of blocks of salt that we finally met someone who knew somethin'. She was a pretty little thing, a tour guide with one of the touring companies. I'd noticed her before at the Laguna Hedionda—the Smelly Lake—don't you just love it? She was leading her troops closer to the flamingoes dotting the frozen pools, pointing to how the birds took off in an almost choreographed display.

But now she waited in the queue for a shower, a towel draped over her shoulder. Anita struck up a conversation first.

—You been working here long?

The woman blinked, then smiled.

—Actually, only about eight months. I'm from La Paz, but I studied languages. The best place to practice my English is with the tourists.
—Like me?
—Exactly.

Anita didn't beat about (around?) the bush.

—Ever meet a guy called Channing?
—The American? Sure, he was a good person to chat to. Used to teach me slang. Not sure I'll ever use it. You know him?

We watched someone leave the first shower cubicle.

—Frickin' icy, the woman said. The element doesn't work.
I'm colder than when I got in.

She stepped past us, wrapped tightly in a turquoise towel, and
her sandals fluffing the sand floor. The guide smiled.

—At least all the showers are working today, she said. All that
driving, you have to clean yourself up, don't you?

We nodded, really wantin' to know more about Channing and
less about the state of the ablutions.

—Are you going in or aren't you? the man behind us said,
looking irritated at the chatter.

The guide shrugged, then moved forward.

—Come join us for a drink, I offered, when we're all done.

The guide's name was Luz and she arrived at our table with
wet hair tied into a tight braid.

—The first time I saw this place, she said as she slid in next to
me, I thought it looked like a funeral parlor.

She was right—all the velvet draping and black Gothic
bedsteads did make the place resemble a mortuary. Out there
in the dining room, where we were sittin' on salt blocks with
cushions, the effect wasn't quite the same. A girl of about
fourteen brought us some crockery—heavy pottery plates and
goblets big enough to knock some poor sucker out. She

twisted the bottle of wine awkwardly, leaving a little cork floatin' to the surface of our glasses.

—So what do you need to know about Channing? Luz asked, sipping her drink.
—Where he's gone, I replied.
—I don't even know if he's still in Chile.
—That's where he went?

Luz studied me. Appraisin'.

—May have.
—Chile's a big place, I said.
—Maybe that's why he went? she murmured.

I wondered if she had loved him. She had a thoughtful air about her that may have suggested it.

—We weren't lovers, if that's what you are wondering, said Luz. Just friends. That guy was mixed up. Frightened of something.
—Did he talk about it?
—He talked, but not about that. He seemed so … lonely. Like an abandoned puppy.
—Well, he certainly doesn't stay in a place for long, said Anita.
—He's a searcher, answered Luz. Never quite settled. Always looking at the next big thing.
—But what for? Anita asked, looking at me.
—Hope, I said. He's searchin' for hope.

Luz gave me a number. The rich man from Chile.

—He offered me a job too, she said, but I didn't want to leave Bolivia. I have a daughter … she's three. My mother takes care of her. I see her whenever I can.

She was babbling a little. Excusin' herself. But unlike Peggy, she kept her baby—even with no man to support her. I admired that.

—I hope you find Channing, said Luz, he needs someone to take care of him. And I wasn't the girl for the job.

August 9, 2004 – Monday

Benjamin had already moved on by the time I spoke to Señor Fernandes.

—That boy, he said, and even over the phone I could hear him shaking his head. He just couldn't settle. He liked the Peninsula, but it was just too quiet for him. He wanted action.

I was getting tired, Anton, I won't lie. How many more phone calls, journeys, plane rides, before I found Ben?

—Where did he go? I asked, almost afraid of the answer.
—Cusco, Fernandes said. And someone there tells me he's met a girl. So don't be disappointed, *querida*, if he doesn't love you anymore.

Chapter 26
15 January 2009. Saturday. 11h00.

Jay takes a breath. This time, there's no choice of a ferry to Koh Phi Phi. The boat was destroyed, and so only smaller speedboats that had been stacked out of the water are moving people back to the island. He's bought some supplies. A tent, which he may or may not need. Food stocks. Clothes. Besides, it's not as though Phuket is *that* far away.

"You're a fool," said Kerese.

"Maybe," said Jay.

"And what about your practice?"

"It'll wait."

"I won't," said Kerese, her arms folded across her chest.

Jay looked at Kerese, his decision made.

"I didn't ask you to," he replied.

The water has been cleared of bodies, but some debris still floats near the beach. Jay looks across at Becky. She doesn't seem to be aware of much except the towering cliffs rising above them.

"It's still beautiful," she says softly.

He doesn't know who she is talking to, but she's right. And when the flattened houses and pier and shops are cleared away, rebuilt, it will be paradise again.

11h04

Jay knows what he is doing here. He's resolute. Prepared. The medical supplies they've brought will be enough until they can appraise the situation better. Liam and Pascale are coming through tomorrow. Pascale's cancelled her teaching job. They want to come too, for a few months. No reason not to.

"I feel useful," says Liam.

He's right; he is. But Jay still wonders if there is something more at the heart of this for Liam. A profundity in busy-ness. Action wiping clean. But Jay doesn't feel he has the right to ask.

Steve's gone. Flew from Phuket to Bangkok. Then who knows how he's getting back to Auckland. Kerese left with Tracy and Mrs McCall. And Rikke and Margot, some sort of medical flight, accompanied by a Norwegian doctor. Jay's not sure the move is wise, but Rikke's parents wanted her home. His mother wants Jay home, but he's not coming.

"I'm not giving up on Nina," Jay said.

"She's gone," his mother replied, almost resolute. "I want you back. You've done what you can."

But he hasn't. He can do more. *That* he is sure of.

Becky seems to have collected volunteers all over Phuket. It's like the responsibility has kicked her into a different gear completely. Complete one-tracked focus. Jay hadn't seen her again until yesterday, but her pamphlets had been dropped off at guesthouses all over the province. The group arriving today consists of local Thais, a few Americans, Brits and some Germans. Like him, the others seem uneasy. Though they've been told the island has been cleared of most bodies and larger rubble from the bungalows, Phi Phi has also been declared uninhabitable. There's a lot to do. A boat coming this afternoon will bring carts and two wheelbarrows Liam has bought. Food and potable water is coming in slowly.

In Krabi Town, rescues and planning are being co-ordinated from a local mosque. Funding is dribbling in. Pockets are being emptied and budgets stretched. But now it's hard labour and medical help the island needs.

Jay looks at the sea. It's still as glass. And though he pretends fearlessness, he can see the worry reflected back. Returning to the UK would have been an easier choice. But not the right one.

They have to jump into the water. The pier is gone and they can't get close enough to moor properly. Jay's shorts are wet through but he welcomes the swim. One by one the passengers descend, passing along suitcases, boxes and supplies, from person to person. Placing everything together, the recruits walk the island to get their bearings.

The rubble is head-height. And some parts of the island are completely inaccessible. Jay thinks about

Murray, his team searching for identities and matching up the lost. They'll do that here too. And maybe he'll find someone who'll know something about Nina.

16 January 2005. Sunday. 09h21.

There's a hotel on higher ground overlooking Loh Dalam Bay. From today it will be the clinic, and as Jay tries to set up his inadequate facilities, people get to work. They lift and carry like leafcutter ants, beginning to clear away basic paths so that the island can start to move again. Becky is co-ordinating identity matches. Nothing with even the slightest clue is thrown away: ticket stubs, passports, drivers' licences, luggage labels, photographs. She's using another room in the hotel, and is typing notes into a computer that may once, a long time ago, have looked new. Sifting through the junk is tiring, and endless people traipse through to Jay with gashes from rusty metal and unexpected sharp edges.

And the Thai people who didn't leave the island are battling with dysentery and untreated injuries. Jay speaks to an old man, a fisherman who won't go back to the water.

"No catch fish. They eat ..."

And he doesn't have to finish his sentence. Somewhere, out there, Nina too may be feeding the fishes. The thought is sickening.

The children who come to him are shocked and unpredictable. Some cry, their heads tucked down, not wanting to be touched by this strange man. Others stare at him, their brown eyes filled with questions. One brings a football he has found. It's soft and needs to be pumped. If a doctor can't fix this, then what can he fix?

They'll need to rebuild the school. And the tourist shops. People need jobs and motivation. And they can't be afraid. Jay looks at the water, picturing the oncoming wave from this height. Wilfred, the hotel manager, has only been in Koh Phi Phi a few months. But he saw the wave from up here.

"It was like watching the end of the world," he says.

Wilfred, like Liam, is practical. He can fix things. Mend pipes. Reconnect wires. There aren't any tourists to pander to so he puts things back together. And unlike Jay, he's travelled. Whereas before this trip a travel conversation might have bored Jay, now he finds he is interested. Especially when Wilfred talks about places mentioned in the diary. Sometimes the writing has been so accurate, he feels he already knows what Wilfred will say.

When the waiting room has cleared, Jay walks to where Wilfred is tinkering. They need to fix a water pump and unblock the drains. The first job is technical, but not overly taxing. The second is vile, and they need to take breaks. All nature of things is stuck in the pipes, and in some places they have shattered completely. French drains are full to overflowing and effluence rots; stinking sludge. Jay and Wilfred wear masks, trying to block the smells from their nostrils. It doesn't help much.

Despite his background and training, Jay finds he doesn't *want* to be inside all day. As the five-foot rubble begins to descend and life starts in embryonic, but visible ways, he likes to be outside. There are more than 150 businesses needing help re-opening, but what Jay doesn't expect is to see Tom. He almost doesn't recognise him. Right after the tsunami he seemed resolute, stubbornly selfish, but what he has witnessed over the last two weeks has changed him. He looks worn thin, worn down. The cavalier don't-give-a-shit attitude replaced with something warmer.

"You're back, bro," Tom says. "Any news of your sister and Kerese?"

Jay updates him, hoping that Tom might have more to offer him.

"They found Kelly, first of January. I discovered some of her stuff as well. A few older journals. Some of her photos. I sent them to her parents. I didn't even know she was much of a writer."

"Was she?" asks Jay, intrigued.

"I always found her a little mysterious. That's probably what attracted me to her. Always some hidden secrets. She was married a few years back. Can you believe she wouldn't have told me something like that?"

"Married? Maybe she wanted to forget about it."

"Well, all I can say is I thought I knew her. I didn't. And now …"

"Now we are all starting a new phase," says Jay.

"Are we?" asks Tom. "I suppose so."

Jay nods, motions towards the clinic where some people are gathering.

"I have to go," Jay says.

"Sure," says Tom, "maybe later we can catch a beer."

25 January 2005. Tuesday. 10h00.

Liam and Pascale are working on the construction of the daycare centre. They've helped raise funds for the building materials, which have come by boat from Krabi town. Forty-six kids need looking after while their parents dedicate themselves to rebuilding Phi Phi. Over the past week, they have cleared the small piece of land allocated to the project and the governor from Krabi has come through for an official visit. They walk past the clinic, stopping to see Jay administering tetanus shots, and handing out the odd lollipop.

Jay has hardly chatted to either Liam or Pascale, but he can often see Pascale in the distance, surrounded by children. It's obvious they like the way she smiles, and somehow she has the patience required to make things happen. Unlike a few of the Americans who have offended some of the Thais with their wild gestures, or the Europeans who touch – or kiss – them inadvertently, Pascale is gentle and distant. Over the past weeks, she's perfected the art of observation, mimicking the Thais to cause the least offence. She *wais* appropriately and the older Thais like her respectful bows, her hands clasped high.

The volunteers have mostly found accommodation, and Jay has given his tent away. People are sheltering in tent villages, under canvas shelters, waiting for the government to complete some more permanent housing. But despite this, the stories he hears are heart-rending. Families wiped out or, even worse, lone family members surviving. In fewer than five minutes, more than one hundred children lost one or both their parents.

It's incredible to be this busy and yet so out of touch. He pictures London, wintry and cold. And he thinks about Kerese, whose life has continued without him. He doesn't miss her in the same way as he thought, but she was a constant presence, now no longer available.

The first shop planned for re-opening is a jewellery shop. No-one comes to Koh Phi Phi except to help or because they live there. Everybody, however, realises that survival depends on tourists making it back to the island. And they won't unless it starts to look like something again. So the clearing is essential – without it they can't rebuild.

But Jay can't rebuild *himself* yet. Not until he knows what happened to Nina. And Becky, who is pulling together a survivor and victim database, has nothing more to offer him. He'll have that beer with Tom, he thinks; perhaps he'll point him in the right direction. Someone on that Similan trip has to know something.

Chapter 27
August 27, 2004 - Friday

But it's not Cusco, is it? This time, I'm skipping a few continents, wishin' I could speak a bit more than English. He was there. That's true. For a month or so. But the girl. They tell me she's real cute, dark hair, almond eyes, and she wasn't stayin'. Got some job planned in the East somewhere and he decided to tag along. You got to know, right, that a mechanic will find a job any place. Don't have to speak much. And from what I hear he was besotted. Nice to hear Ben has finally found some happiness. A soul mate. I just hope he doesn't get disappointed. Sitting in airport after airport, I've had a lot of time to think. And I've got a lot of real happy memories, Anton, but they're cloudin' with the lies.

I warned Eleanor. Told her not to say anything to Bill. And she won't. Two sons and only one accounted for in a Charleston grave. She wants Ben. Sometime I think more than she wants Bill, and I'm getting closer. I can feel it. He can't move much more. He must be gettin' as tired as I am. Everybody wants to settle sometime.

I didn't even stay in Cusco long. I'm a little sorry. It was real pretty—a stone city set in a deep bowl surrounded by some awesome mountains. But when I got there, I checked my emails. I wasn't expectin' much. Nothin' actually. And then I saw a surname that made me stop. Colbert. But it wasn't Ian.

He told me he wouldn't do more. And I believed him. It was Daniella. And even in the ugly typeface, I could feel she was nervous. Checkin' behind her, waitin' for someone, something to pounce.

Something came today in the mail. Maybe I shouldn't be telling you but I know you need to find Benjamin. He's in a little town called Lìjiāng. Couldn't help himself. So he's in love, he wanted someone to know about it. I looked the place up on a map. It's in China. I'd never heard of it. Please don't reply. Ian doesn't know about the latest card and I don't think I'm going to tell him. This is between you and me. Despite what people say, I'm not selfish. And I can still think for myself.

Like I can, Anton. I'm thinkin' your brother is more of an enigma than even I first thought. Is he running? Or is he just seeing the world? Until now, he doesn't seem to have made any real friends, but things have changed haven't they?

We're headin' into September. The card must have been sent a few weeks back, and Daniella's email is almost a week old. I hope Ben's still there. I'm flyin' to Beijing, then through to Kunming, which isn't even particularly close to Lìjiāng. Could your brother have chosen a more inaccessible place? Oh right. He chose Tupiza. So I guess I'm in for another one of his fun journeys. Oh Lord, please not another bus ride. Please?

September 1, 2004 – Wednesday

Darn it. I am so cold. I'm writin' here in this Chinese-style hotel hoping the sun will come up. But at least I'm off that wretched sweat factory. That bus was so full of packages, you had to stand on 'em to reach your bunk. And thank God I was on the top. Hacking and phlegm and spit tricklin' down onto the suitcases below. A woman eyed my bunk, and she could 'want my bed' all she liked. She wasn't getting it. The roads were as bad as in Bolivia. And the cold stuck in my bones, so that now, as I try to get a cup of tea goin' I can barely move my fingers.

The hotel seems to be in the old city of Lìjiāng. Difficult to tell in the pitch dark, but what I do know is, it's far too early to be awake. The hotel owner met me at the door in her dressing gown. Thick flannel.

Outside the window, I can hear someone callin'. Then cart wheels roll alongside the wall on the stone pathways below. They shake and rattle. I won't be able to sleep. I know that. Everythin' is so foreign that I am unnerved. I've looked at a map. Lìjiāng is a lot bigger than I expected. The rebuilt old town is big enough, but what about new Lìjiāng? It stretches on forever. And I don't really have a startin' point. Thank God this place is a tourist town. Someone's gotta speak English. Otherwise I'm going to get nowhere pretty fast.

Later

It's gorgeous here. At least your brother chose some beautiful places. My hostess, Wei, doesn't speak one word of English. Not that I blame her. We *are* in China. But it's just so darned frustrating. She brought me an electric blanket, laid it on the bed with much gesticulatin'. I won't be cold tonight. I left the hotel at first light. I was too wound up to sleep.

The main landmark in Lìjiāng seems to be twin wooden water wheels rotating from one of three river tributaries located here. Thank heavens for them; the winding passageways and paths are so confusin' you could get lost for hours. Just near the wheel, I noticed the goldfish sellers. You buy some, release them and they catch 'em again further downstream. That's recycling, Chinese-style! I ended up walking to a more residential part of Old Lìjiāng. Locals trundled along pushing bicycles or carts, and a woman in Naxi traditional dress leaned forward as a young man loaded her canvas sack with sand. Loaded up, she walked the steep incline, leaving the man behind.

It was near there that I bumped into Li.

I was watching some women who were kneeling next to a river, one scrubbing her laundry with a brush and detergent, and another using the same water to rinse out her cabbage leaves. I guess my face must have registered what I was thinking, because Li started laughing a great belly laugh, from an enormous belly. Li, I soon found out, loved her food, and to her everything was 'velly' delicious.

She gestured to me straightaway.

—Come, she told me. We eat.

I wasn't particularly hungry, but at least she spoke English. And it wasn't like I had much choice anyways; I had to start somewhere. Nodding, I tracked Li—although I didn't know her name then—right out of Old Lìjiāng into a more modern part of the city. Outside the shop, bamboo stacks on the boil emitted huge gusts of steam, but we didn't sit there. Instead Li took me to a windowless back room offering me a chair so close to the ground, it made my bad leg hurt somethin' awful.

And the food: sweet dumplings filled with nuts and brown sugar, pork dumplings dipped in soy and vinegar and then bean curd porridge. My stomach flipped, with tiredness, hunger, nerves. I sure was glad to have the bowl of green tea to wash it all down.

Li didn't talk much while she was eating. She slurped up her meal, smacking her lips then grinned like a possum eatin' bumble bees. Seeing my bowl emptying, she loaded it up again. I was near 'bout sick by the time she were full. And that was when she started talkin'.

Turns out she used to be a teacher. Made more money as a tour guide, so that's what she was still doing. Most of her English was self-taught, blended using input from the different people she met along the way. Despite this, she was easy enough to understand.

—I see you lonely, Li told me.
—Alone? I suggest.
—Yes! Yes!

But actually, the way she continued suggested she thought I needed some company, so maybe I did look lonely after all. She wanted to take me on some tours—to see a Naxi Village, or perhaps a trip to Tiger Leaping Gorge. Her face registered instant disappointment when I shook my head.

—You no like travel, see China?
—I can't, I said to her. I'm looking for someone.
—Ah, she said. Who you look for?

I didn't tell her everything, and I certainly didn't tell her I was in love with Ben. I learned my lesson on that one the last time. Despite this, she was obviously intrigued.

—So this man, this Channing, he live Lìjiāng?
—I think so.

Li nodded, decided.

—You need translator and guide. I help you, she said.

When we left the restaurant, it was quite clear she expected me to pay for the meal. A small price, I thought, knowing I could never do this without Li's help.

September 4, 2004 – Saturday

It's been three days since Li and I met. If nothing else, she's teaching me the art of patience. I've not stopped looking myself, but mostly I've been stopping Europeans who speak English. Like me, most of them were planning to be in and out of Lìjiāng—a tourist stop—nothing more. They'd never met Channing, but liked the idea of my search. Some said they'd keep an eye out and leave a message at the Tea Horse Naxi Family Guesthouse, where I was staying. I wasn't holding my breath.

I had settled on paying Li a daily rate. Every evening, we would meet in the New Town Market and usually I would be the only European there. I was starting to get used to the odd looks from the locals. But it was taking me a little longer to grow accustomed to the food projectiles landing on the floor around us as rejected food was cast off the tables.

Li always ordered. I always paid. Her lack of progress was frustratin' and I must admit, I was beginning to wonder if she was taking me for a ride. As she helped herself to the port rib hotpot and the trays of noodles, I listened to her slurp and suck.

—Tomorrow, she said, looking at me with a triumphant smile, we go Zhi Yue Monastery, just outside Lìjiāng. There is someone to meet you.

September 5, 2004 – Sunday

The Cultural Revolution had taken its toll here, the buildings were too new to have any real history. Li waved her arms around.

—Been rebuilt last twenty years, she said.

Outside the main entrance to the temple, were stands of magnolia and gingko trees—and if what she said was true, they were probably older than the buildings themselves. Hens and roosters clucked around the bushes, peckin' at seeds and insects.

—Taoist temple, Li said, no eating the chickens.
—Then why are they here? I asked.
—Spirit guides, she said, for children who die young. Need protection.

I liked the idea of that. A spirit guide. I wondered if only children could have one of those. Li indicated I should take off my shoes. I did, putting them slightly away from the chickens that were approaching them enthusiastically.

—Temple has Dongba spiritual leader, Li told me, meditate three years, three months, three days, three hours. Not just religion. Study Naxi culture and lifestyle. Very wise man.

Was this the man I was to meet? Li moved through the temple pointing out the different gods that people worshipped.

—Good business. Having baby. Safe travels.

Missing person? It sure was a strange combination—of ornaments, modern photography, glitz and statues. But it appears this wasn't where we were actually headed.

—We go now, Li said, Buddha kitchen.

We went inside a small room where a fire was burning under a blackened kettle. Two yellow-garbed monks greeted us, but a bit distractedly. They were watchin' a soap opera on TV. It seemed a little unmonastic, but when another monk swept in, they scuttled away, the television instantly turned off.

I knew enough not to touch the monk. But he nodded, then grinned, displayed an incomplete set of teeth and a few blackened remains. The man seemed to speak no English, and it appeared Li was going to translate. I didn't rightly know where to start. But I didn't really have to. The monk was going to do this for me. He gabbled away, but even as he spoke he hardly moved his hands.

—You look Mr. Channing, Li said, after the man had exhausted enough words to fill a book.
—Yes.

The man nodded. Continued. I felt a little uneasy. Each time he looked at me, I felt like he was lookin' into my soul.

—Who he to you? Li asked for the monk.

This time, there would be no lies. Except, maybe, the lies Ben might have told.

—Channing is my husband's brother. My husband died. I need to tell him what happened.

The monk nodded to Li's reply.

—He told me once he had brother. Very close. One day. Then big separation. Make very sad.
—I never met him before, I told the monk. But I would like to.

Li looked at the monk. His expression was concerned, as though he was considerin' me.

—Mr. Channing velly good man. Big man. He help with machines. Fix. Fix.

I nodded.

—Yes, he is a mechanic, I have heard he is talented, I said.

Li's head was cocked, just like one of the chickens outside.

—He do bad things once, now he change. He regret.

I watched the monk as Li spoke. There was such a sense of peace about him that I could tell that Ben hadn't hidden much. It would have been difficult to.

—His mother misses him, I said to the monk.

The monk nodded again.

—A child very valuable. Connected always. Beginnings and endings.
—She asked me to find him, I said.

The monk frowned.

—He doesn't want anybody find him. He has new life now, Li explained for him.

I couldn't believe it, all this, and then a reply that offered no hope at all? Li and the monk broke into a detailed conversation that despite the body language, I could not keep track of. I wanted to cry. Is this all it would amount to?

But then Li spoke again.

—We come back tomorrow. The man big thinking. Will pray and consider. No disturb Mr. Channing without spirit guidance.

I wondered if he had his own chicken to help *him*.

Chapter 28

1 February 2005. Tuesday. 17h21.

They've managed to clear a section of the beach so that they can use it. Volunteer divers have pulled out the wreckage in this area and are gradually working their way beyond. The waters are not in the state they were before the wave, but they are getting better. Some are superstitious, nervous to approach the ocean, and others study it tentatively, dipping in a toe. A leg.

It's hot. There are many who look at the water, eyeing it appreciatively. To be cool again.

Jay wants to swim. He can't be afraid forever. And when Liam trundles a blue wheelbarrow past him, he invites him along. They're wary of causing offence, but the island *was* paradise once. And one day shouldn't be allowed to transform them all forever. Although of course it has.

When they dive in, onlookers gather, as though expecting the water to rise up again and punish their defiance. But nothing happens. The wind blows. The clouds move. The water stays cool and still. And then the children run. One after the other they gambol into the water, thrusting arcs of droplets into the sky.

The party is impromptu. They've worked hard. The group is tired and strained. Some are cut, bruised. Others are simply beyond pain; they are wounded from lost loves, lost children, lost friends. But the water can heal, as well as hurt.

Wilfred lights a fire on the beach. It's a veritable pyre. They have lots of wreckage to feed it. Becky and Pascale pull along a crate of beers on Liam's wheelbarrow. Rice is cooked up in large pots, and then some noodles too. And vegetables and meat brought in from Krabi. The spices permeate the afternoon breeze, subtle, drawing people in.

Jay hasn't met everybody yet, but he knows most of them. He's pleasantly surprised to see Harry. His boat is destroyed, but his spirit isn't. He's going to buy another boat.

"The tourists," he tells Jay, "they come back one day. Me ready."

Becky has started to dance. Her body moves, undulating. Lithe and strong. She twists and turns as a drum beats. Someone has a guitar. Jay looks over. It's the Nigerian; they haven't met. But their eyes have. Dark chocolate in the whitest eyes Jay has ever seen. Soulful eyes. Sad eyes. Jay wonders who he has lost. Another guitar, played by Sammy the Thai man from the mountains who fed him and Steve from the giant pot. And Becky starts to sing. Her movements, her voice, frenetic, frenzied. But oh so beautiful. Jay is transfixed. She's like an ocean siren, drawing him in, but he won't stand up. Jay doesn't dance. Never with Kerese. Not now. Or so he thinks.

Becky takes his hand, pulls him towards her. He should be leading her, but isn't. Her body's rhythm takes him, stirs him. Jay is shirtless, his hair still wet from the ocean. They are dancing in the shallows. Shifting. Whirling. And Becky seems so comfortable, her black bikini against her pale skin. It's beaded. Shimmering. The water laps over their toes. His heart is pounding. She's close, then distant. Her body brushes his, making him tingle. He pulls her back to him, she slips away. She's not singing any longer. She looks at him. He studies her. Their faces close once more. Close enough to kiss. A moment. A hesitation.

Then Pascale has taken on a new tune. Her voice is a lullaby. Sweet and delicate. Like her. Becky lets Jay go. Smiles. Jay looks at Liam. His attention on his fiancée, nodding. His face alight. Becky has slipped away. *What happened?* Jay wonders. *What is happening?* Becky has opened a beer, sips it down. Her eyes catch his. Jay's stomach surges. The drums start up again, the beat quickens. Becky's red hair is reflected in the flames, the curls springing around her face. But she isn't dancing. Isn't singing. Then suddenly she turns.

Jay watches her walk away, back through the rubble; a slight wave as she disappears.

2 February 2005. Wednesday. 10h00.

But now that he has seen Becky in this way, Jay can't switch her from his mind. Typing away in the office nearby, her database of victim and survivor statistics growing, she seems to have forgotten the night before. She hasn't changed towards him. Neither positively, nor negatively. He begins to think he has imagined it all. His glances aren't held. His questions answered only neutrally. She's busy. Cataloguing. Phoning. Filing.

Liam visits, his eyebrows raised quizzically.

"Swim?" he asks Jay.

And Jay follows him to Loh Dalam Bay, a towel over his shoulder.

They dive into the sea, toss a ball between them. Dunk each other, and fling armfuls of waves across the still depths. By the time they return to the shore, Jay and Liam are panting. They sit next to the shallows, their feet dipping into them.

"What's going on?" Liam asks.

"What do you mean?"

Liam looks at Jay, then laughs.

"You and Becky, last night you looked just about ready to screw each others' brains out."

"That obvious?"

Liam laughs.

"You're not with Kerese anymore. You probably need a good shag."

"I wasn't the one saying no."

"She said no?"

"She didn't say anything."

"Give her a chance. There's something about her that's hurting."

Jay grins, slapping Liam on the back.

"I'm a doctor. Sure I could make her all better."

Through February

But it isn't easy as that. There are things to do. And though the evening beach parties become the regular meeting place, the dancing doesn't happen that way again. Jay has resigned himself. It was a once-off thing. A mistake. A near-miss. For her anyway. But something about Becky intrigues him. She doesn't talk about herself much. Her words are guarded. And she's mentioned leaving. She's spending a lot of time with Wilfred, and Jay finds that despite himself, he's jealous. Does she *have* to help with the broken generator? And is it really necessary for her to go with Wilfred to Krabi? Why can't Liam go? Or Tom? Or Harry? He wants to talk to her, but what is he going to say? *What happened that night? Did I do something wrong?* There's really nothing to discuss. It was a non-event. Wasn't it?

He hasn't chatted to Tom again. The man seems high on something most of the time. God knows where he gets it. The dive school shop is coming along. Tom recovered a lot of his stuff after the wave. The rest was insured. And when he's not working on rehabilitation, he's out in the bay, pulling out junk. Harry helps him in his new boat. They load it up together. And sometimes Tom brings in things for Becky to look at. And even this irritates Jay.

The way Tom flirts with Becky. The way she flirts back. If he didn't know himself better, he would think he was jealous. Oh hell, who is he kidding? He *is* jealous.

But Tom is oblivious. He doesn't mention Kelly, although sometimes he seems pensive. And when he's like that, Jay wonders what he is thinking about. They do eventually talk on the beach. It's been a long day. A section of rubble collapsed on two of the volunteers. They are not unconscious, or dead, thank God. But a few limbs are broken. Harry and Jay took them off to Krabi. They needed X-rays and plaster casts.

And now Jay is back. He's tired. Worn out. And he hasn't eaten. He's had a few beers. Four? Five? He can't remember. And on an empty stomach, he's a little dizzy. Tom is puffing away on something, his eyes glazed. They sit next to each other, staring out to the ocean.

"You're a good guy," Tom says.

"Am I?"

"Sure, after what happened between me and Kerese, I would've thought you wouldn't talk to me again."

Jay stops, his heart sinking.

"You and Kerese?" he says slowly.

"It was a once-off thing. She was hot for it, but just that time. You know what it's like."

Jay studies Tom, who seems completely unaware of the change in mood.

Jay stands up. He wants to tell Tom about Kelly's offer, but doesn't. He won't lower himself to Tom's level.

"Kerese never told me about your once-off thing," he says coldly. "And maybe you should have kept it to yourself."

Jay walks away back towards the hotel.

"Oh shit," he hears Tom behind him.

25 February 2005. Friday. 09h21.

How long will he stay here in Phi Phi? He's spent time on the phone to the boat charter company that Nina had used for the Similans. But everything seems in such disarray. His Thai is limited to greetings and food names, and no-one seems to know what he is asking in any event. He feels like the girl in the journal, moved from pillar to post, increasingly frustrated. And tired. Maybe it's time to go home. But he hasn't really done enough. The head office for the charter company is in Krabi. At least he got *that* out of Tom before his bombshell. He's phoned, tried to visit. Nobody is ever there. But he can't just leave it at that. This is his *sister* he is talking about. This is *Nina*.

He'll need to ask Harry. Someone to translate for him. They could stay a few days. Ask around. Jay will pay Harry. He could probably use the money. And Jay's just not feeling strong. Becky hasn't even said good morning, and his self-esteem is cracked. And he wonders if Tom and Kerese used a condom. They were probably too slammed to think about one. Should he get an HIV test?

Jay closes up the clinic. Right now he doesn't care about much. He's hurt. Exhausted. He'll sleep. Go to Krabi tomorrow. God knows why he's so upset about Kerese. It wasn't as if he loved her anymore. *It's the grief kicking in,* Jay tells himself, *the shock.*

Kerese and Tom.

A once-off thing.

It doesn't matter really, does it? What difference does it really make?

Chapter 29
September 6, 2004 – Monday

I have this box, Anton. The monk decided to give it to me in the end. Ben left it behind, and the man won't tell me where he is. He told Li he doesn't know exactly. I wonder if monks are allowed to lie? Li was concerned. I could see the furrows on her forehead.

—No velly good, she told me. What we do with box?

But it's something. A link to Ben. He was here and I'm not chasin' rainbows.
Li left me alone. She touched her ample stomach, and left for lunch.

—Later, she said, you come my house. You want?

I didn't know what I wanted, except to look inside this box.

I took each item out. Bit by bit. Photos. Tickets. A baseball cap. Set of screwdrivers. A wrench. A bicycle tube repair kit. I'd traveled halfway across the world for this? There was a T-shirt in the box too. I pulled it out. I don't know why, but I put the shirt on. All this way, and somehow I wanted to be part of him. Benjamin is not a small man. Ben's broader than you are. Even you would have swum in these clothes. And the red wouldn't have suited you. So even now, he's different. I

284

scratched through the photos, expectin' something useful. But the pics were of scenery. Rock formations. Crevices. Caves. Mountains and deserts. I almost passed out when I saw one of them. I'd stood next to that exact rock somewhere out in the Atacama, the hectic wind blowin' me sideways.

I didn't know Ben, but in some ways now I do.

I only found the photo when I opened up the repair kit. It was creased into a tiny square, and I wondered if Ben had even remembered it was there. The faces were so bent and battered that I might not have recognized them. I bought a magnifying glass—Li helped—and as I focused on the figures, somethin' real strange was coming clear.

The photo reminded me of somethin'. That picture of the three of you, full of laughter, your arms round one another. Smiling. Happier days. But this one only had two people. Ben and Peggy. Anton, honey, you were nowhere to be found. And I've seen that look before. The one that passes across a room lettin' everybody know that you're taken. Your brother, Anton, hornier than a two-peckered billy goat on a hill full of ninnies. And Peg, well your girl Peg whatn't sayin' no either.

My stomach lifted, collidin' with my throat. I felt as though I'd been kicked. So I trusted her. Pom-pom Peggy. Aren't I the fool? Gullible enough to gobble up the first story that she fed me. She was hiding something. *You slept with him? I slept with Anton, but I was getting to that.* Of course she slept with Ben. Any fool could see that. I just wondered how much you had known.

I didn't go to Li's house. I had to think this through. It was already dark outside and I found myself walking. Aimlessly.

Why would Peg lie now? I would have thought it was so long ago she would've admitted the relationship and been done with it. And did she know more about the night of the fire than she said?

Who was the person in the car, the one all of Atlanta thought was Ben?

And why had Ben killed him?

I walked past the Naxi theater. I could hear a deep voice talking in Mandarin, then the screaming from the orchestra. Even after a few days here, the instruments still didn't sound like music to my ears. Drums. Bells. Cymbals and gongs. Chanting and banging. Further down next to one of the tributaries, Chinese students lined up beers on a table for a night of heavy drinkin', singin' merrily. *Music good for long life*, Li had told me. The idea made me smile.

I'd seen the Naxi girls selling them before, but tonight I felt I needed some good luck. I bought a candle boat, placed it reverently in the water, then watched it float downriver. Tomorrow would be a better day.

It had to be.

September 6, 03h12

Nightmares. The helicopter whirled around in the clouds, just like it did the day you died. I'd blocked it out my mind. Falling out the sky, the look on your face as you tried to get control. I think I'd resigned myself at the time. *At least we're together.* But my stomach churning, my clenched teeth woke me up. I realized I was caught in this. I wasn't going to leave this mystery unsolved, but I was trapped in that darned spinnin' chopper, about to hit earth.

I phoned Stan Colicchio. He seemed kinda surprised to hear from me.

—So where are ya, anyways?
—China.
—That boy's in China?
—I don't know where he is.
—You gotta move fast, girl, he's slippery.

I sighed. He didn't have to tell *me* that.

—Did you know Peggy Lott Gibson? I asked.
—Name's familiar. Triggers somethin'. Why?
—I think she was the girl Ben was seein', the one you saw him kissin' at the back of the gas station.
—Is it important? Stan asked me.
—It's the only clue I have at the moment.
—I'm goin' to Atlanta tomorrow. My daughter's havin' a baby.
—That's great.
—Yep. I'll be a grandpaw next time we chat. But there's only so much nappy-and-puke talk I can do. I'll leave them ladies to coo-coo, and head to the school. Check a yearbook.
—You will?
—Sure. Peggy Lott Gibson, you say?
—That's right.
—Well I ain't gonna call you. Not in China. I'll send you an email.

I slept better then.

Mornin' time, I'd try again. Now that I thought Peg was some ways involved, it could change the situation just a little.

Chapter 30

26 February 2005. Saturday. 09h22.

But it's not just Jay and Harry in the boat; Liam comes too.

"You look like a ghost, Jay," Liam says. "I'll come with you."

"What about Pascale?"

"She's painting the daycare centre. She's happy for me to go."

They walk to the building. It's amazing how it has sprung up from almost nothing. And in such a short time too. Pascale smiles, then wraps herself around Liam.

"*Bon voyage, chéri,*" she says, painting a dab of purple on his nose.

Their kisses are so intense that Jay looks away. His girlfriend cheated on him with *Tom* of all people, for God's sake. And Becky barely talks to him. His ego is shot to hell. Seeing Liam and Pascale makes him feel even worse.

"Harry," he calls. "Shall we get our stuff to the boat?"

But Pascale doesn't let him leave that easily. She runs to him too, her hands on both shoulders as she looks into his eyes.

"It will be OK, Jay, *bonne chance.*"

The touch makes him falter. He bites his lip.

"You need a dolphin on this mural," he says with a smile, "a dolphin jumping."

Pascale looks back at her design studying it carefully.

"You're right," she says, touching a blank area to the left, "come see it when you return."

11h34

They stand at the pier. Harry chats quickly to one of the boatmen there, who shrugs theatrically. But the next person they speak to points down the way to a little shack. It's quite a bit away from the sea, and looks so dilapidated Jay wonders if it survived the waves. Although compared to Phuket and Phi Phi, the damage looks much less extensive. He's heard that at Ao Nang nearby, the waves only went up the beach for twenty metres, so although there'd been some buildings destroyed, nobody had lost their lives there. Krabi Town seems to have been blessed with a similar fate.

They walk up to the shack and a man greets them. He's wearing a blue cap and a shirt with the sleeves ripped off.

Jay looks at the man's confusion.

Why have you taken so long to get here and ask around?

Many countries have lifted the bans on all but essential travel to Thailand, and though the hotels are only at most ten percent full, the mood has already changed from one of sadness to new optimism.

Jay understands the guy, although they haven't exchanged one word. He's been on the phone every day. His posters are up at every site possible and he's been in touch with his Embassy. Yet the look from the man says he could have done more.

What does he know? Jay thinks in irritation.

He'd only got the name of the charter company out of Tom two days ago. But of course Jay could have done more. Isn't that always the case?

Despite this, they are directed to an office somewhere between the bus station and the Phomka Temple.

A slight reedy man sits behind a desk. Laid out in haphazard piles are brochures showing different boats and along the wall are flyers in separate display units for tours. He stands up immediately. In the corner of the room, a stack of worn lifejackets has fallen over, trailing belts and buckles. The room smells vaguely of saltwater.

"I am Khunpol, you want charter?" he says, *wai*-ing deeply.

Jay takes out his photo of Nina, slides it over the desk.

"I'm looking for my sister," he says, "she was on a charter taking a dive group when the tsunami hit. I haven't heard from her since."

Khunpol nods thoughtfully.

"Which trip you say?"

"I didn't say. She was in the Similans. Left Christmas Day. It was a full boat. "

"Many boats that day," Khunpol replies. "Not good records. Some drown in water."

"Surely you would know how many of your boats came back?"

"Not know everything about this. Not here that day. Week away Pai. Visiting girlfriend."

"Is there someone else you suggest I speak to?"

Khunpol hesitates, then nods again.

"My father," he says. "You speak to him."

Jay realises soon enough that the hesitation is not about speaking of the boats, but more about his father. When Harry leads him and Liam into a massage parlour, Jay thinks he must have made a mistake. But when a few exchanges result in an oiled-up man appearing, his erection still visible under the folds of a towel, Jay feels slightly ill. Unembarrassed, the man tells them he will come back after he has dressed, pointing across the road to a restaurant.

"Why didn't you tell us?" Jay asks Harry, who shrugs.

"No big thing. Good Thai ladies. Medical check-up each month."

Liam just laughs.

When the man sits down opposite him and Liam and orders an iced watermelon juice, Harry leans forward to translate. But the older man waves his arms disconcertingly, indicating he will answer for himself.

As Jay tells Nina's story, the man listens. Despite his obvious age, his hair is still jet-black, and his face almost unlined. He looks about twenty years younger than he probably is. *Living proof,* Jay thinks, *that frequent sex might just be an elixir of youth.* And Jay isn't getting any.

"Only the one boat destroyed," the old man says, "at Phi Phi."

"And in the Similans?"

"That boat come back. Injuries. Maybe some deaths."

"Do you know who was on the boat?"

"Big wave. Big water. Washed list off boat, and list in Phi Phi gone too. Not know every name."

"Can I speak to someone who was on the boat?" Jay asks.

The man sips his juice, the straw seeking liquid and finding air. He sounds like a vacuum cleaner.

"One tourist. He still here. From Brazil, I think. Nice boy. Name Gabriel."

Jay remembers Nina's excitement the day she left. Could this be the same guy? They listen to the old man's directions. Harry will find the place.

13h13

The Brazilian watches them from the makeshift goalposts. He's surrounded by teenage boys who whoop and whistle, their feet kicking towards the ball. They're wearing team shirts, some yellow and some blue, but the action moves so fast from one side of the field to the other that Jay hardly knows which way each team needs to score. Gabriel smiles at their approach, but his eyes are focused on Jay.

"Do I know you?" he asks.

"I was there the day you left for the Similans. On Christmas."

The man nods.

"That's right. You seemed familiar."

"I'm looking for my sister."

"Your sister?"

"She left on the boat with you. You survived, so I'm hoping you're going to tell me she did too."

Jay hands him the photo.

Gabriel looks at it, his eyes dark.

"Nina?" he says.

"You remember her name?"

"Her and I ..."

Jay is glad about one thing, then. Nina got her man. If only for a short while.

"What happened?" he asks.

Gabriel checks his watch.

"Fifteen more minutes," he says, "I'll finish up early here and then I'll tell you what I know."

Chapter 31
September 6, 2004 - Monday

I sat in the bed, the electric blanket on high, and a cup of green tea next to the bed. I don't much like the stuff, but at least it warms me from the inside. I laid out everything I knew. Wrote down names, connections, drew them into columns and then again into some strange spider diagram where everythin' links up. Nothin' made sense to me anymore. If Ben and Peg were lovers, where did that leave you, Anton? Did you know about it? And why did Peg lie? What did she have to do with the whole episode?

I spread the note I'd found in Peggy's box out.

I'll do anything for you, my angel. You know that. And if it means I have to hurt my brother, I'll do it. I love you. Passionately. I have from the first moment I saw you.

I'd assumed it was from you, the writing was similar enough. But maybe it wasn't. Maybe it was from Benjamin. And if that was true, was he only talking about their relationship? Or was it something more sinister?

My heart was really hurtin'.

Was Peg's baby really Ben's? And when I had my miscarriage were you grievin' a second baby or a first? Was this the reason you were so silent on the subject of Ben? It was just so confusing and all this thinking wasn't bringin' me any closer to finding Ben. Was he still in China? And if not, where could he have gone next?

Li came by earlier this morning. She's asking around but nobody is forthcoming about anythin'. Li says she'll keep on looking. She may have to. I barely want to leave the guesthouse. I'm blue. Real blue. I sure don't want to go back to Eleanor with a cold trail, but at the moment, I'm losing hope. I miss my life. My old life with the old you. But that's gone. And what do I have to go back for anyhow? A waitressing job in a dingy bar so I can paint and blow glass, and sell my stuff for nothin'? What a mess. My leg is aching somethin' mean. It'll rain tonight. I guarantee it. This darn leg only aches like this with the rain.

September 7, 2004 – Tuesday

Wei from downstairs is worried about me. I just sleep and sleep. She brought me bean curd porridge for breakfast, and gestured it was time to open the curtains. She spoke to me loudly, banging open a window to let fresh air in. That fresh air was frozen and I pulled the blankets up over my head. No dice. Wei tugged on it like a madwoman. The only word I understood was Li. So she'd put her up to this. Darn it to hell. What was the point in gettin' up? I didn't have a single lead.

I only left the guesthouse to get Wei off my back. She stood there at the main door, her arms folded over her chest, and a huge pile of my washing next to her feet. The fact that she had shoved me in the shower too made me feel a little self-conscious. I didn't want to explore really, but I didn't know what else to do. I took a cab to Black Dragon Pool Park, not realizing I could just as easily have walked there. Li had mentioned its beauty, but this was only really revealed an hour or so later when the clouds cleared. In the meantime, I was cajoled into sitting for a photo opportunity. A husband-and-wife team had set up a swinging seat on either side of which they'd tied a peacock. Beneath the seat was a trail of plastic flowers.

As I sat, a fake photographic grin plastered on my face, some school children gathered.

—Hello, hello, hello, they called to me, tryin' out their English.

A boy of about ten approached me.

—My name is, he said, then added, good morning.

They all wanted to be in the photograph. I don't suppose I minded. What did I want a photo of myself for anyways? By the time the posing was finished, I found I had been adopted, and was being dragged around the garden. Loud music blasted around the pool, and some Chinese girls in a rowboat, spotting us, waved furiously, and shouted greetings. I didn't know where I was being taken, but we left the gardens, and disappeared into Lìjiāng's back roads. The older boy seemed determined and eventually he led me to what must have been his family home. Outside two women were scraping dried corn from the husks. The kernels were pilin' up around them and a stack of turnips near the wall seemed ready to topple. A girl of about two stared at me in mistrust, a trail of green snot danglin' from her nose.

Soon we were in the family kitchen. A hotpot for rice stood to the one side next to a stove fed by carbon blocks. Near the corner of the room, a fire burnt, a kitten warming itself by the flames. And then, on a bench, sat an old man, his face deeply grooved and his teeth black or missing. And unlike the others, he spoke English.

—My grandson thinks I need visitors, the man said.

I smiled. The kitten, now warmed, stood up, stretched and slipped into the old man's lap.

—So he brings you fresh tourists from Black Dragon Pool? I replied.

One of the women scuttled inside, stirred a pot on the stove, then left again.

—Oh from anywhere really, but the pool is closer.

He laughed.

—Your English is excellent, I said.
—I owned a trading company once. English was important.

My eyes must have betrayed my surprise.

—Hard times, he told me, bad investments. So here we are. Until a year ago I taught Mandarin at the Learning Center. Now I rest and talk. Tell me where you come from.

So my journey came out, little by little, and it was only after I spoken for a little while that I noticed the expression on the old man's face.

—Your travels sound so familiar, he says. Like I have heard them before. About two months ago, I met a couple. They

were walking along the road to Héilóngtán Gōngyuán, when
my motorbike broke down.
—He fixed it for you? I guessed.

The man nodded.

—He lived in Canada for a while. I couldn't speak to his
girlfriend much, I didn't understand her accent.
—French? I said, trying to hide my excitement.
—I am not sure. Perhaps. They came here for dinner. My
wife, he indicated towards the doorway, she cooked. Local
Naxi food. Some Chinese, Lìjiāng speciality.

I pictured the food for myself, the pork hotpot, and trays of
tofu and vegetables. Giant fluffy mushrooms. Green bean
jelly. Chicken feet stew. Naxi sandwiches with fried eggs,
goat's cheese and tomato between pieces of baba flatbread.

—He wasn't from Canada. I can't tell the difference from
American, but he told me that, the man continued.
—Were they living here?
—Yes, but in the Old Town. When I met them, they were
thinking of leaving. I can't remember where they were going.
We talked about places. Guilin. Xian. Beijing. Shanghai. And
then they talked about Vietnam. Hanoi. Saigon.
—Were they on holiday?
—They were not settled. But they had been in Lìjiāng for two
months. What do you call it? Itchy hands?
—Itchy feet.

The man nodded, then looked at me, his eyes clear,
penetrating. He was silent. Appraisin' me. Then the man
stood up, walking to a little cupboard, with drawers to the left.

Extracting a postcard in Benjamin's unmistakable hand, he handed it to me.

—You'll find them, he said. You've got this far, haven't you?

Chapter 32
26 February 2005. Saturday. 14h31.

Jay watches Gabriel with the kids. It's easy to see they like him. They stare at him with open-mouthed admiration, and even when he sends them dashing across the field until they look exhausted enough to fall over, they still smile and cheer. He's also made an effort. Every now and then, he scatters in a few Thai words, and he calls each child by name. As the kids finally peel off down the road, muddied and spent, Gabriel watches them with a trace of pride.

"Good kids," he says, "they try hard."

Jay nods.

"You want to go somewhere?" Gabriel says. "I have an apartment down the road."

There isn't much to it. A bedroom, a basic lounge with a kitchen and a bathroom. A TV is on a stand tuned into the sport. A pan next to the sink is soaking, bubbles frothing, and a coffee machine has clearly been recently used because the coffee granules are spilled over the surface.

Gabriel walks into the kitchen.

"Drink?" he offers, extracting some bottles of beer.

Liam shifts.

"You want to chat without us?" he asks. "Harry and I could wait outside."

But Jay shakes his head.

"We've come here together," he says. "Please stay."

They sit, an uncomfortable silence filtering through the room. Jay is sitting on something. He shifts, extracting a diving bootie, which has caught in the cushion.

"So where do you want me to start?" Gabriel says, his eyes focused on Jay as he places the bootie on the floor.

"I want to know everything," Jay replies. "I need to, I mean."

Gabriel nods, sipping his beer.

"I wish I could tell you better news ..." he starts.

The trip had gone well. Comfortable boat. A sense of camaraderie. Good kit. They'd stopped at an island. Gabriel couldn't remember the name of it, but it was beautiful. They'd done a dive. *A wall dive – it was like watching a movie, we barely had to kick and this underwater paradise just opened up.* Nina was leading the dive. She'd briefed everybody well, helped one of the girls get down. *She couldn't equalise, I think she was just a bit panicked.* They were under almost forty minutes. Early lunch on the island. A fish barbecue. And piles of Phad Thai. *I liked Nina immediately. She lived in her skin. You know what I mean? Comfortable being her. We talked. She seemed a little sad. I asked her what was wrong and she mentioned your brother. Daniel was it?* The sunset was amazing. Just a few clouds to turn pink. A few drinks. Rum and Coke. More beers. They got a little tipsy. Not drunk. *Just chilled, you know?* And there was this attraction. They shared a cabin. *She was really passionate, but I guess you don't want to hear about that. I thought at the time this was really a girl I could get to know. The looks between us in the morning. We were so happy.* Breakfast on the boat. Pineapple, cut up, on sticks. He was hungry, it had been a big night. *The others were teasing us. Nina took it well, laughed about us rocking everybody to sleep.* She went back into work mode, co-ordinating. He helped her with the tanks. They laughed a lot. Everything seemed perfect. They all went on the morning dive, all except for the boat pilot. *I can't remember his name, it didn't seem important, until ...*

Jay nodded, waiting for Gabriel to continue.

When the tsunami hit, most of them were under the water. The girl who couldn't equalise and her boyfriend had surfaced early. *It was so confusing. One minute I was at 20 metres, the next, I was sucked down to 40. My ears felt like they were going to explode. There was just sand and reef and water. There was no visibility. I couldn't even tell which way was up. I tried to calm myself, breathe slowly to save my oxygen. There was someone else in the water near me, but I couldn't see who it was. We tried to swim to each other. I was shit-scared. So was he. We held onto each other. Weighting each other down. I was watching my air. It was going down fast. So was his. We needed to surface soon. I don't remember too much after that. We got out of the water, onto the boat. Nobody knew what was going on. We couldn't communicate with the mainland. There were 15 of us, including the pilot. But only 14 of us after the wave. We waited. Refilled the tanks and I was getting back in to find Nina.*

Then the next wave came. We were terrified. She was the most experienced diver by far. If she hadn't come up by then, we knew she wasn't going to. It was sickening. I think she drowned in the first wave. She must have hit her head or something. But we didn't find her. I wanted to let you know, but you'd left Phi Phi and I only remembered Daniel's name. The pilot did all the official stuff, but we didn't know Nina's surname. She told me she lived on Phi Phi, so I wasn't even sure of her nationality. I don't know why. I thought she was Australian.

Jay nods, a thick lump forming in his throat. He'd thought Nina was dead, and now that this is confirmed, he feels completely hollow. Jay stands up, his stomach tightening. Without a word, he walks out of the apartment. It's too small. Too narrow. He needs to breathe. Stumbling down the road, he can hardly focus. He walks, and without realising it, is approaching the sea. So much loss. So much destruction. The aquamarine carpet laid out for miles. Still. Unruffled. There's a wall. It's mostly unfinished brick, and layered with graffiti. Jay sits, his sobs rising and exploding until his chest hurts. He aches. The tears coursing and wet on his cheeks. Images of Nina flicking through his brain. Jay finds he can't stop. It's as though the shock and hurt of the last three months has been unbottled, and it won't be put back. Daniel and Nina. Kerese gone. His own nightmares of the approaching wave.

He doesn't recall Liam sitting down next to him. But when he looks up, he finds him there. And Liam doesn't say anything at first. Just sits. This solid reassuring presence, waiting. Just waiting. Liam doesn't touch him. He looks out to sea with Jay. A boat passes in the distance.

"It's better to know," Liam says finally. "This is the worst part. After this it can only improve."

"My mother," Jay says.

"You'll call her."

"I'm the only one left."

"Then thank God she has you."

Jay studies his fingers. Wipes his face with the back of his hand.

"I think I knew all along," says Jay. "Maybe I expected this."

Liam nods.

Harry and Gabriel are walking towards them. Their approach is tentative. Reluctant.

"I'm sorry," Gabriel says.

"I know," says Jay.

Harry's reaction is different. Distinctly Thai. He offers a broad smile. Even in suffering, a smile like this is possible. Jay and Liam stand up. Gabriel shakes Jay's hand. He gives Jay a card.

"My contact details – if you need to speak to me again."

Jay pulls a pen out of his backpack, writes down his mobile number and email address. He touches Gabriel's shoulder, then hands him the paper.

"I'm glad she met you," Jay says.

Gabriel nods.

"And I am glad I met her. We have a saying in Brazil. *Curta que a vida é curta.* Enjoy every moment because life is short."

"That was Nina," says Jay.

"This is a bad time for all of us," Gabriel says, "but one day it will be better."

They walk to the boat. Jay silent. Tense. He wonders when that day will be.

Chapter 33
September 10, 2004 – Friday

I was walking on air. The trail had opened up again. And this
time, I wasn't going to lose it. I held the postcard as though it
contained the secrets of the Pentagon. Thank goodness for the
chance meeting. But was this *really* chance? I've read about
somethin'. It's called synchronicity—and maybe that was
what this was actually about. Right time. Right place. I'm
meant to find Ben. If I don't, I can't carry on my life. It's like
I'm stuck in some kind of time lapse. I'm travelin' and
travelin' and the world goes on. But I can't.

The news was too wonderful not to share. There was an
Internet center next to the Sakura restaurant. I logged in,
waiting to type up an email to Eleanor. She'd set it up at
home. Bill had no idea about it whatsoever. And knowin'
what I know now, that was probably the best decision we ever
made.

There was an email waitin' from her, two days old. '*Any news?
You've been quiet. Are you alright?*' Isn't it funny that after all our
mutual dislike we have finally got to a place where she
actually cares? I know I'm the route to Ben, but even in her
emails, I have sensed a change. She told me when I was in
Cusco that she might have given up by now. She admired my
determination. And praise from your mama was somethin' I
never thought I'd get.

The email from Stan Colicchio came in as I was at the terminal. I didn't expect much. In my heart, I knew Peg was the girl at the gas station. Somethin' about it just made sense. Her edginess. The way she led me through the clues. Lord alone knows how many things she took out that box before she let me in it. She just didn't see the note. And I wouldn't have either, except for having emptied out the entire box and shaking it. Synchronicity. See what I mean?

Subject: Blonde gal

So you were right. The kisser was Peggy Lott Gibson. Unmistakable. His age, I wouldn't have minded a bit of her myself. Hey, wouldn't have minded a piece now. But wasn't she supposed to be with Benjamin's brother???

I dug around a little longer. Somethin' I thought you might find interesting. Checked your husband's class's yearbook, some boy went missin'. Name was Kim Harrison. Was a bit older than the rest of the group. Guess he flunked out once or twice. Went out one night, and didn't come back. Had threatened to leave a thousand times. Finally did it. Parents looked. He'd stolen a stack of cash, could have been on the run for months with no trace.

I know the headmaster at the time. Hadn't seen him in a coon's age, but I chatted to him. Said Kim was a terror. Stole a car once, wasn't charged. Caught with all sorts of bad stuff in his locker. His father

```
Harold paid the school off. New library
even—the Harrison Wing. And that was before
he disappeared. I'm putting two and two
together. You reckon I may be right?

My daughter had a little girl. Cherry-May
Oliaro. Purdiest little thing you ever did
see. Am I excited! If things get any better,
I may have to hire someone to help me enjoy
it.
Good luck and keep me posted.
```

Could this be the missing link? Kim Harrison. I wondered why the name hadn't come up before? Today's news seemed too good to be true. A new lead and a puzzle piece—in one day. I did a quick search on the Net. Harold Harrison. Where do parents get these names from anyways? Made his money in mining. Not sure of the details, but he's originally from Texas. Now he deals in heavy machinery. Heads up a big company that sells the stuff all over the world. Some of the production happens in China. What d'ya know? He travels a lot. There are little pieces on him in papers all over the States.

And as for his son. Trawled a little. They did some sort of projection of how Kim would look now if he were still to be found above ground. That was for the tenth anniversary of his disappearance. It's been another two years. There were photos of him at school. A big guy. And then a short description. Missing money. Kim only reported gone on the twentieth, but had been missing about six days. What parents wait that long?

'Kim often went off on his own. He was a loner,' Mrs. Harrison said. 'We didn't suspect anything was wrong immediately.' Of course they didn't. If he was the troublemaker Stan says he was, then they were probably glad for the break.

The dates fit. I wondered if Stan still had a copy of the yearbook. Maybe there was a photo of him with Ben or Anton? But you had to have known each other, right Anton? That school of yours wasn't all *that* big.

I looked a bit more. Heyward. Harrison. One little article in the *Atlanta Star* in 1982.

Atlanta Remembers Double Tragedy

Tragedy hit two of our cherished Atlanta families this year. A death and a disappearance. Colonel William Heyward, the father of Benjamin who died in June, has since been stationed in Charleston. "We're just trying to get on with our lives. You don't get over the loss of a child overnight. We are focusing on keeping our remaining son Anton close and loved."

The circumstances of Benjamin's death were both mysterious and heartrending. Benjamin died in a fire, which has been confirmed as an act of suicide.

But for the family of Kim Harrison, the mourning process can't really begin. Harold "Harry" Harrison, the father of the young man who disappeared earlier this year says, "Our son is with us in our hearts. But we are never going to give up on finding him, and bringing him home."

A reward is still being offered for any
leads that help the Harrison family recover
their son. Please contact the Atlanta Police
Department to pass on any information you
may think relevant. Says Detective Cannon,
"No fact is too small. Many cases have been
solved on what the general public might have
deemed irrelevant information."

Well, this wasn't irrelevant to me.

So Benjamin killed Kim. It's a possibility, isn't it? Now I just
have to find him to ask him face-to-face.

Chapter 34
27 February 2005. Sunday. 02h57.

Jay can't sleep. His mother's agony down the phone too much to contemplate. It's bad enough to *think* someone is dead, but excruciating to confirm it. He slips on his bathing suit, walks softly out the building. His sandals waft up dust, but protect his feet from random nails and bits of sharp wood that are still lying on the path.

A mosquito buzzes noisily at his neck. He slaps it, drawing blood. The moon was full only two days ago, so although it's waning, it's bright enough to light the flat isthmus between the two beaches. He trembles, wondering what to do next. What would be the point in going back to England other than to comfort his mother? Here, he is doing some good. It isn't going to change what happened to Nina, but it will keep him busy. And his mother doesn't need him. Not really. She's busy with her bridge club and her morning walks, her charities and her garden. And as for his practice, it's doing fine without him. The locum can stay on for a few more months – she'd be happy for the extra time. And cash.

The breeze has shifted. At the edge of the water, white foam coats the beach in undulating trails. Jay takes off his shoes, tossing them behind him over his shoulder.

"Ouch," he hears behind him as the sandal collides with something solid.

He jumps, then jerks around. It's Liam.

"What in God's name are you doing?" Jay asks.

Liam lifts his hands up and past his shoulders in a gesture of surrender.

"I'm sorry. I know I'm intruding, but I wanted to see if you needed some company."

"I don't want to talk about it," Jay says.

"I didn't say we had to talk."

Jay shrugs, "I was going in. I couldn't sleep."

Liam strips off his T-shirt, dumps his shoes.

"So what are we waiting for, then?"

Jay doesn't know how long or hard they swim, but the pull and push of the ocean is not enough to hurt him this time. He's out of breath and even his aching muscles don't block his emotions. Ducking and swimming, he drags himself through the water. The sea is so dark and mysterious that he can't see the bottom of it. He blocks the thoughts of the creatures that could be swimming below him, hurling himself faster and faster. Fighting, punching. When he finally hauls himself out of the depths, Liam close behind him, Jay begins to cough. His chest throbs and he leans over, a hand on each thigh as he supports himself. His whole body heaves as he splutters and chokes. And behind him, Liam stands, waiting.

When the coughing subsides, Liam hands Jay a towel. Then, digging in his bag, he pulls out a hip flask, passing it over too. Whatever is in it burns. Jay sips again, trying not to cry. They sit, their feet in the sand, sharing the liquid between them.

How long has it been? An hour? Two. Nothing but silence and terrible thoughts, and the fire in his gullet blazing all the way down. Liam puts the flask in the sand. Looks up to the stars, which are fading in the light of the almost moon.

Finally, Jay speaks.

"So how did you get to be so damn nice?"

Liam turns to Jay.

"Nice?"

"I've never met anyone who *gets it* the way you do."

"It's taken me a long time to get *anything*," Liam says. "I didn't get on with my father. I don't think he even liked me. That's a hard start, you know."

"My father has Alzheimer's. At least he doesn't remember anything."

"My father is mean and violent, with an important job that makes him think he rules the world."

Jay studies Liam. Never, in the whole time he has known Liam, has he said anything unkind about anybody else.

"And what about your mother?" Jay asks.

"I haven't spoken to her in more than ten years. I miss her, but it wasn't something I chose."

"Do you think I should go back to England?" Jay asks.

"Do you want to?"

Jay picks up the flask. Sips again. "I don't feel like I'm finished here."

"Then don't leave. It'll be months before Phi Phi is back on track again. We'll get funding. Build it again. Give people their lives back."

"Are you staying?"

"I've travelled a lot, Jay. And sometimes you find a place that needs you more than you need it. Pascale and I aren't finished here either."

Despite himself, Jay leans forward, touching Liam on the arm.

"The only good thing about the tsunami was meeting you both on the roof."

Liam smiles.

"Your life can change completely in a few minutes."

Jay nods, wondering for a moment, if Liam isn't talking about the wave.

10h43

The morning is a little easier. Yesterday's news doesn't hurt him any less, but it's closure. He wonders about a memorial service for Nina. His mother didn't mention it but of course it will have to happen now that they know for sure. It's just a matter of when. Nina's friends are scattered all over the globe. She didn't stay in one place very long.

Ironically, she seemed most at home where he is now – on this island.

Jay doesn't see Liam until almost lunchtime. But he isn't alone. A boat has come in from Phuket, and with it is Margot. Her hair is windswept, and her eyes clear, but there is something about her that makes him stop. Margot walks towards him. And she doesn't really need to say it, but she does.

"Rikke died two weeks ago. There was a clot. They say the flight home was probably the worst thing any of us could have done for her."

Jay nods, takes Margot's hand, between his. He doesn't say anything for a moment.

"My sister died too," he says eventually. "In the Similans."

"I've come back. I had to keep busy. My studies don't start for a few months, and I've collected some sponsorship in Norway."

"You want to stay here in Phi Phi?" Jay asks.

"I want to help, but I'm not completely self-sacrificing. We left a lot of stuff behind. If we can find some of it ..."

"It's not likely."

"Of course it's not. I'm not holdin' out for anything. Did I tell you I write? Well I do. And that stuff you can't replace."

Jay looks at Liam.

"Can we ask Wilfred if Margot can stay here too?"

Liam nods.

"He was at the beach when the boat came in. He's already told me where to get some keys."

Jay takes Margot's suitcase from her.

"You should speak to Becky," he says, "she's cataloguing anything we've found – from plane tickets to passports."

"Liam tells me Pascale's been workin' on the daycare centre."

"You know Pascale?"

"Only from the hospital in Phuket."

"Well, she'd love the help, if you're up to it."

"I'm not here to wallow; I'll get my hands dirty if you need me to."

Margot pulls off her T-shirt, stuffing it in her suitcase. Her breasts are barely covered by her nearly-there bikini top and Jay does his best not to focus on them. But Margot doesn't seem to care either way.

"I may as well get a tan while we're at it," she says. "Think this'll do it?"

Chapter 35
September 22, 2004 – Wednesday

I went straight there. No need to ask every person I saw along the way if they knew who or where Channing/Benjamin was. The postcard was picked up directly from the hotel where he was staying and posted in town. Which town? Well, Anton, I skipped out of China and am now in Vietnam. A cosy little place called Hoi-An. The border crossin' was fun. I had to get from Pingxian to the border by tuk-tuk driven by a woman who spat and whose motor clearly needed replacing. It was icy and muddy, a terrible combination. By the time I got through the first hurdle, I was spattered head to toe, my hands bloodless from dragging my suitcase. I stood before the customs official, my nerves in shreds while he studied me. I thought for a moment he wasn't gonna let me out of there. He did. Eventually.

And then I was handed over to the Vietnamese, couriered like a parcel from the urine-stench of the passport control to an overloaded minibus taxi headin' for Hanoi. Even from the frontier, Vietnam seemed more chaotic. Our driver picked up stray passengers all the way—schoolchildren, three soldiers, a man on crutches and a young couple with a baby who abandoned their scooter on the side of the road under a tree. I loved the khaki pith helmets the taxi drivers wore. Here, the women wear conical hats like somethin' out of *Sleeping Beauty*. They tuck their long floaty robes under their fannies as they cycle down the road, draping the material from the front over the crooks of their arms.

I've only been here a short while, but Vietnam already seems more light-hearted than China. The architecture is so darned different. China was controlled, a little grey. But here the buildings are four stories high and painted in brilliant colors: pink, green, red and blue.

Hoi-An is on the water. And I haven't a clue where Ben's hotel is yet. So much for my wishful thoughts. Seems the taxi procedure here is to nod and then take your tourist where you want her to go. *Not* where she has requested. And Lordamighty, by the time I got here, I was too tired and grubbed up to care. I saved a day or so with the flight into Danang, and who'm I kiddin' anyways? In all likelihood, your brother and his phantom girlfriend are already on the move. See, Anton, I *am* tired. Yesterday I might've sounded more hopeful …

September 23, 2004 – Thursday

I left the hotel. I was surrounded immediately.
—Lady, lady. Would you like visit my shop?
—Velly good tailor. I promise you. We measure you. Good body hug!
—Cyclo, Madame?
—Motorbike? I give you discount.

Women lingered on doorsteps, gesturing me inside. Others approached more boldly, thrustin' business cards in my hands. It was impossible to avoid them. On every street was a row of tailors, alternated with an occasional tour operator, hotel, or Internet café. Though you never used to say I was a big shopper, this little place might have been the exception. The clothes laid out were so beautiful, with silky pyjamas, funky trousers, chill-out wear and business suits if I were so inclined. And the souvenir shops—loaded with prints, woodwork, handbags, paintings and postcards.

Eventually, I stumbled on the Thu Bon River, leadin' to the beach almost one and half miles away. Women rowed tourists briefly up or downstream, fishermen repaired brightly colored boats and people on bikes cycled the lengths of what my map called Bach Dan.

It would've been easier than pie to forget why I was really here and get sucked into the atmosphere. But armed with my postcard, I walked into a little café—'we speak English!'— ordered a ginger tea and waited for a bit of conversation. The waitress brought the mug to the table, pointing at the menu. I asked for fruit and pancakes, hoping her English was going to be better than my Vietnamese. As she was about to turn, I showed her the card.

—I'm lookin' for this place, I said.

The waitress nodded, took the postcard and disappeared into the kitchen. This was not good. Right at that moment, the address was a lot more valuable to me than my wallet, and I wasn't going to let it out of my sight. I stood up, chasing after her, but an older woman emerged from the behind the swing doors before I could get inside.

—You looking for hotel? The woman asked me, her amusement at my panic obvious.
—Yes.

—You like hotel? My brother owns good hotel. Water view. I give you good price. You won't regret.
—No, I said. I'm looking for this hotel. *This* one.

I extracted the postcard from her extended fingers, my irritation obviously more visible than I wanted it to be. The woman shrugged. *So I tried*, her body language said. She clicked her fingers.

—Okay. I show you. Tonight you come back. Cocktails. Cheap. Special all night.

Later

I guess Benjamin was on a budget. The place was off the main track and a good walk into town. It was clean, noisy and flanked by tailors on both sides. At the reception desk, I wrote down Ben's new name. W. CHANNING. Told the guy he was my brother.

—I'm meetin' him, I said.
—You meet brother. Mr. Channing?

That's what I said.

The man tapped his fingers on the lacquer surface.

—You late. Mr. Channing no say you come. No say I keep room. Rooms not have.
—It doesn't matter, I just want to see Channing.
—I say you late. Mr. Channing, he leave this morning on bus.

You've got to be kiddin' me.

—Do you know where the bus was going? I asked, my heart sinkin' right into my shoes.
—I not asking. Maybe airport?

I looked at the man, his face blank, unhelpful. I turned. So this was it. The end of the road. Bound to happen sooner or later. I just didn't expect it today.

—Did he leave me a note? I asked at the door. Stupidly.
—No messages. No expecting you.

Then I was seized by a moment of inspiration.

—Has his room been cleaned?
—No clean. Just left.

I walked back to the desk, slapped a hundred dollars on the table.

—I need to see Channing's room, I said. Right now before you clean it.

The man brightened, slipped the money into his pocket, then bowed.

—I get keys. You wait, Mr. Channing sister.

Chapter 36

13 March 2005. Sunday. 10h00.

They're planning a Saint Patrick's Day festival. It'll be on
the beach. They'll drink too much, play loud music, and
raise money for the Phi Phi orphans. In between all of that,
they're going to play volleyball in fancy dress. Jay is going
to be a pirate and much as this isn't original, it's the best
he'd prepared to do.

"I'm English," he protests, "I don't *do* dressing up."

"Yes you do," says Becky. "It's for a good cause.
And I can help you."

Margot is pulling the whole thing together, though
she is far from Irish. She does, however, have a fondness
for beer and is happy to help set up a casino and games
area in Ernesto's bar for the evening. That makes her the
perfect logistics manager. Though most of the time she
shows her happy side, she is as quiet as she was on the boat
when they first met, writing often in a notebook. Rikke's
absence in Margot's life is obvious, even to Jay who didn't
know her at all well.

With the destruction of Phi Phi, the locals are
worried. RICH MAN COME FOR LAND, POOR MAN
MUST GO, some graffiti apparently says in Thai on a half
building.

"What if investors come, build big hotels and chase us away?" Harry wonders.

"They can't do that," Jay says.

But Harry looks doubtful.

"Anything is possible. Tsunami come. We not expect that."

14 March 2005. Monday. 07h00.

Jay wakes up to the sound of Pascale and Liam laughing in the room next door. *Why am I still here?* he wonders. *What am I waiting for?* He'll need to set a deadline. Go home. Back to work. Back to his real life. But he wonders if he will ever truly go back. The last few months have changed him. He's more profound, yet more lighthearted. And willing to challenge his comfort zones… to a point. And yet like the journal girl, he's still searching, for what he's not really certain. He picks up the book, the handwriting now as familiar as his own.

See what I'd been reduced to, Anton? I was diggin' around in Ben's garbage, like a homeless person. He and the girlfriend sure are neat. They bought a few things. Baggies. T-shirts. A dress (V-neck) and a pair of leather trousers. I hope those weren't for Ben??? They don't smoke. One of them left a book behind. John Irving's The Fourth Hand. *Guess it must be finished. I didn't take it though. I didn't want to steal anything. I just wanted a clue. Somethin'. Somethin'. Lord alone knows how I was going to do that. There was a pair of torn shorts in the dustbin. An empty shampoo bottle. (L'Oréal— detangling—so one of 'em has long hair.) Mosquito repellent. There was still a little in it. A few bananas on the counter and a bottle of water with only the dregs.*

And then I found it. I did. It was folded into the novel, obviously being used as a bookmark. A booking form for Mr. W. Channing. One double room—king-sized bed. In, 25 December 2004 (late check-in) and out 5 January 2005. The Phi Phi Chalets, Thailand. Oh my God! Oh Lord! I'd nailed it. I finally did. So all I had to do was get there. And wait. Some time off on a sandy beach. I could learn a new hobby. Something energetic. Different. A new focus! Finally, Anton, I had my life back. Right until Christmas. And then everythin' would be solved. For me. For Eleanor. And I could go back home.

I'm chugged full of happiness. I really am. So I'm off to Thailand. There're a lot worse places I could've had to wait. But right now, I think I'll drink a few cocktails. Sure there'll be someone to celebrate with me. And if not, who cares?

I'll drink on my own if I have to.

Jay turns to the next page. The booking form is stuck in, the dates highlighted in bright yellow, and next to it, a smiley face has been drawn. It folds in perfectly. But then the writing stops, as though with the discovery, the almost-obsessive collective of business cards, travel tickets, and souvenirs has been put aside. There are only a few pages spare, saved perhaps for the meeting in Thailand. The final showdown. He wonders if it happened. Did Channing appear on Christmas, as she expected, or was it a case of yet more disappointment? A change of plan? A cancellation? He hopes not. The tsunami didn't give them much time to find each other. That's for certain. But lots of plans changed the day the tsunami came. That's why he's still here.

Isn't it?

09h00

Jay walks down to the daycare centre. Pascale is already there. The colours wind around the building; giant coral, and fish, shells and seahorses carousing. Pascale smiles.

"I'm sorry if we make noise this morning," she says. "Sometimes Liam gets a little carried away."

Jay laughs.

"It wasn't early."

Pascale studies Jay.

"You seem thoughtful today."

Jay grins, "Don't I always?"

Pascale shakes her head.

"Some days you are *practique*, today you think very hard."

"I'm wondering when I should go back to England."

Pascale frowns.

"Not soon?"

"Maybe soon."

"What's happening soon?" Liam asks.

He walks up to Pascale, encircling her waist with his broad arms, but lets her go almost immediately.

"Maybe Jay is leaving."

"You can't do that," Liam says. "We need you here. And right now Becky's gashed her foot open. She's bleeding like a stuck pig."

"How in hell's name did she do that?"

Liam shrugs.

"Where is she?"

"On Loh Dalam. I didn't want to move her until you'd seen the damage."

09h17

Jay runs to where Becky is lying. She looks at him, an expression of relief crosses her face.

"So doc, what d'ya think?"

Although Becky is usually pale, now she looks washed out, the colour in her cheeks completely absent. She bites on her lip and he can see she's in a lot of pain. She's dressed only in her bikini, her hair still wet from the water.

"What was it?" Jay asks, casting his eyes about for her towel.

"I was runnin' after my swim. Kicked a buried piece of corrugated iron. Next minute, I was pumping blood all over the place. Lord, it hurts."

If he doesn't do something soon, she'll go into shock. Clearly Liam had no idea how severe this injury is. His announcement of it certainly didn't give him any idea to expect this. She's hit a vein, and possibly an artery too. Hard to see with all the blood. Jay touches Becky's face.

Feels her pulse. She's clammy, her blood pressure low. Jay takes off his shirt, holds it against the wound.

"Okay. We're going to have to elevate this leg."

He sees her tog bag a little down the beach, nods at a little child standing nearby to fetch it for him.

"Don't move."

Extracting her towel out the bag, he covers her with it, then uses the bag to lift her foot. He puts his shirt back against it. She has started to shiver, and a crowd gathers around them. Jay spots Harry.

"Call Margot, tell her we need some blankets and a stretcher for Becks."

Harry nods, hurries off.

"It's not a biggie," Becky says. "Sure'll be fine in a moment."

"You will, because I'm going to take care of you."

Her eyes start to close. She's lethargic, limp. They don't have anything for a blood transfusion, but if he can get her back to the clinic, he can put her on a saline drip. He checks her airways and breathing, turns her head to the side.

When the stretcher comes, they'll move her fast.

09h26

"Jesus, Jay, I'm sorry," says Liam. "If I'd known this was that serious, I would have acted slightly differently."

They carry the stretcher together. Becky is still conscious, moaning softly.

"She'll be fine. I'll get her on a drip and suture this."

Becky mumbles as they move her onto the bed.

14h33

"Every time I open my eyes, you're still here," says Becky.

Jay shifts.

"You had me worried."

"Come here," says Becky, patting the bed.

He stands up, moves from the chair to perch next to her. Becky lifts her hand, traces the contours of his face.

"I kinda like havin' you closer," she says.

Jay's been down this road with Becky. He's spent enough times studying her, wondering if she even thinks about him. Since the time they danced together, she's kept her distance. And he's vowed to keep his. But her hand moves down his arm, to his hand. And then she threads her fingers with his. The touch is just enough to bring those feelings from the beach back again. He tries to disentangle himself. He's had enough heartache the last few months. And he isn't really sure he can deal with any more.

But Becky doesn't let go.

"I'm sorry if I hurt you," she says. "Did I hurt you?"

Jay looks away. "I'm all grown up, Becks. I can take a few games."

"Wasn't a game."

"One dance. One night. What does it matter?"

"Sure mattered to me. It's just—"

"Becks, we don't need to have this conversation. I'm happy to help you. That's what I do."

Becky's eyes register her disappointment, but she nods. Closes her eyes and turns away.

"Think I'll go to sleep now, Jay. I'm plumb tired."

15h03

Jay walks outside to where Liam is pushing a wheelbarrow.

"Now what?" asks Liam, then abandons the rubble to follow Jay down the path to the beach.

"I'm a complete and utter tosser," says Jay, skidding a pebble into the sea.

"Becky?" asks Liam.

Jay nods.

"I totally screwed up in there," he says.

"You didn't move on her in that state did you?"

"That's entirely the problem. I didn't and she clearly wanted me to."

Liam grins, slaps Jay on the shoulder.

"Heck, am I glad I'm getting married," he says. "Sex on tap ..."

"Yeah, right," says Jay.

Chapter 37
14 March 2005. Monday. 19h12.

Despite the incident, Jay can't actually avoid Becky. Margot has helped her shower off the saltwater and wash her hair. She's back in bed, her red ringlets drying against the pillow. Dressed in loose trousers and a pink shoestring strap top, her face clear and innocent, she's more beautiful than he has ever seen her. Becky smiles at him when he comes in, exposing her arm so that he can monitor her pulse.

People float in and out of the room to call on Becky as he checks up on her. They chat to her, offering her fruit, or magazines, chocolate bars or photos to scrutinise. A little girl sits with a hairbrush studying the task at hand with extreme seriousness and dedication. Jay realises Becky's made a lot of friends here on Phi Phi – before and after the tsunami. There's something candid about her. A loving quality he's never really noticed in anybody else. Kerese was always so hard and self-serving. Over the last few weeks, as far as Jay knows, Becky hasn't done *anything* for herself.

Becky chats easily to her visitors, eating the rice and vegetarian green curry Margot has brought for her. Jay sits to the side once he's done, crowded out. When he leaves the room, he wonders if she has even noticed.

Not that she has any reason to.

15 March 2005. Tuesday. 00h17.

He's tried to sleep, but no matter what he does, he won't drift off. What is it with this island and insomnia? He stands up; paces. Switches the light on and does a few push-ups. Another night swim? Yet this time he knows what he wants to do. He wonders if he has the guts to do it.

Jay taps at Becky's door. Her light is also on. He touches the door, stepping carefully inside. Becky looks at him. She's sitting up, her foot still elevated.

When he kisses her, he knows she's been waiting for him, her kiss back powerful, answering his. They haven't said anything. Their locked eyes say everything. Their lips sear each other's faces, necks, ears. Jay's tongue traces the hollow at Becky's neck, making her groan. He travels lower to the rise and fall of her breasts. She holds his head against her, urging him down. He kisses, licks, touches. Jay lifts his head. He's face-to-face with Becky, their breath mingling.

Becky pulls off Jay's shirt, her hand caressing his chest, his nipples. He's almost hairless, his tan from the months in Phi Phi a shocking contrast to her marble skin.

"You're gorgeous," he says, trailing a ringlet around his finger.

She kisses him and her excitement makes him want to move faster.

Jay leans to take off her top. She lifts her arms to help him, her nipples swollen and hard. He lifts himself over her, his chest to her cool soft skin. *God, it's good to feel himself against her.*

He can feel her under him. She's twisting, lifting her groin to grind against his. And she doesn't look so innocent any longer. Just that look in her eyes could make him come. Becky shifts.

"Am I hurting you?" he asks.

"I want these off."

She's shimmying out of her trousers, underneath him. Takes his hand to the cleft between her legs. It's moist and warm. *Slow down. Slow down.* He'll burst like this. Jay stands up, pulls a condom out his pocket then slips out of his shorts. Becky takes it from him, rips the wrapping off with her teeth. Her hand grasps the shaft of his penis, cups his balls.

"I can't wait," Jay says.

He sheathes himself, moving back over her. Becky looks at him. Smiles. She's holding his back, then her hands slide down to his buttocks. She's pushing him into her. *Oh fuck. Oh my God.* He moves his finger down between them, touches her. Becky whimpers, her face almost crumpling.

"Are you okay?"

Becky lifts her head, kissing him, over and over.

"Better than."

Jay can see Becky's expression change, her eyes fix on his.

He can't wait either. When the rush comes, he can see it travelling across her chest in red heat. Wide eyes. It feels so good, he wonders why they waited so long.

05h39

They use the whole night. Waking, talking, exploring each other. They make plans. Beyond the now. Beyond Phi Phi.

"I thought you were hot the first time I saw you at Tyt's," says Jay.

"Did you? But I gave you such a hard time."

"A bit like this?" says Jay, making Becky laugh.

"You wish," she says. "Another unavailable man with a steady girl. So what happened with Kerese?"

"We were over before we even left England. I just didn't realise it. And what about you?"

"Oh he lied. And lied. I still haven't worked'em all out."

Jay traces Becky's breast. His back is against the cold wall.

"I won't lie to you," he says. "I can promise you that."

"Thank you," Becky says. "I think that's what I liked about you. Your honesty. And your buns."

Jay laughs, kissing Becky. They fit.

"So what happens next?" he asks.

"Ain't that meant to be *my* question?"

Jay hesitates, wondering if she thinks he's going too fast. Becky touches his jaw.

"Jay, don't look so serious. I'm not off anywhere without you."

"You were making plans to leave the island," Jay says.

"I was aimin' to volunteer in Sumatra. We've done our bit here, and I think we can do more."

Jay blinks.

"Jay, I didn't know what to do. I liked you, but my mind was so messed up, I reckoned it'd be better if I left. And then when you heard about Nina… I wanted to comfort you. But how?"

"This would have worked," he said.

"Don't be so sure."

Jay kisses her, his lips travelling down the length of her body.

"You're probably right," he murmurs. "But I think we should make up for lost time."

10h33

By the time they both emerge, Becky hopping on one leg, knowing glances are cast their way. But they are so entranced, entangled with each other, they don't really care. Jay borrows a wheelbarrow so she doesn't have to walk.

Pascale is doing the finishing touches to the underwater scene when they arrive at the centre. She looks at them, smiles, but doesn't say anything.

Liam, however, can't help himself.

"Y'all have fun last night?"

But they don't even have a chance to answer. Harry is running along the path, Gabriel behind him.

"You won't believe what I found out," Gabriel says as soon as he sees Jay, "You just won't believe it."

Chapter 38
15 March 2005. Tuesday. 19h00.

He's in a plane, care of Thai Airways. Becky came all the way with him to Phuket. She didn't cry at the airport, but he could see she wanted to. When he kissed her goodbye, it was almost impossible to pull himself away.

"I'm so happy for you," Becky said, but everything about her was stricken. Disappointed.

They didn't make any promises. How could they? Jay's world had been toppled, or righted. Neither of them was sure which. He didn't know what would happen once he got to Bumrungrad Hospital. What to expect.

Jay looks out the window, remembering his first flight to Thailand. His distress and uncertainty. He's found Becky now, and he realises he's in love with her. Last night was magical. Unforgettable. Why did he wait so long? Jay has always been hesitant, testing the waters before he jumps in. But Becky is brave, outrageous. Everything he's not.

His suitcase broke as he was trying to pack what little clothing he had. The zip simply detached itself from the material and the only way he was going to get it to Bangkok was by duct-taping it.

Like always, Liam was the constant, reassuring presence he needed him to be.

"Wait a moment," he said, then returned with his own suitcase. "This will do, won't it?"

So the clothes were shoved over from one bag to the next. No debating or hesitating.

"We go quick-quick," said Harry, beaming from ear to ear. "This good news, I like it."

Gabriel sits next to Jay. He smiles, not realising the agony twisting Jay's heart. He found out about Nina. He gets to go too. Jay misses Becky already and he finds his emotions switching from joy to misery in instants. And he's left Liam and Pascale behind.

There were no deaths in the Similans. That's what made Gabriel wonder. The military were patrolling in the area. How were they to know who Nina was? She'd hit her head, taken in a lot of water. When they picked her up, she wasn't even conscious. A serious case, severe trauma. Both legs broken. Damage to her internal organs. She didn't speak Thai and they didn't speak English. Not that they would know that for a month or so.

Gabriel's Thai is basic but passable. He hails them a taxi. It's almost ten o'clock, but the traffic snakes into the city, cars and buses daring each other between seemingly non-existent lanes. In comparison with the silence of Phi Phi, Bangkok is frenetic. Jay's stomach churns. He looks at Gabriel, who smiles. Jay wonders why Gabriel is here with him. Can one night change everything? For Gabriel too?

23h06

There's an accident across one of the roads. Hooting and cacophony. Jay wonders if it is too late to get into Bumrungrad. Visiting hours must have finished ages ago. But they'll go. God knows where they're staying tonight. He hasn't even booked a room.

Gabriel nods at him as the taxi turns into the entrance.

"We're here."

The building towers above them, floors and floors of concrete. The entire complex is massive. Big enough to get lost in. But it seems their story has reached the media, and as Jay and Gabriel emerge from the taxi, their surprised faces are captured in the bursting flashes from cameras angled towards them.

"How are you feeling right now?"

Right now, Jay feels ill. He has no idea what he's walking into, and all these people are standing around to find out what he doesn't know either.

A man stands at the door. He's dressed in a lab coat, his black shiny shoes sticking out below. He was on his way to a dinner when he heard they were coming. Or so Jay understands.

"I'm Doctor Khan," the man says.

"Doctor Gifford," Jay replies.

The man's eyebrows rise.

"One of us," he comments. "Then I won't have to warn you not to expect too much."

Gabriel nods at him.

"Gabriel," he says, not offering anything more.

He looks at Jay.

"Do you want me to wait until you have seen her?"

It's exactly what Jay wants. But he doesn't want to say so. It appears, however, that he doesn't have to.

"Where can I buy a sandwich?" Gabriel asks. "I'll come up when I'm done."

23h33

The lift hums. Claustrophobic. Jay taps his hand against his thigh. He has so many questions, but he doesn't know what to ask.

"When did she come here?" he says.

"Mid-February. She was always in Bangkok, but they didn't want to move her to Bumrungrad until then."

"Why didn't I know," Jay asks, "what did I miss?"

"It wasn't you," Doctor Khan says. "The paperwork got mixed up. She was registered as Amina Griffiths. I don't know how it happened. She was in a bad state when she came in. Damage to her jaw. I suppose they didn't hear her properly. And she had no ID."

Was that supposed to make Jay feel better?

"So what happened?"

"That man, Gabriel, he called us. One of the many hospitals I understand. He heard about the rescue teams. Took a chance your sister had come out with them. Identified her by her body art."

"Will she know who I am?"

"I hope so. She's had short-term memory loss, but her longer-term memories are still in place."

23h42

There's a balled-up figure in the bed. Jay remembers the morning Daniel died. Nina just like this. Tucked away in her own world.

"Nina," he says, almost afraid to see her.

At first she doesn't hear him. She's probably been asleep for hours. But then her head emerges. Her hair has grown longer; it's curlier than he remembers it. She looks at him, her eyes wide.

"Jay."

It's a whisper. A statement.

Jay bends down to the bed, takes his sister in his arms. She's fragile now, like the skeleton of a leaf. Disintegrated over time. The last few months have aged her. Pain is etched into her forehead which once, before all of this, never even used to have a worry line. And now he looks closer, there are tinges of grey at her temples. As he hugs her, he can feel her wince. But she doesn't say anything. Jay lets her go. He's tentative, wary. When he looks into his sister's face, he knows he won't abandon her. The tears trickling down her cheeks prick deeper into her than any of her tattoos.

Chapter 39

26 December 2005. Monday. 12h30.

Jay walks down the steps from the Banana Beach Hotel. A row of pot plants surrounds a hole on the stairs where the wood has worn away, right near the restaurant. Like the Thai people he has encountered since his arrival in Phuket two days before, the hotel seems indestructible. It's bruised, a little battered, but nevertheless still standing.

Jay wonders why he has chosen to stay so close to the water. It doesn't matter now that the waves swept over the opposite end of the bay and that this hotel was never touched. What matters is what happened beyond it. And in the ten months since he has been home, he hasn't quite felt the same. It's just one of those things you can't quite forget.

His mother refuses to understand why he needs to be here. She couldn't tell him not to come, but he knew she wanted to. Yet of all the thousands of lit candles stretching along Patong Beach, he wanted at least one to be his. For Rikke. Deng. Laura. Finn. Pete. The man he put in the helicopter. And the piles of bodies who were once people, with families. And life. It isn't risky to be here, but his mother is keeping him closer than she needs to. She seems to have forgotten that he never was the *real* risk-taker. Between Nina and Dan, he never needed to be.

Jay walks across the cacophony of tuk-tuks and scooters toward the beach. Umbrellas stick out the sand like cocktail decorations, and Thai mats are rolled out for body treatments. Foot massage. Thai massage – special offer. Hair braiding. A family collects under a palm, scoffing plates of food, a baby enjoying a handful of dirt. Smells lift from the drain, blending with ginger and kaffir lime and lemongrass – sickly sweet and pungent. It's the scent of life going on.

But not his life.

His life has been in limbo. Becky waited, but she couldn't wait indefinitely. She went to Indonesia as she'd planned. They emailed, but somehow the conversations seemed stilted. Forced. As though the connection had been broken. She let him go, and he let her do it.

After all, Nina needed him more than Becky did.

Jay thinks back to his first days in England. Lining up therapists, physios, more surgeries. Nina wouldn't let him out of her sight without an explanation.

"You didn't come," she told him. "I waited and you didn't come."

He didn't want to explain it all again. The misunderstandings, the red tape. She was right. He didn't come. Not immediately. He should have looked harder. Been more insistent. Like Gabriel was. That's one thing he's learnt to be now. Forceful. Determined. But every now and then the real Jay creeps back to the surface. A little uncertain. Law-abiding. With a trace of longing for something, someone else. He had one weekend away.

Alone in Snowdonia. And he remembered Becky clinging to the rocky outcrop, her legs taut, her movements sure. He missed her the most then. But he'd made his choice. That didn't mean though, that he was entirely happy with it.

Nina didn't ask about his sadness, and she didn't seem to care either. She was punishing him; he knew that. And though he didn't deserve it, it was the only way he could think to do to give her power. She was only just learning to walk again now.

Jay touches the journal in the bag slung over his shoulder. He never found out who it was who wrote it. Perhaps he didn't really try hard enough. Maybe he didn't want to know, especially after what he found out. Who it would implicate.

Jay did advertise on the net, on *www.tsunami26.com* where survivors like him remember or try to forget. The old Nina would have enjoyed his idealism and Dan would have thought him a sap. And even Jay knows he's being silly. The post seems ridiculous, even to him:

I'm looking for an American woman who may have lost a journal during the tsunami in Koh Phi Phi on 26 December 2004.

Who for God's sake would answer a request like that? But he couldn't do much more –contacting Eleanor or her husband might have put *him* in danger.

Although it's been overcast this morning, now the sun has burnt the clouds away. It's so hot, he could do with a beer. But even the idea of this seems somewhat sacrilegious on an anniversary like this. Though if there's one thing he has learnt, it's to live life. He's got the theory perfectly. It's just putting it into practice that he hasn't been all that good at. And he's been carrying this burden. The book itself is light, but there is more to it than that. Honour. Disappointment. Loyalty. Jay's thought long and hard about it, and the only way to do justice to this mystery woman and to his own conscience, is to send her journal to the ocean – where it should have gone a year ago. The diary is still carefully enclosed in its original Ziploc bag, but back in England he paged through it many times.

He's debated writing something in the book himself. A tribute. A goodbye. Yet he doesn't have the woman's way with words and anything he thinks of sounds ridiculous. Farewell. Good luck. *Bon voyage.*

Jay stands at the water's edge, debating how far he should wade in. There are so many people here that somebody is bound to find it, resurrect it. He'll have to swim out, or take a boat. He's probably not the only person performing rituals today, but he just can't decide.

Jay remembers Kerese on their first day on Phi Phi as they tried on some T-shirts and he couldn't bring himself to choose.

"Jesus Jay, can't you even make up your mind about this?"

Jay can, that's what she never realised. He can make a decision when it really matters. And he'll do this today because he must. Jay walks to a vendor; hires a deck chair. He'll leave his bag here and then he'll swim out so far that he will exhaust himself of the emotion building in him.

Goodbye journal girl. Goodbye Benjamin Heyward and the secret I have been keeping for you.

Jay strips off his shirt. If he's going to do it, now is as good a time as any.

He's already in the ocean when he hears the voice behind him.

"Doctor Jay Gifford. Don't you even say hello?"

12h41

She's even more beautiful than he remembers. Her hair is a little shorter, her nose a bit pinker. And when he looks at her, his heart flips. Jay doesn't know how to greet her. As an old friend? An acquaintance? But she doesn't give him a chance to choose. Becky slips into the water next to him, her arms around his neck. When she kisses him, he's already breathless. She hasn't left. Not like he thought she had. Her body against his feels better than he ever recalled. With her sundress floating about her, Becky resembles a water lily. Their bodies crush and they almost topple over.

"Hello," Jay murmurs.

"I hoped you would come," Becky says.

"You could have asked me."

"I wanted you to come without my havin' to ask."

"Well, here I am."

Jay finds Becky's lips. She tastes like watermelons.

"Can we stop wastin' time now, Jay?" Becky whispers.

Jay looks at her, his face creasing into a smile.

346

"What do you have in mind?" he asks.

It's only as they stop at the deck chair to fetch Jay's bag that Becky notices the package in Jay's hand. It's dotted with water, but reasonably unscathed.

"Did I interrupt somethin'?" Becky asks, then her eyes widen as she looks at what he is carrying. "Lordamighty," Becky says, "I thought that journal drowned in the wave."

Chapter 40
26 December 2005. Monday. 12h42.

Jay is incredulous.

"This is *your* journal?" he says.

Becky nods.

"You've read it I suppose?" she asks, her face clouding.

"I'm sorry Becks, I couldn't help myself."

Becky touches his face.

"So now you know everythin' about me."

Jay puts his hand over hers.

"I hope that one day you would have told me."

"I might've," Becky replies, "but since I lost Anton and Ben, I've been tryin' to forget. In Sumatra there were people a lot worse off than me. Villages destroyed. My problems faded a little."

Jay pulls Becky to him.

"I was taking your journal out to sea. I didn't know what else to do. Somehow, I knew it was important to say goodbye properly."

"You always understood me," she says.

Jay kisses Becky.

"Even if I didn't know it was you," Jay replies.

They make love at the hotel and with each touch, each stroke, Jay knows he has to tell Becky the truth. Benjamin's final secret.

"There's someone I think you should meet," he says.

14h51

"You sure about this?" Becky asks.

"Totally. We'll fetch your stuff afterwards. You're checking out. I'm not letting you out of my sight another minute."

She looks at him, then smiles. "Thank the Lord you came back."

Outside the traffic is building.

"Tuk-tuk?" a man cries from the opposite side of the street.

Becky and Jay walk over to him, climb in the vehicle. Jay hands the man an email, the address printed out. He doesn't bother to debate prices; not today.

"Where we goin', Jay?" Becky asks.

He touches a finger to his lips.

"Trust me, journal girl, you're going to want this."

15h20

The tuk-tuk struggles over the hill. They're leaving Patong and heading in the direction of the Phuket Country Club. Jay's read the email over and over. Before seeing Becky again, he wasn't really sure if he would accept the invitation. He had too many doubts – about his own ability to hide what he knew, when everything inside told him he'd been betrayed. About ethics. About truth.

Jay squeezes Becky's hand, feeling her soft hair brush against his face in the wind. Becky looks at Jay, leaning over to kiss him.

The tuk-tuk slows.

"We here now," the driver said, waving towards an apartment block.

"Wherever 'here' is," says Becky.

They take the stairs. Wind themselves up to the top storey and a view of the island. By the time they reach the top, Jay is panting and Becky favouring her good leg. Jay straightens, then strides to the front door. And this time, as Jay lifts his hand to knock, there are no hesitations.

When the door opens, Jay makes his introductions.

"Becky, I'd like you to meet your brother-in-law, Benjamin."

The confusion on Becky and Liam's faces is evident.

"I think y'all better come in," Liam says.

15h26

Pascale scuttles into the kitchen, emerging with a tray of beers, and a glass of pineapple juice. She sits next to Liam, her one hand over his, the other over her rounded belly.

"Do you want that I leave you alone?" Pascale asks Liam.

"Of course not, honey. I'm not hiding anything from you."

Liam looks at Jay, and for the first time since they met, Liam seems uncertain. Wary. A silence pierces the room as everybody waits for somebody to speak. And eventually, it's Liam who does.

"What do you mean brother-in-law?" Liam asks.

"Technically speakin', if Jay is right and you *are* Benjamin Heyward, you're my ex-brother-in-law," Becky says.

"What happened to Anton?"

Liam's face betrays a look of fear.

"I'm sorry. He died in the May of 2004. Helicopter crash," Becky says. "I was with him."

"Your leg?" Liam asks and Becky nods. "I don't understand, Jay. How did you find out? Why didn't you talk to me?"

Jay sips his beer, a gulp forming in his throat.

"I found your name in the suitcase that you gave me. Not for months after I got back. I was too focused on Nina."

"But the name in the suitcase was–"

"William Channing," Jay says. "The person Becky had been looking for since Anton's death."

"William?" says Becky. "Your name is William?"

"Isn't it classic? My father gets me a new identity and I end up having the same first name as the man I detest most in the entire world. I never used William. Except for the official stuff. I'm Liam now, not William."

Liam puts his head in his hands. "My brother's dead, and I only find out more than a year later?"

"Your mama sent me to find you," says Becky.

"She knew all the time I was alive and didn't try to contact me?"

"Actually, she didn't know anythin'. She suspected Bill was lyin' and the postcard… With Anton gone, she couldn't face the questions any longer. She sent me halfway around the world to find you."

"Halfway round the world?"

"San Francisco. New York. Tupiza …"

"Tupiza?"

Liam looks increasingly amazed.

"Cusco–" Becky says.

"Where you and Pascale met on the Inca Trail," adds Jay.

"Lìjiāng. Hoi-An …"

Liam begins to smile. "And I thought I covered my tracks," he says.

"Well, I'm pretty persistent," says Becky. "I was goin' to find you at the Phi Phi Bungalows on Christmas."

"You knew I was there?"

"Sure, I found a reservation form just after you and Pascale checked out of that place in Hoi-An. D'ya like John Irving?"

"Good book," says Liam. "Did you read it?"

Becky smiles but shakes her head.

"The thing is, I never knew your first name. I knew it began with a W. That's why I spent so much time with

Wilfred. I thought you might have been him. With a new surname or somethin'. Come to think of it, I don't think I ever knew yours. And I didn't ask, because–"

"My name began with an 'L'."

Becky nods, then leans forward.

"Did Bill kill Louisa-May Colbert, Ian's first wife?"

Liam's eyes shift. "I want to tell you no, but I actually think he did."

"And what about Kim Harrison?" Becky asks. "Did you kill Kim?"

15h56

Liam looks at Becky.

"I'd like to say I underestimated you, but really if anybody would've figured something out, I might have guessed it would be you."

"With a little help from Stan Colicchio."

"Stan Colicchio?" muses Liam. "He was the only person then who believed in me."

"You've not answered my question, Liam," Becky says. "Did you kill Kim?"

Liam sighs. His face has gone pale, and instinctively he crosses his arms over his chest. Pascale shifts as he moves slightly away from her.

"I couldn't tell you in a word," Liam says. "It wasn't that simple."

"Don't you think I deserve to know? How d'ya think I feel knowin' my husband lied to me every day we were together?"

"Maybe he was trying to protect you."

Becky stands up, paces at the window.

"In case you haven't noticed, *Benjamin*, I've been doin' a mighty fine job of takin' care of myself."

Until this point, Pascale has remained silent, but this time she looks at Becky.

"Do you really want the truth? *Peut-être*, you will find out something you did not want to know."

"About Anton?"

Pascale nods.

"But that's it exactly, Pascale," says Becky, "It just gets my goose. I love Jay now, and I have, no *need*, to put Anton behind me."

Pascale turns to Liam, pulls his hand over her swelling stomach.

"Tell her then, *chéri*; you have kept this secret for much too long."

Liam swallows, then nods. "It's a bit of a long story. But I'm going to tell it right."

I wasn't always like I am now. I had a lot of problems. Anton made friends easier than I did. He was good at everything. Sports. Academics. Girls. I was the older son and everyone used to forget my name. Oh you're Anton's brother. That's how I was defined. I wasn't worth anything on my own. That was for sure. And my father constantly reminded me of how useless I was. Why can't you be more like Anton? *The thing was, I couldn't even fault Anton myself. He was kind to me. One of the few who were. Anton defended me, which only made me seem weaker. Incapable.*

    I spent a lot of time on my own. I was only interested in two things. How machines fitted together and sequences. Numbers. I didn't have to deal with people. I could remember the most amazing things. The order of an entire deck of cards. How to put a computer together – and without any instructions at all. I retreated into my room most of the time. Failed abysmally in class. People thought I was a freak. In a way, I suppose I was. Nobody except my mother took any notice of me. Until Anton brought Peggy home.

Liam stops.

    "You met Peg, I suppose, in San Francisco. She tell you anything?" he asks.

    Becky shakes her head.

    "Not much exceptin' about her and Anton's baby. The abortion."

    "Ah," says Liam. "Well, I'll get to that."

She was beautiful. From what I've seen from the Internet, she still is. Married that shipping guy. She could never tell the truth after that. Secrets. Her bum in the butter. She was different then. At first she tried to be kind to me, for Anton's sake. Took an interest in my machines. Found number games to challenge me with. She's a clever girl that, amazing head for figures. We laughed a lot. Infuriated Anton who didn't get the joke. Strings of numbers. Mind games. It wasn't too long before I started to see her differently. I fantasised about her. Imagined her kissing me. I'd never seen a girl naked, never mind slept with one. Well, one day, she arrived at the house. I was eighteen by then, virtually drooling at the sight of her. I was the only person home. Funnily enough, she seemed to know it. She didn't even ask for Anton. All she did was take my hand, lead me upstairs. We've got two hours, *she told me.*

"But Anton came back early," Becky said as Pascale shifted uncomfortably.

Liam nodded.

"I've never dressed so quickly in my life; I didn't quite make it though. Peg, however, was totally calm. Scattered the cards on the made-up bed. Invented some story about marijuana and strip poker."

"And Anton believed her?" Becky asked.

"Sure. I was always the misfit. Why wouldn't it be my idea? I thought it might be a once-off. A bit of charity for poor, deprived Ben. She was sleeping with Anton, I knew that. He bragged about it to me. I couldn't look at her the same way after that. I'd catch her eye over the Hoppin' John and she stared right back, her hand on my thigh right at the dinner table. I was smitten. We met all over the place."

"At the gas station?" says Becky.

Liam looked at Pascale, patted her hand.

"I guess we got careless. When Stan caught us I didn't know what to say. But I wanted to touch her any chance I got. Luckily he didn't know who she was."

"Not then," said Becky.

My mother probably told you about the gambling. I was good at it. Given it up now but then, people respected me at the tables. I'd clear the decks of cash. Take it home. At the beginning I had nothing much to spend it on. Another machine. Something to take apart. But then with Peg I had someone I loved. I bought her anything she wanted. And one thing I can say about Peg, she liked the finer things in life. But she got what she wanted. I got her. And yet, all the time we had Anton too. I wasn't happy about it. Her sleeping with both of us. But if it was a choice between that or nothing, I chose that. She didn't make promises, but I thought she loved me. And anyway, it was exciting. Beating Anton at something. He was my brother, but I'd be lying if I told you I wasn't jealous of him. West Point was pretty much in the bag. My father was painful. Bragging about Anton at every opportunity. I started to have a bit of a bad run at the tables ... lost some money, but I wasn't in debt. And then stuff started going missing at the house. Of course my mother thought it was me, but it wasn't ...

"Then who was it?" Becky asks.

"I didn't know at first, but finally I confronted Anton."

He was really angry at me, I could see that straight away. For the "strip poker". If he'd known what Peg and I were really up to, he would have had a duck fit. That's when I found out about the baby. My blood ran cold. Whose baby was it – mine or Anton's? Anton needed cash fast, for the abortion. And who cared if he sold off the family silver to pay for it? No ways were his West Point plans going to be wrecked by an "unplanned fucking foetus". *And he wasn't going to tell our parents either. But even then, he didn't have enough cash. And I had none to spare for him. Anton told me I'd have to make it for him, on the gambling tables. He tried his hand a few times at the casino. And now he was in debt. Peggy was selling some of the jewellery her daddy had bought her. I was to take the money and triple it. He didn't even ask me; he* expected *me to do it – as if I owed him something.* You'll do it for Peg, *he said.*

"And what about Peggy?" asks Jay.

I went to find her. I remember I was crying. It didn't matter to me. I loved her. I would marry her, be a dad to the baby. Mine, or Anton's. She looked at me as though I was insane – I love Anton, Benjamin, how could you ever have thought I wanted to be with you?

Turns out the jewellery she sold was everything I had ever bought her.

I left her.

Went home. Vomited into the toilet.

Then got so drunk I don't remember much until Anton drove up to the bar. Marched me out. You think you're going

358

to fuck up my life? You sober up and get me the fucking money! *He didn't ask why I was drunk. He didn't care. The man was deranged.*

Jay looks at Becky who has sat down next to him again. Her hands are drawn into a tight fist on both knees, her knuckles white. She shakes her head ever so slightly.

"What happened?" she almost whispers.

I went with him. He ... led me into the fray. His eyes darting from person to person. I couldn't focus. Couldn't remember anything. All I could think of was Peggy and the terrible things she'd said. I didn't understand why she'd done what she did. Even now, I'm not all that sure. But I'd just lost the one thing I cared about. So I gambled for Anton. The debts piled up. All night long. And Anton, just pushing and pushing. You fix this, Benjamin. Fix it. *We crashed into bed at six in the morning. Anton grim. My head pounding. When I woke up at midday, Anton was gone. Came back with a load of cash from Kim Harrison. Short-term loan. With a mountain of interest.*

So we went back. I didn't want to win the money. If they didn't have it, they couldn't kill my baby. Kim started putting the pressure on almost immediately. He wanted his money back before his father found out. So Anton went out to visit him, some dodgy place out of town. Around noon or so. Lost his temper with Kim. Anton wanted more time. But Kim was insistent ...

Jay focuses on Becky. Her head is in her hands as she begins to cry.

"Then it wasn't you ..." she says.

Liam's eyes are also filling.

"Anton shot him. Twice. Then called me. He couldn't lift the body on his own. Kim was a big man."

"You went?" asked Jay.

"Anton was my *brother*," Liam says softly.

"You went back to the house to fetch Bill," says Becky.

"We didn't know what else to do."

So my dad; he was friends with Major Patrick Davies – you might have heard about him from my mother. They worked out a plan together. It was like some sort of war game for them. Kim was trash. Dispensable. Disposable. And we'd better do what they told us and keep our mouths shut. "I won't lose my son like this," my father shouted. And even as he spoke, I knew he wasn't referring to me. I was going to have to be the one to die. To disappear. Anton was going to West Point.

So when it was dark, they loaded up Kim's body. Burnt it in my car. Put me in some sort of safehouse until they could arrange a passport and get me into Canada. I had nothing. Nothing of my old life. Just a bit of cash from my father and the warning that I should never come back. Never.

"And Anton said nothing?" Jay asked.

"I'd betrayed Anton with Peggy. Perhaps I thought I deserved it."

"And the baby?" asked Becky.

"I heard they went to some quack in the backstreets. Ripped her apart. She blamed Anton. She wouldn't see him ever again."

Chapter 41

New Year's Eve 2005. Saturday. 23h58.

As the sun begins to slip behind the clouds, drifting away beyond sight, the first lanterns lift up from Patong Beach. The atmosphere is frenetic, but celebratory.

It's the end of the year.

Balloons in all sorts of colours are hung like grape clusters outside shops and restaurants. From the hotel, Jay and Becky can see the first lanterns floating upwards. They don't know what they are at first – not fireworks – how could they be? The flames lift, drift, and flicker upwards, then are blown by a slight wind towards the left. At first there are only a few. They can't identify them. A shower of red sparks, then scatters in silver.

Outside the hotel, Christmas lights flash in red and gold, rivalling any display down on the High Street near his home. Giant snowmen guard the entrance to the bar with broomsticks and Santa coaxes his reindeer over the doorway. More fireworks. The bangs are distant, but recognisable. It's the start of a celebration.

As the music reverberates from loudspeakers on the stage above the swimming pool, it drowns out the sound of the rockets – they take off, explode, and adorn the sky with diamonds, rubies, emeralds. But as midnight approaches, even the speakers can't drown them out. Across Patong Bay, they sparkle, sizzle, hiss.

They'll go down to the beach now. It's not the beach either of them remembers – cluttered with motorcar pile-ups and scrap-metal scooters. It's empty of those, but alive with the sound of people cheering.

Laughing.

Beers clinking.

It's 80 baht for a lantern – probably less, although Jay doesn't bother to barter much down from that. Jay and Becky want their own wishes to take off – beyond the palm trees and the lamp posts and the tsunami evacuation escape-route signs.

Jay feels Becky's soft hand in his. He may have chosen Nina before, but Gabriel has come back from Brazil. It's his turn now.

"So you solved it," Becky says.

"You solved it more than I did," Jay replies, "I just filled in the missing piece."

Jay looks at Becky. After only a few days of knowing, she seems lighter. Happier.

"Are you going to tell Eleanor?" he asks.

Becky shrugs.

"Liam is our *friend*. With a baby comin'. And as for Benjamin, unless he decides otherwise, he was finally lost to the waves on December 26, 2004."

She leads Jay close to the shallow water. Pouring paraffin over the waxy base of the lantern, she smiles at him.

"Are you really ready for this?"

He looks at her, his heart filling with a love he never thought possible.

"Of course I am. You?"

"Jay, I was ready a year ago."

Becky slips the lighter from her pocket.

"Hold tight," she says.

He grips the opposite paper corners, as the lantern begin to puff with the first bursts of hot air rising. She stands up, holding the other two corners.

"Wait," she says, "we have to wait at least two minutes."

"Two minutes," he says, "I feel like I've waited a lifetime."

They look at each other over the puffing paper. And he wants to pull her to him.

"Wait," she says, and this time she laughs.

Their eyes meet. They're no longer aware of the midnight revellers, the pumping music from a roadside stall. They don't care about the fireworks and the passage of time, the gongs sounding in the New Year. This time, it's just them.

"Now," Becky says.

And almost as though synchronised, the paper lantern puffs up, then wobbles. Suddenly it whooshes upwards into the sky, straight and true. Their wishes on a paper lantern, carried up into the night sky over the Andaman Sea.

From the author

Thanks so much for reading *Under the Surface*. You've travelled the world, and now you're back in bed, or in your favourite chair!

As anyone who has ever written a book or attempted to will know, writing a book can never happen completely in isolation. This particular novel drew on the many stories shared on websites and forums on the Internet after the terrible tsunami of Boxing Day 2004. Doing this research was disturbing and heartbreaking, and in no way at all was I attempting to make light of the experiences of the victims and families of victims. There were many times, in fact, that I had to switch off my computer and just sit to mull the awful tragedy that, in this modern world, was recorded on so many personal videos and photographs. I also spoke to some people who'd been affected in some way.

Sadly, the death toll was almost incomprehensible. According to Hannah Osborne (http://www.ibtimes.co.uk/2004-indian-ocean-earthquake-tsunami-facts-1480629): "Over 500,000 people were injured by the tsunami, with a further 150,000 at risk from infectious diseases in the aftermath. The exact death toll is unknown, but over 230,000 are believed to have been killed with thousands more missing. Indonesia was worst affected, with an estimated 170,000 dead."

When I travelled back to Thailand in 2008 after the tsunami what struck me most, however, was the resilience of the Thai people. I went to Ko Phi Phi, where much of the novel is set, and I was humbled by the industry and rebuilding that had occurred since the wall of water hit the island. This made me think that rejuvenation *is* possible despite hardship and catastrophe. And that is a hopeful message for others who are suffering right now, whatever they are going through.

The widow's story, on the other hand, was an easier one to write in the sense that she travels over many journeys to places I have visited and loved. Travel is a fundamental part of my life and I hope *Under the Surface* gave you a chance to experience some of my past haunts — although these become altered through the widow's viewpoint. So they are my journeys but seen through a different lens and completed for a different purpose completely.

Finally, if you'd like to learn more about me or my work, you can access my website or email me: paula@paulamarais.com.

I'd love to hear from you!

About Paula Marais

Paula Marais is the author of several books including *The Punishment, Love and Wine* and *Shadow Self*. *Shadow Self* was nominated for the Etisalat Prize in 2015 and won a literary award for its translation into Afrikaans. Paula has a Master's in Creative Writing from the University of Cape Town and is an alumnus of Bread Loaf in Vermont, the oldest and most illustrious writing conference in the US. She lives in Cape Town and is addicted to travel (she's been to more than 80 countries around the world), quality coffee and beautiful views.

For more about her work see her website: www.paulamarais.com or connect with her on:
Facebook: PaulaJMarais
Twitter: @paula_marais
Pinterest: paulamarais

Or if you'd like to join her mailing list (free books, prizes and reading suggestions) or to ask questions, you can reach her directly: paula@paulamarais.com.

Thank you

Under the Surface has taken many years and much effort to come to light.

I would like to thank the following people for their contributions:
Marilyn Marais — my ideal reader
Kara Peters — my champion, my sister and just as an added bonus, an enormously talented designer
Kirsty Savides — marketing guru and friend extraordinaire
My editors/proofreaders — Leonie Duncan, Stephanie Hunt (in the US), Maya Fowler-Sutherland
My launch team
All those who assisted by voting on the final cover and blurbs
And last but not least, my family, but especially Dave, Jed and Cole van Wijk with whom I continue to take the most incredible journeys of my life.

If you'd like to read more from Paula Marais, following are a few pages from her novel *Shadow Self*, which was nominated for the top 100 books in Africa in 2015. But first a quick summary…

Suburban family life can be mundane, but it can also push you over the edge. When Thea Middleton finds herself behind bars for an unthinkable crime, she realises she's become the most hated member of any society: a failed mother. As she, her husband Clay and oldest daughter Sanusha try to repair their shattered lives, their individual accounts form the pieces of a tragic puzzle that will haunt them forever.

Praise for *Shadow Self*

Shadow Self is a good book. Somehow, I feel like saying that is an understatement. But what else can one say about a book one really loves? ~ *The Critical Literature Review*

Every intricate detail penned by Marais takes the reader emotionally and painfully through Thea's journey ~ *Herald Live*

"Written with compelling power and jagged intensity" ~ Tony Morphet

PROLOGUE
How to plead

I'm sitting on a bench in some small room, a cramped musty space. They're coming for you, I hear and I look around. I can't see properly. It's like being asleep and feeling that you need to open your eyes but you can't. The more you try to focus, the more you panic, and the more out of touch you feel. I want to scratch the cataracts from my eyes, but even if I squint it's like the room is moving up and down.

A wave of room. A wave of noise. Clattering.

Jangling.

I sit still, putting my head down between my knees. "It's okay, Thea, I said I was here, didn't I?"

Robbie. My heart is bulging with voices, and my brother sounds exactly the same as ever. I feel seasick, leaning in a glass-bottomed boat, with fish floating around below me all dead and bloodied.

A shark dropping below me, its fin cut off, crimson and spinning. A top, going round and round. And round and round.

Lights on. Lights off. Lights on. Lights off.

"Ma'am, you've got to come now," and I'm not sure if it's the shark talking, but I feel a grip on my elbow, and I push it away. There's a squealing noise, like a piglet, a kettle whistle. Then I'm being lifted, floating in a balloon.

Weeeeeeeeeeeeeeeeeeeeeeeeeeeeeee . . .

"This is the courthouse, mevrou," that voice says. "You need to stand up now. We're going up the stairs."

"Don't want to," I say. "I need to sleep."

"Lady, after what you did, you've got a lifetime to sleep. Not much else to do in Worcester."

371

Worcester? What are they talking about? I'm not in Worcester
– I'm

supposed to be asleep with my kids and with Robbie. Didn't
he promise? "Leave me alone," I say. "I don't like you."

"Lady, I don't like you either."

I peer at him, and his face appears as though through mist.
Fat nose. Stubby eyelashes. Coffee eyes. A peaked hat.

"We're going to have to cuff you, ma'am," someone says, but
I don't think it's him because his lips don't move.

"As in handcuffs?" I ask Robbie.

"I think so," Robbie says. "What else could he mean? Just go,
Thea. Remember how we used to play with handcuffs in the
tree house? Cops and robbers?"

But that was fun and this hurts.

"No need to push me," I say, sounding like Mother.

"Listen, lady, just get a move on now. This magistrate don't
like to wait."

So I walk. I don't like waiting either. And it irritates me when
Clay is late. Clay, my husband. I always check my watch a
thousand times and wonder why he can't respect me by
arriving on time. Always another emergency at one of his coffee
shops.

As I walk, each step is heavy as if my legs are in water. I
wade the stairs.

Up, up.

The chains clank behind me where the policemen are
standing. They're talking.

"So she told me that my son stole my car when I was
attending an accident scene. Dronk, jy weet. And only sixteen. I
found him at Muizenberg Beach. And he thought he was too
old for a klap."

Mother specialised in those. My first husband was more like
her than she would ever have admitted.

Violence. Bodies on bodies.

I shiver. What's that saying again? Like someone's walking over my grave.

At the top of the stairs, I walk into a uniform. The man holds me back.

"Steady on, wait until we're ready."

Go. Wait. Walk. Stop. Go. I wish they'd just make up their damn minds. Below me, the other cops chat on.

"And the car? What about it? No problems with the car? A dent in the front, jong. He's going to rake leaves for a year to pay for it."

Rake. My Zen garden relaxed me. Patterns in the sand. Swirls. Twirls. Until Joe tipped the sand on the lounge carpet and Clay said, Enough of this. I don't like the grit under my feet.

At the top, it's buzzing. Voices up and down. And the lights are so bright.

I blink, blink, blink.

There's a hand coming towards me, and then it goes away. Someone's shouting, "Keep away from the prisoner!"

"That's you," says Robbie.

"I know," I say back. "I can feel my wrists."

My oldest daughter, Sanusha, is there, I think, with her hot olive eyes shouting, why, why, why? And I wish Robbie would just explain it to her. It's better. For Joe. For baby Caitie. For me. Even for Sanusha.

She has her father and he'll care for her. She doesn't need me to save her.

The policeman's pushing me; I could feel his fingers in my ribs. "Ouch," I say, massaging my side.

"There," he says. "Stand over there."

I'm in front of a microphone with the sound turned off. The judge – is that what he is? – is whispering to me. And I look at him, concentrating, trying hard to hear.

"Madam," he says to me.

There's my defence attorney, Tom Harper. I know him, have for a long time. He's smiling at me, nodding gently. But Tom's not gentle and he's confusing me. He says something to the judge and comes closer.

"Just answer the questions, Thea," he says. "What questions? I can't hear him."

"He asked you for your full name."

"Doesn't he know it? He needs to speak up."

"Your Worship, the prisoner says she can't hear you properly."

Then the judge booms at me and he sounds like God, like Ganesha: "Madam, please state your full name for the court."

"Just do it," says Robbie. "Do what he says, and say 'sir'. Show him some respect."

"Thea June Middleton . . . sir."

"And your full address, please?"

"28c Jamieson Road, Rondebosch." (Currently incarcerated elsewhere.)

"Now I do this for the purpose of confirming you are the correct accused, and from the records in front of me, you are."

I realise Tom is standing still in front of me, facing the judge. He has his hands folded at his waist, like a contrite schoolboy. But he turns once or twice to look at me, as though I'm supposed to understand him. As I watch the judge, his mouth opens like someone blowing smoke rings at the bar.

I sniff. The room smells of hate and despair. The judge shrugs and I want to step away, step back and float on a cloud, catch a smoke ring like a Bentley Belt.

"Does the accused speak English? Why isn't she answering me?" calls the red man, man in red piping.

"Yes, Your Worship. She understands you."

"Plead, Mom!" I hear a voice and it sounds like Sanusha. Sanusha under the water I'm drowning in.

"Not guilty," I say. I think I sound firm, solid, but then the big man, Mr Law, says, "Can you repeat that please."

"Louder," says Sanusha.

"Silence, miss, this is a court. We can't have interjections from the observers."

So I clamp my mouth, like Joe used to when he didn't want to lie but didn't want to tell the truth either.

"Not you," says Tom, and now I recognise his voice. "Oh, there you are, Tom," I say.

"Yes," he says, flint-eyed. "The plea, please, Thea."

"Not guilty," I say again.

The lawyers and prosecutors and policemen and judge all jump. They heard me this time and I laugh.

Panty boys.

Before long, the cops are escorting me down the stairs and I see Clay. Lovely Clay looking grey.

He shakes his head at me, but all the time his eyes don't leave me, as though he can't believe it's me in front of him. I wave. Kiss-kiss.

Now I can finally go back to sleep.

PART ONE: PRECONCEPTIONS
Sanusha (aged 5): Important family facts

I am 5 and I know 3 things about Mom:
  1. Her eyes don't match.
  2. Being happy is hard for her.
  3. She doesn't like Asmita Ayaa. (Mom says she does but I'm
  not stupid.)

I know 3 things about Appa, my father:
  1. He's not always at the university when he says he is.
  2. He shaves 2 times a day, so he must be super-hairy.
  3. He has friends who are ladies who are our little secret.

I know 3 things about me:
  1. I'm not beautiful like my mother.
  2. I like numbers the best.
  3. I hate secrets.

3 + 3 + 3 = 9 important family facts.

If you take 9 and make 3
groups, there are 3 in each
group. Also, a polygon with 9
sides and 9 angles is called a
nonagon. See?

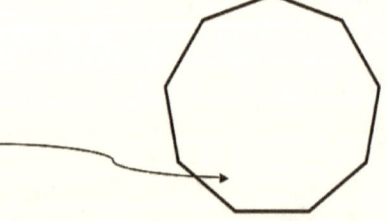

    There are 9 planets in the solar system: Mercury, Venus,
Earth, Mars, Jupiter, Saturn, Uranus, Neptune and Pluto, plus
the sun, which is actually a burning ball of gas. Pluto is the
furthest away from the sun. Mercury is the closest.

Cats have 9 lives. (But our cat, Marmite, has only got 7 left. Appa rode over him once, and once he landed in the swimming pool and got his head caught under the pool net.) Beethoven wrote 9 symphonies, but I don't care. I hate classical music, but I love Abba, especially "Money, Money, Money" because it's about counting.

Also, 9 sounds a bit like "new". And Mom taught me 9 is neuf in French, nueve and nuevo in Spanish and neun in German.

I like the number 9.

It takes 9 months to grow a baby. So this means that when I count to 9, I can make a new start.

I would like a new start.

Mom cries a lot. We're still in this godforsaken garden flat with not enough room to swing a cat (but Mom says don't swing Marmite).

Oh, there's another thing I also know about Mom. $3 + 1 = 4$

She's smoking in the garden under the blue gum that Appa wants to pull out because it's Australian. Appa doesn't like Australians. Also smoking. He says Mom smells like an ashtray. She carries Stimorols in her handbag to make her breath sweet but they're burny and they make my tummy growl. Appa says she'd better give up the cigarettes, or else. I'm not sure what else, but I think Mom knows. She still smokes sometimes, but she tries not to. That's another secret I have to keep.

Mom's lungs are going black inside her body, but she told me it helps her relax. Relaxing is good, but smoking is not good.

I think I should rub her feet, but she doesn't sit down long enough. Mom walks up and down the cottage like a trapped animal, peeking out the window. I don't know what she is waiting for. Sometimes Annie comes down the path, and Mom's eyes shine. When Annie leaves, Mom's eyes are dull like my shoes after a long day in the dust.

I have another granny, but she and Mom aren't friends any more so she doesn't want to meet me. Mom says I'm not missing anything, but it feels like she is lying. There are 5 things I think I am missing:

1. The other granny's beautiful house, which Mom talks about some-times.

2. The other granny's cooking. When Appa isn't around, Mom some-times makes food from recipes. I love oxtail, which is meat, but Appa doesn't ever eat meat.

3. Mom's old toys. She says when she was little she kept them care-fully in a big wooden box at the bottom of her bed. Mom says this granny probably chucked them out, but I don't think so. Why would someone throw away toys?

4. Other photos of Mom's brother whose name was Robbie. He died when she was small. Mom only has one photo, which she took the night she left that granny. (Appa says Mom got kicked out.) So Robbie only looks like Robbie in that one photo. I don't think anyone looks the same always, even if they're dead.

5. The tree house Mom's dad made for her and Robbie. Mom says that granny chopped it out of the tree, but I saw it. One day, Mom thought I was sleeping in the car, and she drove to

this big-enormous-gigantic house and then she stopped and looked at the tree for a long time. She drove away quickly when the gates started to open. When she got home, she gave me to Asmita Ayaa, and got into the bath to cry.

When I cry, and I don't cry nearly as much as I did a long time ago when I was 4, Mom holds me tight. She tells me she is filling me with love from her skin to mine. Sometimes she holds me too tight so I can't breathe nicely, but I like the way her body feels, so I turn my face to gulp some air. Appa taught me that word "gulp". He also taught me "polygon" and "nonagon". Fishes gulp in the water. Snakes gulp down whole frogs. I saw that on TV. I like TV but my grandmother, Asmita Ayaa, says I must only watch for 1 hour total a day, and because it is her TV, I have to listen to her for my obedience star on my chart. I've been thinking about it. 1 hour is 60 minutes, and there are 60 seconds in 1 minute, so 60 x 60 = 360 seconds in 1 hour.

So it's 360 seconds of TV a day. That sounds like more than 1 hour. That's why numbers are better than words, but there are a few words

I really like:
1. Smile
2. Kangaroo
3. Aeroplane

They make me feel like hot chocolate in my tummy.

Mom has been acting a bit funny. She is sad all the time. She wakes up sad. Even sunshine doesn't make her happy. I love sunshine – it's better than rain. When I go to see Mom, I open the curtains to let in the sunrays to make her feel happy, but it doesn't work. Sunshine always works for me. And chocolate, and bubble baths, and making biscuits in Asmita Ayaa's kitchen, because Mom's kitchen is too tiny.

I heard Appa talking to Asmita Ayaa. He was very angry with Mom; really, really furious – like when I spilt paint on his computer when I was supposed to be helping Mom hang up the washing. Why is he angry that Mom is sad? Why doesn't he hug her and make her better? Asmita Ayaa found me behind the door and told Appa he must calm down. He pinched his mouth together and picked me up, but he didn't send me love through his skin.

Appa doesn't enjoy cuddling me, but he likes cuddling my teacher at Humpty Dumpty's. He thinks I don't know. When she looks at him, her eyes are all gooey like in the cartoons. Appa doesn't get all gooey. He's got lots of ladies who like him. Once he saw some ladies on the side of the road and he stopped to say hello. Their boobs were popping out, and they had long silky legs and very high shoes. They looked in the window. One of them was chewing gum. Mom says chewing gum is not for children because they can choke. The ladies had shiny bits of gold in their smiles. I liked their make-up. It was pretty, like in the movies.

I also said hello.

One of the pretty ladies' faces changed.

"What kind of a jerk are you?" she said. "With kids in the [...] car?"

She said a bad word, and I wasn't "kids". There's just one of me. "Calm down, love. I forgot she was here."

So that hurt my feelings. I was driving with him all afternoon telling him my news about the plastic containers we need for collecting but-tons, and Melanie's new doll that has hair that really grows. Also, I was telling him that "dog" begins with "d" and rhymes with "frog". I know all about rhyming, you know. 1 = fun.

"Well, I have kids and I don't bring them out here, mister. Go home to your wife."

Appa drove away and then he looked at me.

"Your mother can't even fetch you from school," he said. "Doesn't she know how busy I am? Now, don't tell Mom about this. It's just our little secret, okay?"

Years ago, when I was actually 3, I slept in the same room as Mom and Appa in the cottage. But then I heard Mom saying, "No, no, no." They were playing wrestling. Appa was on top of Mom and she pushed him back so he hit his head on the wall and then he said a naughty word and smacked Mom on the face. She cried very quietly but then I got out of my bed to hug her and tell her I was awake.

"I love you, Mom," I said. "Do you know how much I love you?" Mom wiped her tears and smiled for me, but it didn't look like a real smile because there was blood coming from her lip. She said, "I love you too, poppet."

Appa said nothing. He lay back on the bed and switched off the light. He grunted like a piggy pig. Mom took me outside and we looked at the moon. She smoked a cigarette, but I didn't tell Appa. When we got back to the cottage, he was snoring. I don't like that because he sounds like a train going through a long tunnel.

I didn't fall asleep the whole night. Seriously. Children can do that, you know. I got up in the morning and I wasn't even a tiny bit tired. I don't know why I always have to go to bed so early.

I'm not allowed to sleep in the cottage any more. Asmita Ayaa made up a pink room for me in the house. Mom and Appa said I needed my own space.
These are the things in my bedroom:

1. Bookshelf with 5 shelves

2. Bed

3. Cupboard

4. Fairy lamp

5. Bedside table

6. Toy box

7. Art table

8. Blackboard with photos stuck on

9. Kiddies chair (purple)

10. 13 stars on the ceiling

I like my room, but Mom can't understand why we can't get our own flat where we can all be together in the same building. She doesn't actually mean all of us, because she wants to leave Asmita Ayaa and my grand-father Kandasamy Ajah behind, and be just 3:

1 = Mom

2 = Appa

3 = me

Appa gets cross when she says this, because why waste money when we have a perfectly good place to live and we're all very comfortable? Money doesn't grow on trees, and why doesn't she bring in some cash of her own and stop lying in bed feeling sorry for herself? Then Mom says she's 24 and married 5 years and we can't be tied to Appa's parents forever. Then

Appa says she knew what he was like when she married him, and after 5 years she still doesn't make a decent curry.

I like Mom's curry.

Some days are very bad. Every day when I wake up, I always run to the cottage to say good morning, but sometimes Mom doesn't even open her eyes. I know she's not dead, because I can see her breathing with her lungs. Her lungs are inside her body getting rid of the bad air and giving her blood beautiful fresh oxygen.

Appa is normally gone when I wake up, but sometimes he has breakfast with my grandparents and me. When I don't have Humpty Dumpty's on Saturdays and Sundays and holiday time, I like to crawl into bed with Mom. She moves over without waking, but I can hear her sigh. Moving over for me is good.

I can hug Mom as much as I want to, even if she doesn't hug me back.

~~~

Enjoying *Shadow Self*? Purchase the rest of the book at your favourite online bookshop or contact info@logogog.com for more information.